New Year's Resolution:
Resolution:
HUSBAND

About the Authors

REBECCA BRANDEWYNE is a self-proclaimed "country girl with a dash of big city sprinkled in for spice" who has gone on to write 16 consecutive bestsellers with appearances on the *New York Times, Publishers Weekly* and *Los Angeles Times* lists. She sold her first novel when she was only 23, making her at the time the youngest published romance writer in the U.S., a record that lasted for ten years. A member of the *Romantic Times* Hall of Fame, Rebecca has over 8.5 million copies of her books in print and is published in over 60 countries worldwide.

ANNE STUART has been writing for more than two decades, a great deal of that time for Harlequin. She has won every major award in the business, and, as she says, "prides herself for being a model of decorum at all times."

CARLA NEGGERS is the *New York Times* bestselling author of many novels of contemporary romance. She has received the *Romantic Times* Reviewer's Choice Award four times and has been praised by *Publishers Weekly* for her "highly entertaining" writing. *Affaire de Coeur* has said, "One is never disappointed by anything written by Carla Neggers." The daughter of a Dutch immigrant and a Southerner, Carla lives in Vermont with her husband and their two children.

Rebecca Brandewyne
Anne Stuart
Carla Neggers

New Year's Resolution: HUSBAND

Harlequin Books

TORONTO • NEW YORK • LONDON
AMSTERDAM • PARIS • SYDNEY • HAMBURG
STOCKHOLM • ATHENS • TOKYO • MILAN
MADRID • WARSAW • BUDAPEST • AUCKLAND

For Suzi, for wilder days and happy endings. With love.
—Rebecca Brandewyne

For my pals on GEnie. Moral support, critical advice, business acumen,
and the best friends anyone could find anywhere. —Anne Stuart

 To Pam and Paul Hudson. —Carla Neggers

NEW YEAR'S RESOLUTION: HUSBAND

ISBN 0-373-83312-1

Copyright © 1996 by Harlequin Books S.A.

The publisher acknowledges the copyright holders
of the individual works as follows:
THE ICE DANCERS
Copyright © 1996 by Rebecca Brandewyne
KISSING FROSTY
Copyright © 1996 by Anne Kristine Stuart Ohlrogge
HUSBAND FOR HIRE
Copyright © 1996 by Carla Neggers

CONTENTS

Rebecca Brandewyne

The Ice Dancers

Dear Reader,

I hope you enjoy this novella, *The Ice Dancers*. Ice-skating is one of my favorite sports, and since I can't ice-skate myself, I really admire those who can—not to mention that it's simply one of the most beautiful sports in existence. Something I will always remember is being one of the judges for the Miss USA 1990 pageant, for which Olympic ice-skater Robin Cousins was also a judge. It was such fun for me to chat with him and get a glimpse of an insider's viewpoint of the sport.

As for New Year's resolutions, well, I suppose I should confess that I don't actually make them for myself—mainly because I suspect I wouldn't keep them anyway! Perhaps that's because I seem to celebrate each new year differently. New Year's Day is, to me, like that first blank page I stare at when beginning to write a new work: the year, just like the work, will become whatever I make it.

Mariah and Alek were in my head for a long time. I'm so glad I had this opportunity to introduce them to you! If you'd like to write to me, you may do so at the following address: c/o Ms. Margaret Ruley, Jane Rotrosen Agency, 318 East 51st Street, New York, NY 10022.

Have a wonderful New Year!

Rebecca Brandewine

The Ice Dancers

Like a phoenix, love rises from the ashes
Of an old but not forgotten flame.
It begins again, with "Do you remember when
You whispered low my name
And held me close in the darkness—"
Which one of us was to blame?
It seems so unimportant now.
We are changed, no longer the same.

So come to me urgently in silence.
On this wintry night, we will start anew;
And when all of the old memories awaken,
As they are bound to do,
We'll bury the worst in the past,
Keeping only the best, we two.
So, come, love. Dance forever with me.
We are changed; still, this ice isn't new.

We have trodden it before, you and I.
We know each rut that e'er led us to grieve,
And every fragile patch along the perilous path.
So this time, do not leave.
It is only the lucky ones who are given
A second chance, a reprieve.
And sometimes, dreams really do come true.
We are changed—if only you believe.

Chapter One

An Old Flame

"I thought I told you never to mention her name to me again." Alek Khazan's voice, while low, contained an underlying note that warned of his anger. A muscle flexed in his set jaw, as well, a sure sign of the turbulent emotions he held in check with difficulty. Anybody else in the world of figure skating would have backed off at this point, Alek's black Russian rages being notorious. But Jules Straetham was not just anybody.

"Alek, be reasonable." The former Olympic gold medalist turned coach exhibited not the least sign of fear in the face of his protégé's wicked temper and ill mood, having himself equally strong emotions and an equally imposing, well-muscled physique, despite the fact that the older man was more than twice Alek's age. "Although I wish Cissy nothing but happiness, her quitting ice dancing to get married *does* leave you without a partner. And no matter how you feel about it, the fact remains that the only one available to you at the moment is Mariah.''

Alek winced again as he heard the name of his former ice-dancing partner—and former fiancée. *Mariah!* For his own sanity and self-preservation, he had tried determinedly, desperately, to forget her. Despite all his efforts, he had never gotten over her. She still haunted him.

It had not helped that, with both of them being ice dancers, albeit skating now with different partners, they had inevitably run into each other at competitions during the more than two years since their highly publicized professional and personal breakup. Whenever they met, mindful of the watchful cameras of the media, they nodded and greeted each other politely, as though they were practically strangers. But every time, Alek was seized inwardly with a fierce, wild desire to snatch Mariah up, to carry her away to the nearest private place and to fling her down and make endless passionate love to her, as he had used to do.

He was drawn irresistibly to watch her performances on the ice—in the arms of another partner—and he was consumed with jealousy at the sight. Until the automobile accident that claimed the life of Mariah's new ice-dancing partner, Worth Deverell, Alek had longed to throttle him, even though Worth had been a friend, and not responsible for taking Mariah away from him. No, if anyone was to blame for their breakup, it had been Alek himself. He had driven Mariah away, pure and simple. Deep down inside, he knew that, although he was unwilling even now to admit it to himself.

"I can't skate with Mariah," Alek instead insisted stubbornly to his skating coach. "Even if we didn't have a personal history between us, she's just not willing professionally to devote the necessary time and practice to her ice dancing."

Jules snorted scornfully to demonstrate just what he thought of this remark.

"That's terribly unfair, Alek—and, what's more, you know it! With the exception of you, there's nobody harder-working or more devoted to her art than Mariah. Cissy, for all that she's sweet and talented, isn't half the skater Mariah is. Yet you were never as tough on Cissy as you were on Mariah. The truth is, you allowed your personal feelings for Mariah to interfere with your professional relationship, Alek. And I must shoulder a portion of the blame for that, as well, because I saw what was happening, and I didn't put a halt to it. Like you, I wanted Mariah to be not just the best, but perfection personified on the ice. It was too much to ask of anyone—and you *demanded* it, Alek, as you demand it of yourself. But Mariah wasn't you. She wasn't me. We should have realized that...realized, too, that she wanted, that she was *entitled to,* a life beyond her work. You pushed her too hard, and I let you do it. But we won't make that mistake this time around, will we?"

"No, because I'm not going to skate with her again—and nothing you say or do is going to change my mind about that, Jules."

"Then you must have plans of which I'm unaware, Alek." Jules's craggy, handsome face went suddenly still. "Are you thinking of quitting ice dancing, too, then, like Cissy? Of...of *retiring?*"

"You must know that if I were, I would have informed you of that fact," Alek said stiffly, the muscle in his jaw still throbbing ominously.

"Well, then, have you discovered some fresh, unknown talent you've invited to be your new partner?"

"If I had, I would have told you about that, too, Jules."

"So...you're not retiring, and you don't have a new partner I don't know about. I have to

confess you've got me stumped, then, Alek."
Jules scratched his head, as though purely puzzled. "Just how are you going to ice-dance without a partner? Have you bought one of those inflatable dummies, maybe? Do you plan on tying its feet to your ice skates or something, and hoping the judges won't notice your partner's not exactly too lively?"

"No." Alek's mouth turned down sourly at the sarcastic humor. The more Jules hammered at him, the more Alek realized how unreasonable he was being. If he wanted to continue ice dancing—and he did—he had to have a new partner. And whether he liked it or not, Mariah Nichols was the only one available at the moment. Still, he made one last-ditch effort to squelch the idea. "She won't skate with me," he declared flatly.

"How do you know?" Jules pasted on his best poker face, so that his excitement and triumph would not show. He had won. He knew it. Still, Alek was just volatile and unpredictable enough to get in a huff, to quit ice dancing altogether and to stamp out of the rink forever, if he spied his skating coach openly gloating. "Have you asked her?"

"Don't be ridiculous!" Alek's tone was sharper than he had intended, and he had to force himself to modulate it. "Except for the polite inanities we've exchanged for the benefit of the media's cameras, Mariah and I haven't spoken to each other in years."

"Then how do you know she won't skate with you?" Jules paused for a moment to allow his question to sink in. Then he continued. "Look, Alek, she's had a hard time and a tough break— one a hell of a lot worse than losing her skating partner to the dingdong of wedding bells. It's only by the grace of God she wasn't killed in that accident, along with Worth and Richard. At least neither your partner nor your coach is lying dead and buried in a cemetery. And you haven't spent some weeks in a hospital, recovering from such a traumatic experience."

"I know...I know..." Alek replied softly, running one hand raggedly through his shoulder-length black hair. He had been stricken when he heard about the fatal automobile accident. For a moment, he had felt as though his own heart had stopped. It was only when he learned Mariah, although injured, was alive that he had become aware of his heart lurching to life again, of its beating in his chest, albeit far too hard and quickly. He had sent flowers to Mariah at the hospital, along with an awkward letter that did not even begin to express his innermost feelings. Mariah's choreographer, Lanie Prescott, had responded with a short but courteous note, thanking him on Mariah's behalf for the flowers and reporting, to his relief, that Mariah, while not yet up to speed, was expected to make a full recovery.

"I almost went to visit her at the hospital, you know," Alek confessed. "But then I decided she...she probably wouldn't want to see me. And even though we both need a partner, Jules, my gut instinct still tells me Mariah won't want to skate with me again, either."

"Well, your gut instinct is wrong, Alek," Jules announced bluntly, playing his trump card. "I've talked to Lanie several times, including late last night. It seems Mariah is willing to give your professional relationship another chance, provided you're willing, too. If you agree, I'll coach you both, of course, and Lanie will come on board as the team's choreographer. So, what do you say, Alek? Shall I call Lanie back and give her the go-ahead...or not?"

The question hung in the silence of the rink, and in that moment, Alek had a strange, nebulous impression that he was standing at a crossroads in his life, uncertain of which path to take. Before his dark, handsome face, his breath formed tiny clouds in the air, and he had an unreal sensation that he could see Mariah in the mist, a miniature figure turning and gliding like a fairy princess across a frozen pond, so small that he could have held it in his palms. Her long black hair was loose, falling nearly to her waist, and she was dressed in the white feathered costume she had worn for the program they had once danced together to music from *Swan Lake*. She was beautiful—and he was honest enough to acknowledge the fact that, despite everything, he still wanted her.

"Yes," he at last uttered slowly, huskily. "Tell Lanie to tell Mariah I said yes."

After that, Alek removed the blade protectors from his skates, then stepped out onto the ice. The rink was cold, as always, so he kept on his heavy sweater and gloves while he warmed up, then began his practice session, executing chassés and mohawks and other movements fluidly. But the fact that, more than once, Alek missed a more intricate step informed Jules that his protégé's mind was not on his skating, for it was unlike Alek to make a string of careless mistakes. Normally, Jules would have been pounding his fist on the rail of the rink, shouting rebukes and instructions. Today, however, the older man was compelled to hide a grin of satisfaction. Abruptly he strode from the rink into the corridor beyond. On his cellular telephone, he dialed Lanie Prescott's number, a victorious smile lighting up his face.

Chapter Two

It Begins Again

She was going to skate with Alek Khazan again. As she gazed at herself in the mirrors of Lanie's dance studio, Mariah Nichols could not believe she had agreed to such a thing. She must have been out of her mind, she thought as she stretched her slender body out over one long, graceful leg, which was positioned on the bar that ran along one wall. She grabbed her foot, holding the pose for several long counts and remembering to breathe normally as she did so. There was still, now and then, an occasional twinge of pain when she forced her leg muscles to respond. But, for the most part, she had fully recovered from the automobile accident that had left her hospitalized for several weeks and had killed her ice-dancing partner, Worth Deverell, as well as their skating coach, Richard Underwood.

The three of them had been returning home late one night after a skating performance when their car was struck by a drunk driver. Even now, months later, Mariah had only vague, horrifying memories of the accident. It had been raining, and the car's wipers had made a squishing sound against the windshield. Wisps of mist had drifted across the road, and the wet highway had shimmered in the glare of their car's headlights.

At first, Mariah and the others had thought it must be some trick of that same mist and headlights that made it appear as though the oncoming pickup truck had veered from its own lane into theirs. Too late had they grasped their peril. Richard, cursing with rage, fear and disbelief, had tried frantically to steer their car out of the truck's path, onto the shoulder of the road—to no avail. The impact had been sudden and violent, the brutal crunching of glass and metal sickening. Richard had been killed instantly. Worth had died in the ambulance en route to the hospital. In the curious, ironic way of things, the drunken driver of the pickup had walked away without a scratch.

Over and over, as she had lain in her hospital bed, not knowing if she would ever walk again, much less ice-dance, Mariah had replayed the deadly accident in her mind. She had wondered endlessly whether there had been any chance of avoiding it, although she had known deep down inside that Richard had done everything humanly possible to attempt to prevent the terrible collision. There had simply been no escaping from the wildly speeding, weaving truck that barreled toward them. She saw it still—in her dreams.

More than once since the accident, she had awakened from a deep sleep, screaming and feeling the cool rain drizzling down on her as the paramedics had worked frantically to save her life, and then the ambulance attendants had lifted her onto a gurney to transport her to the hospital. Only after her heart had slowed and her mind had oriented itself following the nightmare did Mariah realize she was lying in her own bed, that the wetness on her face was tears, not rain.

In addition to the nightmares, she still experienced moments of unexpected shock, dazedness and panic. She thought it must have been during one of these times that she agreed to ice-dance again with Alek Khazan. Mariah could not explain her having consented to their reunion, otherwise. She didn't *want* to skate with him. She did not even want to *see* him! He had pushed her professionally with a single-mindedness that bordered on monomania, sacrificing their personal relationship in the process. He had broken her heart. That its shattered pieces still ached for him was all the more reason to avoid him.

"Earth to Mariah ... Earth to Mariah ..." Lanie Prescott's voice, followed by her soft, musical laughter, rang in Mariah's ears. "Sweetie, if you stay bent over like that much longer, you're liable to freeze in that position. Are you regretting your decision already? Is that why your mind isn't on your work this morning?"

"Yes," Mariah admitted reluctantly, with a rueful smile, as she rose and changed legs, continuing to stretch her muscles. If it weren't for the fact that her and Alek's first performance together would be a Christmas Eve benefit for the Letters to Angels program for the All-Children's Hospital, she'd have had Lanie call Jules Straetham back and tell him she'd changed her mind about skating with Alek. "But how can I refuse to help a program I believe in so strongly, Lanie? A fact I'm sure you counted on when you proposed this match made in hell!" Mariah shot her choreographer and dance coach a knowing, accusatory glance that spoke volumes.

"As I recall, it used to be a match made in heaven—or so the press always claimed. Nichols and Khazan were the dream team of the decade, the American hope for Olympic gold, Mariah—

and, what's more, you know it! Oh, you and Worth skated well together, yes. But let's face it, the two of you never achieved on the ice that indefinable quality you and Alek shared. You and Alek had something special together, Mariah. You had *magic!* A magic each of you lost when you started skating with Worth and Cissy."

"Worth was a marvelous ice dancer!" Mariah protested, stung.

"Oh, sweetie, I know he was." Lanie's eyes, like Mariah's own, were abruptly shadowed with grief. "But the two of you were only good friends, not lovers . . . and so the chemistry was just missing from the mix—not to mention the fact that Worth's style was as different from Alek's as yours is from Cissy Howland's. The pairings produced competent, professional performances, yes. There's no doubt about that. But the heart and soul that elevate the excellent to the magical just wasn't there, Mariah—for you *or* Alek. And *that's* what makes a performance outstanding and memorable, what brings the audience to its feet and prompts the judges to hand out sixes. Because it's so rare to see that. Only a handful of ice dancers have brought it to the rink—Torvil and Dean, and Klimova and Ponomarenko among them."

Mariah sighed at the mention of these fellow ice dancers, because of all the competition she and Alek had faced during their time together, she had always known that these couples, especially, set the standards for everybody else in the past decade or so, elevating the art with their dramatic and innovative performances. Marina Klimova and Sergei Ponomarenko, especially, were Mariah's idols.

"Much as I hate to admit it, I know you're right, Lanie. If you want to know the truth, I always felt in my heart that Worth should have been paired with Cissy. Still, that doesn't make the prospect of skating with Alek again any easier. Despite everything, I still have...feelings for him, Lanie—and I'm not sure if I can sort out all my emotions and tuck them into neat little compartments for the sake of my art. But I'm not going to back out of the commitment now, if that's what you're worrying about. Letters to Angels is a wonderful program to benefit an extremely worthy cause, and, of course, it goes without saying that the All-Children's Hospital is something I'm proud and glad to support."

"Good," Lanie said briskly. "Then, if you feel like you're warmed up, why don't we get to work?"

Because of Alek's Russian heritage, he and Mariah had developed a practice routine that relied almost as heavily on dance—ballet, especially—as it did upon their actual skating. As a result, after their breakup, Mariah had continued to spend nearly as many hours in the dance studio as she did upon the ice. It was not enough just to learn a dance or program. It took weeks, months, of development, training and refinement to bring a performance to its peak. Although ice dancing lacked the jumps that characterized both individual and pairs skating, it was in other respects more difficult than either, requiring extremely precise footwork and exceptional grace of movement. Ice dancers also had to conform to the regulation that required them not to be physically separated for more than very brief intervals on the ice.

Of course, in a benefit performance such as she and Alek would be doing for the All-Children's Hospital, they could skate any kind of program they wished. Even so, it would be a good place to try out routines they planned to skate later on in competition. So today she and Lanie were going to work on a few ideas to propose to Alek and Jules tomorrow morning, when the four of them were to have their first meeting.

Mariah's heart pounded at the thought of seeing Alek again, of skating with him. The prospect so unsettled her that she flubbed several steps in a row. She could not understand why Lanie merely shook her head and smiled. Lanie had said Alek had agreed to the proposed pairing, but Mariah knew nothing about the telephone conversation her choreographer had had earlier that morning with Jules Straetham—during which he had related to Lanie that the normally cool, arrogant Alek Khazan had just taken a most uncharacteristic spill on the ice, landing flat on his backside.

But even if Mariah *had* known that, she would not have believed it. In the world of figure skating, Alek was frequently referred to behind his back as the Ice Man, because nothing ever unnerved him. Nothing at all. He was as cold as the ice he skated on. As a result, it was absurd that just the thought of him should make her feel so strangely hot and flushed, as though she were melting inside. Absolutely absurd.

Chapter Three

Memories Awaken

It was in the dark, predawn hours that Mariah and Lanie made their way to the local ice rink where Mariah, Alek and various other well-known skaters, both amateur and professional, regularly practiced. Both Mariah and Alek had always preferred the quiet of the early dawn to begin working. It was one of the things that had drawn them together initially as ice-dancing partners, and that was something Mariah could not help thinking about as Lanie pulled the car to a halt in the still-lit parking lot and shut off the engine and headlights.

"Are you ready, sweetie?" Lanie asked, glancing over at Mariah. Wisely, the choreographer had neither chattered like the proverbial magpie nor remained absolutely mute during the drive to the rink. Instead, she had carried on a perfectly normal conversation, speaking when she had had something to say, while at the same time not rushing to fill natural silences.

Mariah nodded, slowly unfastening her seat belt. The fact that she was wearing her seat belt the night of the automobile accident had, she knew without a doubt, saved her life. Neither Worth nor Richard had taken the time to buckle up on that fatal night. Now, even if she were going no more than a block, Mariah always fastened her seat belt, as did Lanie.

Outside, the early-winter air was cool and crisp, with a hint of rain. Dead leaves blown by the wind from the deciduous trees into the parking lot crunched beneath Mariah's feet as, after retrieving their gear bags from the trunk of the car, she and Lanie walked to the building that housed the rink. As Lanie opened the door, Mariah took a deep breath, trying to quell the racing of her heart, the jumping of her nerves. She thought yet again that she had been crazy to agree to this professional reunion of her and Alek. It was all she could do not to turn around and run back to the car, insisting Lanie drive her home. Despite the cold, Mariah's palms, clenched into fists inside the pockets of her bright down ski jacket, were sweating.

Inside, the rink was hushed, its lighting dim, its ice empty. She and Alek were to have the place all to themselves this morning. Mariah marveled that, after this and all the other arrangements had been made, word had not yet leaked to the press. She had expected a horde of media cameras in the parking lot. Instead only Alek and Jules were at the rink. Alek had clearly completed his stretching and other preliminary warm-up exercises, and he was in the process of lacing up his ice skates. At the sight of him, Mariah felt her mouth go abruptly dry and her heart begin to throb deafeningly in her ears. Impossibly, he looked even handsomer, sexier and more potently masculine than ever. He was tall, dark, lean, and superbly muscled, like some sleek, predatory animal, and as she glanced at him, she could not prevent the rush of memory that assailed her, the memory of how those sinuous, hard muscles had felt, bunching and rippling against her naked, sweating skin. To cover her sudden confusion, Mariah turned to Jules Straetham, who had been her own skating coach, as well as Alek's.

"Hello, Jules," she said quietly, holding out her hand. "It's good to see you again."

"Mariah!" The older man's voice boomed as, smiling broadly, he flung out both arms warmly in welcome. "Now, surely, you're not going to stand on ceremony with me!" Then he grabbed her and gave her a big bear hug that, had she been a smaller, less physically fit woman, would doubtless have crushed her.

Against his broad chest, Mariah could feel tears stinging her eyes. She had always liked Jules tremendously and had been very sorry to lose him when she and Alek parted ways. Although she had also liked Richard Underwood, he had been Worth's coach before becoming hers, and she had never felt she and Richard meshed the way she and Jules always had. Grateful Jules held no hard feelings toward her, she hugged him back fervently until he finally released her.

"You're looking as beautiful as ever, Mariah," he declared. Then, as though he sensed Mariah and Alek would prefer to exchange their greetings more privately, he turned to Lanie, standing to one side. "And you, Lanie! You're a sight for sore eyes!"

"Jules, you old rascal, you!" Lanie exclaimed in response.

As though by mutual, unspoken consent, the two coaches strolled away toward the rink, leaving Mariah alone with Alek—despite her urgent, pleading glance in Lanie's direction. Mariah had no choice then but to address Alek himself. Having finished lacing up his ice skates, he had risen to his feet. The blades made him even taller, so that, even though she was a tall woman, he appeared to tower over her, reminding her somehow of a panther poised to spring, animal magnetism and menace seeming to emanate almost tangibly from him.

He had his long, glossy jet-black hair tied back in a ponytail, as he had always worn it at practice, exposing the tiny diamond stud earring in his left ear. His startlingly green eyes glinted like fiery emeralds when caught by the diffuse light, contrasting sharply with the dark stubble of beard that shadowed his face and that Mariah could remember grazing her skin when they had used to make love. The cable-knit sweater he wore matched his eyes, and his black practice pants hugged his legs tightly, emphasizing the superior, powerful muscles that corded his thighs and calves. Despite herself, Mariah could not help but think about how those strong legs had once entangled with her own as he had taken her to the heights of rapture and back.

"Hello, Alek." She nodded in his direction, not offering her hand, wanting to postpone as long as possible the moment when he would touch her again. Her pulse was jerking erratically at the memory of the warmth of his hands, of his skin, of his breath. She could feel a blush creeping into her cheeks as she wondered whether Alek guessed what she was thinking. Somehow, he had always been able to tell.

To hide her discomfiture, Mariah sat down on a bench and shrugged off her ski jacket. Then she bent over the bag in which she carried her gear. Unzipping it, she removed her ice skates and gloves, which she set to one side. After that, she began her stretching and other preliminary warm-up exercises, telling herself it was only these that made her breath come fast, her heart beat too quickly in her breast.

"Hello, Mariah." Alek's voice was low, serrated by emotion he could not quite conceal. Seeing her again, being so close to her again, had affected him deeply. She was, as Jules had noted, as beautiful as ever, he thought as he watched her stretch and bend her body, loosening up her muscles.

Mariah had the figure of a classic ballerina— tall, willowy, with small, high, round breasts and long, graceful arms and legs. In sharp contrast to her gorgeous blue-black hair, her skin was very white and luminescent, like fine porcelain, so her large, liquid midnight-blue eyes seemed to dominate the delicate planes and angles of her face. On the ice, she could appear like spun sugar, like a fairy princess gliding or a swan floating over a still, serene, misted pond—qualities she and Alek had always capitalized on when they had skated together. They had made an extraordinarily striking couple.

Today, Mariah had her long hair twisted up in a French knot, exposing her swanlike nape and throat, to which Alek used to press hot, impassioned kisses. At the remembrance, it was all he could do to prevent himself from bending over her and planting kisses there now as, finished with her exercises, she began to tug on her ice skates.

"I want you to know how sorry I was to hear about your automobile accident, Mariah, about Worth and Richard," he stated awkwardly, instead. "I . . . wanted to come visit you while you were in the hospital. But I—I thought that perhaps you wouldn't want to see me."

"I didn't want to see anybody, actually," Mariah confessed, her head bent as she pre-

tended to concentrate on lacing up her ice
skates—a task that did, indeed, require close attention. Improperly laced ice skates would not
only provide inadequate support on the ice, but
could also prove dangerous, since a dangling lace
or strap could get caught under a blade, sending
a skater sprawling. "It was a very difficult time
for me. But I—I appreciated the flowers and note
you sent, Alek." She did not add that, upon re-
ceiving them, she had wondered if, deep down
inside, he still harbored some feelings for her, as
she did for him.

Finished lacing up her ice skates, she at last
glanced up at him, her breath catching in her
throat at the intensity of his gaze. For a long
moment, silence stretched between them, taut,
expectant, fraught with significance.

"Hey, you two!" Jules shouted, abruptly
breaking the hush, the tension. "Are you going
to gab all morning over there, or are we going to
get some work done here? We only have the rink
for so long, you know, and time's a-wasting."

Alek cleared his throat. "Well, I guess we'd
better get going, or else Jules is liable to have one
of his infamous conniption fits," he said.

"How well I remember those!" Mariah managed a small laugh as she got rather shakily to her

feet. "More than once, I went home in tears after a day of Jules's tirades." She paused briefly, remembering. Then she continued. "But I've been through a lot since then, and I'm no longer the woman I was then. I'm much stronger now, Alek," she asserted, looking him straight in the eye, putting him on notice that neither he nor Jules would find it so easy to intimidate her these days.

But, to her surprise, Alek did not take up the gauntlet she had cast down between them.

"Good. I'm glad to hear that," he replied shortly instead. "You were always much too sensitive, Mariah, too easily hurt, because you took things so much to heart. And in this business, as you know, you've got to be tough to survive. Still, I do hope that, in the process of becoming strong, you've not grown hard, as well. Your femininity, your softness around the edges, was always one of your most appealing qualities."

For an instant, he did not trouble to conceal the heat in his eyes when he gazed at her, and Mariah felt her heart turn over in her breast. Oh, God, she had been such a fool to agree to this reunion, when she knew in her heart that she could not trust herself to keep her emotions under

control when it came to Alek Khazan. Just one
look from him—and she already felt as though
she were melting into a puddle at his feet! So
much for the strength of which she had boasted
only minutes before! With difficulty, she forced
herself to gather her wits and composure.

"Jules and Lanie are waiting," she reminded
him, a trifle breathlessly, as, pulling on her
gloves, she stood and walked toward the rink.

Slipping off her blade protectors and laying
them aside, Mariah stepped out onto the ice,
briefly testing it with a few movements that sent
her sailing gracefully across its hard surface. It
was not new ice, for which she was inordinately
grateful. New ice was brittle, prone to rutting
from the sharp blades—after which it was all too
easy to hit a rut or catch a blade in one. And one
thing she did not want to do this morning was fall
flat on her posterior in front of Alek Khazan.
Presently, he joined her on the ice, his own
movements strong and clean.

"Okay, why don't the two of you get warmed
up?" Jules directed as he watched them. "After
that, the first thing I want to do this morning is
run through some of the technical programs.
We'll do the Starlight Waltz and a couple of others . . . see if you remember any of your old pro-

grams together. Then we'll discuss new routines. You're going to need at least two for the benefit. Lanie, I know, already has some great ideas."

"Yes, I do," the choreographer confirmed.

Mariah and Alek spent several minutes warming up on the ice, skating individually for the time being, for which Mariah was grateful. Since the accident, she had developed a fear she had previously lacked: that her legs would give out under her, that she would slip and fall on the ice especially during a performance. It was an irrational fear, she knew. Now that she was fully recovered, her legs were as strong as ever, despite the occasional twinge of pain—and even those were increasingly few and far between. Besides which, all skaters fell; it was part of the price of the sport. And even though it was extremely unusual for an ice dancer to fall during a performance, it still happened. In ice dancing, more than a matter of score deductions or losing a competition, it brought a feeling of having failed your partner. And since Mariah had always striven to do her best, she loathed the thought of giving any less than that.

Alek, of course, was so single-mindedly driven that, at times in the past, his ambition and determination had frightened her. Now, having worked with Worth, she understood Alek's purposefulness better, because deep down inside she'd known Worth lacked that fine, sharp cutting edge that separated the good from the best, the best from the brilliant.

"All right, Alek...Mariah..." Jules clapped his hands together to get the two skaters' attention. "Lanie's finally all set up now, so let's try the Starlight Waltz, shall we?"

This was the moment Mariah had been dreading—and yet perversely awaiting, too—the moment when Alek would touch her again, when they would skate together again. As always, it was cold upon the ice. Still, she felt heated after her warm-up—although that was not the only reason. All the while she had been skating, she had been all too aware of Alek's proximity on the ice. Now, he was moving toward her—taking her in his arms, in preparation for the Starlight Waltz. He could feel the tension in her body. She knew that when he spoke.

"Relax, Mariah. I'm not going to bite you."

His words did not help, because, of course, there had been a time when he had bitten her, nipped lovingly at her ear, her nape, her shoulder....

"I *am* relaxed," she insisted, although she knew her words for a lie. "Or at least, if I'm nervous, it's got nothing to do with you, Alek! I haven't skated with a partner in a while—or had you forgotten that?"

"No. Yes. Sorry," he said tersely.

A muscle pulsed in Alek's set jaw. His hand tightened involuntarily upon Mariah's waist, so she was aware of his sudden anger at himself. For a moment, holding her in his arms again, he *had* forgotten the accident. All he could remember was the feel of her.

As the opening strains of the waltz drifted over the ice, Mariah felt as though she had somehow been transported back in time, as though she and Alek were once more dancing this technical program in a competition.

Alek was as masterful on the ice as he was on a dance floor, leaving his partner in no doubt as to who was leading whom. As though it were only yesterday, the moves came flooding back to both him and Mariah, as they executed the chassés and mohawks that formed the basis of the Starlight Waltz, following the prescribed pattern, from which there could be no deviation. Even so, each couple had its own individual style, movements and lifts, and Mariah and Alek were no exception to that rule. It was these they now remembered, as though the two of them had never been separated as partners, as though Worth and Cissy had never been.

Watching Mariah and Alek, Jules sighed deeply with satisfaction. Whatever "it" had been—rapport, telepathy, chemistry, magic—the two of them still had it together. They had not lost it, as he had half feared.

"They still look like the couple on top of a wedding cake," Lanie observed softly, echoing aloud the skating coach's thoughts. "Oh, Jules ... This is a good thing you've done. I do think that if you hadn't called me to propose this reunion, Mariah might have given up ice dancing altogether—and it would have been such a pity, such a crime to deprive the world of her talent. She and Alek together have the ability to rank right up there with the very best in the sport. It's not too late."

"No, it's not too late," Jules agreed softly. "We've got a few years to prepare for the next Winter Olympics. Meanwhile, the benefit is an excellent place to begin."

"And I've got some good ideas for choreography, as well as for music and costumes." The music for the Starlight Waltz at last faded to a halt, and Lanie inserted another cassette. On the ice, at Jules's direction, Mariah and Alek started the technical program to this particular music.

As they went on skating fluidly together, Mariah's confidence in her performance, at least, grew steadily. She had until now, she realized, almost forgotten what it was like to skate with Alek, having been compelled these past few years to accustom herself to Worth's style instead. Now she recognized how Worth's affable, easy-going nature, his "Hey, we'll be great, babe" attitude toward his skating, had subtly affected her own performances, eroding her sharpness, her assertiveness, making her as nervous as Worth himself had always been underneath all his bravado. Subconsciously Mariah had always been half-afraid Worth would accidentally drop her during a lift—even though he never had, and had never even given her good cause to suspect he might.

There was just something about Alek's own self-confidence, however, that seemed to communicate itself to her. More than one reporter had remarked that Alek had nerves of pure steel, not to mention incredible strength and stamina. Like Elvis Stojko, Alek had a background in the martial arts, which made him extraordinarily focused when it came to his skating.

But although her confidence in her performance had increased, Mariah's faith in herself had not. Pairs skating and ice dancing were, in many respects, extremely intimate, the male's hands often on his female partner's body in ways and places otherwise familiar only to her husband or lover. Every time Alek's arm brushed her breasts or his hand clasped the inside of her thigh during a lift, she remembered how he had touched her when he had made love to her, and her pulse jerked, deeply unsettling her. She wondered if he, too, was assailed by memories of them lying naked and sweating together, their hearts pounding as one. But she could not bring herself to ask. If she meant nothing to him now, Mariah did not want to know.

For his part, Alek put the slight tension he continued to feel in Mariah's body down to the fact that, as she had reminded him, she had not skated with a partner for a while. Even so, that did not quell the wild desire he had to run his hands over her body in ways that had nothing to do with the technical program the two of them were currently skating together.

Once, late one night after practice, when the rink was dim and deserted, they had made love together on the ice. It had been a mad thing to do—cold, wet and awkward, with both of them shivering, freezing and laughing until, grabbing up her discarded clothes, Mariah finally leaped to her feet and fled, with Alek in hot pursuit. They had wound up in the women's locker room, which had at least been infinitely more comfortable than the ice. But, despite his memory of how chilly the ice had been against their nude skin, Alek was still seized by an urge to throw Mariah down upon it and make love to her then and there.

So it was with both annoyance and relief that he heard the music come to an end at last, and Jules's voice ordering the two of them to take a break. Jules and Lanie were, it seemed, ready to discuss future routines, music and costumes.

"Good skate, Mariah," Alek commented as they left the ice.

"Thank you. It's...very kind of you to say so, Alek—especially since I felt rather wobbly at first."

"That's understandable, I think. You've... had a hard time, a tough break—and I know it can't be easy for you, working with me again, either. I'll be honest with you, Mariah. I wasn't certain how I felt about our skating together again myself. Frankly, I'm still not sure—although, obviously, since we're both here, we're at least willing to give it a try." He paused for a moment, collecting his thoughts. Then he continued. "Earlier, you said you've grown stronger. Now, I'd like to tell you I hope I've grown . . . more tolerant. Since it looks as though we're going to be spending a lot of time together, I just wanted you to know that. I realize I was perhaps . . . too demanding in the past, that maybe I pushed you too hard, too fast. I, ah, don't want to make that mistake again, Mariah. I'd like us to build a good relationship, professionally at least. We had a chance before at Olympic gold, and now, we might have that chance again. So if at any time you feel I'm asking too much of you, I hope you'll let me know."

Mariah was momentarily caught off guard by his words. She had not expected to hear them. The Alek she had known in the past would not have spoken them.

"I . . . don't know what to say, Alek—except that I hope you didn't say all that out of . . . out of some misguided sense of pity for me. Because

I couldn't bear that. I don't want pity, yours or anybody else's. I've got no reason for anyone, least of all you, to feel sorry for me, do you understand? I was the one who survived, remember?''

"Yes, I do—and believe me, what I feel toward you isn't pity. I just wanted to get a few things straight between us right from the start, that's all. There's no real reason why we shouldn't work together, why we *can't* work together, just so long as we understand each other and we're not each at the other's throat all the time. I simply thought things would be easier for us both if we laid out some ground rules, right up front.''

"You're right. Of course, you're right,'' Mariah replied at last as, reaching the edge of the rink, she picked up her blade protectors and slipped them onto the blades of her ice skates. Sitting down on the bench she had used before, she withdrew a towel from her gear bag, wiping off her face and throat before slinging the towel around her neck. She tugged off her gloves, and took a drink of mineral water. "It's the sensible course of action.''

"And that surprises you?'' Alek, too, had opted for the bottled water over the coffee Lanie had offered him. Upending the container, he emptied it in three long swallows.

"A little," Mariah admitted. "The Alek Khazan I used to know wasn't particularly concerned about whether or not he trampled on other people's feelings. He was always more interested in taking first place."

"I suppose I deserved that."

"No, you didn't, actually—and I was sorry I said it the moment the words left my mouth. It was a low blow, uncalled-for under the circumstances. I guess I'm still slightly on edge and, to be honest, kind of thrown for a loop by your behavior, Alek. It's . . . not what I expected. We hardly parted friends."

"No, we didn't. But we can hardly go on being enemies if we're going to work together. So, what do you say to our letting bygones be bygones and starting afresh?"

"I say that's a deal."

"Are you two done yakking over there and ready to pay attention?" Jules asked gruffly, interrupting their conversation. "It's like I keep telling you, we've got work to do!"

"That we do, Coach," Alek agreed as he sprawled in his seat, stretching out his long, muscular legs and crossing them at the ankles.

"Yes, let's get back to work," Mariah urged. "Tell us what you and Jules have in mind, Lanie."

"Okay." After putting on her reading glasses, Lanie produced a sheaf of notes she had made to herself. "You'll be doing two numbers at the benefit, and since this will be your first appearance together following your reunion, I believe people are going to want to see if the two of you still have 'that old black magic' together. Jules agrees with me. Neither of us feels a program to music that's peppy and popular is going to be particularly conducive to proving that. On the other hand, since Letters to Angels *is* a program to benefit children, we don't want something classical or operatic, either. It might win points with the judges, but it's not going to be particularly appealing to children. We have an additional problem in that we've got a lot of ground to cover, a lot of work to make up since your separation, so we really can't afford to waste time developing programs you might only skate once or twice." Lanie paused, shuffling her papers, and, with a pencil she took from behind her ear, made additional notes to herself on them. Then she continued.

"I've got two possible songs and a third song I believe we definitely ought to use. The first two are both Whitney Houston songs, slow and emotional enough that we can put together the type of dramatic routine the two of you used to skate together and that I think people will be expecting. One is 'The Greatest Love of All,' the other is 'One Moment in Time,' and personally, I'm inclined toward it. It's a very inspirational number from the '88 Summer Olympics. Might remind people of your Olympic potential." Lanie grinned. "The third tune is entitled—appropriately enough—'Mariah.' It's an old country-western song, but it can be reworked with a hint of blues, perhaps."

Again Lanie paused to jot down notes on her papers. Then she went on. "Now, as to costumes...I'm open to suggestions for the Whitney Houston number. I do, however, have definite ideas about the costumes for the 'Mariah' routine. Alek, I'd like to see you dressed totally in black. We might use some bugle beads on your shirt and down the sides of your pants, put a bandanna around your neck to give you a 'lethal gunslinger' appearance. Since you, Mariah, will obviously be the wind they call Mariah in this number, I see you dressed totally in white . . . something light, airy and flowing. I'd like your hair to be loose, too, so we can really give the impression that you're a wild, western wind and that Alek is the only man brave enough to attempt to tame you.''

"Well, I like the sound of that," Alek drawled insolently, glancing speculatively from beneath lazily hooded lids at Mariah, by his side. His green eyes glinted, as though twin flames burned in their depths, as his gaze raked her slowly, lingering on her mouth, her breasts.

To her dismay, she could prevent neither the blush that crept up to stain her cheeks, nor the strange, electric tingle that coursed through her body at his appraisal. Surely he could not think that, just because she had agreed to work with him again, she would also consent to sharing his bed once more! Earlier, he had addressed only their professional relationship. He had not mentioned their personal one. And no matter what her feelings toward Alek Khazan were, Mariah had no intention of becoming involved with him again. He had broken her heart once. She was not going to give him an opportunity to do that a second time!

"I agree the tune has good dramatic possibilities, Lanie," Mariah said to cover her confusion. "But shouldn't the wind triumph in the end? I mean, after all, the wind is far stronger than any mere man." She allowed her words, with their underlying meaning, to speak for her to Alek.

"I think we need to see some of the choreography Lanie has in mind for the number before we make any concrete decisions about just how it will play and just who will prevail over whom," Jules declared tactfully. "So, why don't we do this... you and Alek get together, Mariah, and decide which one of the Whitney Houston songs you like best. Also, I'll want to hear both theme and costume ideas from you, once you've picked one of those two tunes. Meanwhile, since it seems we're all in agreement that we will do the 'Mariah' routine, why don't we meet at Lanie's dance studio tomorrow morning, and she can show us exactly what she has in mind for it."

"Excellent suggestions, Jules. Are we done for today, then?" Alek asked, slowly straightening in his seat, his hands already moving to the lacings on his ice skates.

The older man nodded. "Yes, we're done."

"Then why don't you have Lanie run you home, Jules, and I'll take Mariah with me. We can grab some breakfast somewhere, listen to those two songs together, and start working up some ideas to present to the two of you tomorrow morning. I can drop Mariah by her place later, when we're done. If that's all right with you, Mariah?'' Alek turned to her inquiringly.

She knew him too well, however, to be fooled by his seeming innocence. How cleverly and smoothly he had maneuvered things so that he could get her alone with him. But did she truly have cause to be suspicious of his motives? she wondered. Perhaps, because of her past experience with him, she was reading more into the situation than was warranted. After all, following their breakup, Alek had kept his distance from her; he had not sought to pursue her again. And how on earth was she planning on working with him if she insisted on having a third party present whenever they were together? That was just plain foolish. It was not as though she were afraid of Alek . . . not exactly. She just did not know if she was indeed strong enough to resist him if he turned the full force of his devilish, sexy charm on her again—especially if, as it appeared from his words earlier, he had changed in ways she had always hoped and wished for.

''Sure, that'll be just fine, Alek,'' Mariah answered his question at last, forcing herself to speak casually, and shrugging her shoulders slightly to show she could not have cared less, one way or another, what the car-pool arrangements were. "We have to start somewhere, sometime, and I guess it might as well be here and now. We don't have that much time. If the benefit is to be broadcast on TV on Christmas Eve, I assume we'll be taping before then."

"Well, get your ice skates off, then, and let's hit the locker rooms." Alek was already putting his own ice skates into his gear bag. "Lanie, Jules, we'll see you two later. Oh, and, Lanie, don't forget to leave us those two tapes."

Lanie handed them to Alek. "Mariah, sweetie, why don't you give me a call when you get home?"

"Will do," Mariah said.

Gathering up all their paraphernalia, Lanie and Jules departed, so that all too soon, Mariah was left alone with Alek in the dim, deserted building. Just as she had been on the ice, she was acutely aware of him, even though he was not now touching her. Once she grew accustomed to being around him again, she was sure, the sensation would pass. He was just a man, like any other—except that, for her, there was no other and had been no other for more than two years.

Well, she would just have to get over him, that was all. Resolutely she put her ice skates in her gear bag, then zipped it shut and slung it over her shoulder. At her abrupt action, Alek, too, stood and, without speaking, they headed for the locker rooms.

Chapter Four

This Ice Isn't New

In the past two years, when she entered the women's locker room at the rink, Mariah had only occasionally thought about the night she and Alek had made love here. But this morning that memory, like her others of Alek, was uppermost in her mind. As she stripped and showered, she recalled standing naked with him beneath the warm spray of the shower head, after they had made love, and how they had laughed together and soaped each other leisurely, becoming aroused again, and he had taken her once more, this time against the shower wall.

Mariah wanted to wash away those memories. Still, they came, flooding over her like the water that streamed from the shower head. She had a mental image of Alek in the men's locker room, standing in the men's shower, nude and separated from her only by the tiled wall between them. When she closed her eyes against the spray, she could see every plane and angle of his tall, dark bare body, sleek and powerful with hard muscle, his broad chest dusted with fine black hair, his flat, firm belly, his lean hips and buttocks, his corded thighs and calves. She wondered if he was even now picturing her as she was him, and her breath caught in her throat at the thought. What would she do if he suddenly came striding into the women's locker room, naked and dripping wet, to press her against the shower wall again?

She simply *must* stop thinking about him like this! Mariah told herself, silently but sharply. It was over between them—and even if they were ice dancing together professionally once more, she could not, *would* not, let herself get involved with him on a personal level again!

Stepping from the shower, she toweled herself dry, then dressed in fresh clothes, rolling up her practice garments and stuffing them in her gear bag. When she exited the women's locker room, she saw that Alek was already waiting for her in the corridor beyond.

"I thought we'd go to the Irish Coffeehouse," he told her. "You always liked their Top of the Morning breakfast, and one of those sounds pretty good to me right now, too, after the workout Jules gave us."

"That . . . that would be fine, Alek," Mariah replied reluctantly as they left the building and started toward his car in the parking lot. She would have preferred to go somewhere else, someplace that did not hold so many memories. She wished Alek was not being so courteous, that he did not recall her favorite breakfast—or anything else about her, either. It would be easier— much easier—to hold him at arm's length that way, to tamp down the emotions and longings roiling inside her, to tell herself he had never truly cared for her, that they would never have made it together as husband and wife. But if she suggested the two of them eat breakfast elsewhere, Alek would surely suspect why she did not want to go to the Irish Coffeehouse. Perhaps he was even testing her again, trying to determine her feelings toward him. "I could use a cup of hot coffee, too, right about now." She forced herself to speak casually.

"Good." Taking his key ring from the pocket of the black wool topcoat he now wore, Alek popped open the trunk of his British-racing-green Jaguar XJ6, stowing his gear bag and

Mariah's own. Then he slammed shut the lid and opened the passenger door for her.

Even his car evoked memories for her, she thought as she slid into the rich buckskin-leather seat, drawing the seat belt across her body and fastening it. She had ridden in the Jaguar countless times before now, in the days when she and Alek were an "item" in the world of figure skating, and even before then, when they were involved only on a professional level. They had been friends before becoming lovers. She remembered that, too, as he opened the driver's door and slipped into the seat beside her. That had been one of the most devastating things for her when they had parted ways: She had not only had her heart broken, she had also lost her best friend.

Inserting his key into the ignition, Alek started up the car and pulled away from the parking lot, which was no longer so deserted, now that other skaters were arriving. Mariah had to quell the sudden, wild urge she had to crouch down in the seat, so that nobody would observe her and Alek together.

"It's only a matter of time until everybody knows about our professional reunion, Mariah," Alek remarked, somehow reading her mind, as he always had.

"Was I cringing that obviously?" She laughed softly, ruefully, trying to make light of the uncanny intuition it seemed he still possessed where she was concerned.

"No, not really. It's just that I haven't forgotten, either, what it was like for us. Living under the telescopic lenses of the media. Always having to be 'on' for the cameras. These days a relationship is difficult enough, without that added strain. I suppose it's no wonder so many marriages between celebrities fail."

His implication was that their own marriage, had it gone forward, would have failed, too, sooner or later. Mariah wondered if this were his way of hinting that, even if he might be interested in sleeping with her again, he would not have marriage in mind.

"Yes, I suppose so," she agreed slowly, after a moment. "But then, I believe that any two individuals these days, whether celebrities or not, have to be very much in love, very strong and committed, to make a marriage work." She knew there was a wealth of underlying meaning and rebuke in her words. But somehow, Mariah could not make herself stop speaking. "Life itself has become a competition, Alek, and the pressure is tremendous, with much more than an Olympic gold medal at stake. It's hard to be friends, much less lovers, if all the hours of all your days are taken up with trying to be the king rat in a race that has no finish line. If at night you're so tired that all you want to do is fall into bed and sleep forever. And if when you think of your partner at all, you feel guilty for thinking of him or her so little.

"I know it sounds like a cliché, but there really *is* something to be said for taking time to smell the flowers while you have the chance. Because, otherwise, you're bound to wake up one morning and realize it's too late. And I feel certain that, when you finally *do* come to understand that, all you've achieved is outweighed by your regrets. Worse, not taking that time somehow seems like a sin, when you think of all the people who never have that time allotted to them. Kids, especially, like so many of those at the All-Children's Hospital. Kids who are dying before they've ever even had the chance to live. Kids who will never know what it means to grow old with someone they love—" Mariah broke off abruptly, tears unexpectedly stinging her eyes and a lump rising in her throat, choking her.

Pretending to have suddenly spotted something of interest out the window, she quickly turned her head away so that Alek would not spy her tears. She wished she had her hair down, loose, so that she could hide behind it, so that he could not see her face, even in profile.

Not only had she revealed too much of her own feelings toward Alek, her own regrets about their failed relationship, but she absolutely hated and deeply mourned the fact that any child should die. Life was short enough as it was—and so terribly unfair. Death was for those who were too old and too tired to care about living anymore—not for children, who were young and vibrant and eager to live.

"Each of us does what he or she can, Mariah," Alek said quietly. To spare her embarrassment, he spoke as though the thought of the kids at the All-Children's Hospital alone were the cause of her tears, although, deep down inside, he knew that it was not, that he had hurt her deeply. How he regretted that—now, when it was perhaps too late for them. "With our ice dancing, we'll not only be entertaining those children, but also raising money to benefit them. The Letters to Angels program will make some of those children's dreams come true, at least."

Mariah nodded. "It's such a wonderful program ... and so thought-provoking sometimes, to learn what the children have wished for in their letters to their 'angels.'" She was glad her voice quavered only a little as she strove to speak normally, to recover her composure. "A lot of them want only to go to Disney World before they die. But some of them ask for a horse and a pasture to ride it in, or a fishing hole in a little woods, or a vacant lot with a baseball diamond on it. When I hear all those kids' dreams, I can't help but wonder what those boys and girls might have become if they hadn't been stricken with a terminal disease...whether they would have grown up to become scientists or politicians, artists or builders. And I wonder what the world has lost because those children will never reach adulthood." Mariah paused for a minute, dwelling on the terrible tragedy of that loss. Then she continued. "I'd like for our Whitney Houston number to be something really special for those kids, Alek. Do you have those two cassettes Lanie gave you?"

"Yes, I do." Reaching into his coat's inside pocket, he withdrew the two tapes. "Why don't we go ahead and give them a listen?" he suggested. "We've got some time before we get to the Irish Coffeehouse, seeing as how we seem to have caught the tail end of the morning rush-hour traffic.'' He grimaced wryly as he nosed the Jaguar forward, down one of the town's busy main streets.

Mariah put the first tape in, and within moments, the strains Whitney Houston's beautiful voice filled the car as she sang about the greatest love of all. Alek and Mariah did not talk while the tune played, each of them instead listening intently to the slowly building music, envisioning the way in which they might ice-dance to it. When it had ended, Mariah removed the tape and popped the second one into the cassette player. The minute she heard this song—"One Moment in Time''—she knew her choreographer's instincts were right on target, that this was the one she and Alek should dance to. Not only was it a powerful melody, but the lyrics just seemed inordinately appropriate, since they were all about wanting just one moment in time, when dreams were only a heartbeat away and you were the best you could be. After all, that was really what the Letters to Angels program was all about, Mariah thought, giving those kids just that one moment in time when their dreams came true and they were on top of the world.

"That's it. That's the one," she declared firmly.

"I think so, too," Alek agreed as he pulled the Jaguar into an empty space in the parking lot of the Irish Coffeehouse. "So let's eat—and talk about costumes, why don't we?"

Open twenty-four hours a day, the Irish Coffeehouse, decorated with lots of hanging plants, brass pots and Irish paraphernalia, was a popular restaurant. But since the workday had finally begun, the place was largely empty now. Mariah and Alek waited briefly until a table by the large windows that flanked three sides of the building was cleaned. Then the hostess led them to the cheerful dark green vinyl booth, handing them each a plastic-encased menu. Mariah barely glanced at hers before she laid it aside. Moments later, Alek tossed his menu on top of hers.

"So...what thoughts do you have about costumes?" he inquired as he shrugged off his topcoat and folded it up beside him on the seat.

"I'm not sure, really." Mariah slipped off her ski jacket and laid it aside. "Two ideas came to mind while we were listening to the song. The first is that we wear something really bright and jazzy, in a fabric with swirls of color that make it look like a rainbow. I think that would be appealing to the children, at any rate.''

"Yes, very appealing, I should imagine." Alek nodded. "But do you really think rainbows suit the tempo and mood of the song? They always make me think of cotton-candy clouds and wizened leprechauns, of four-leaf clovers and pots of gold.''

"True. But then, pursuing dreams can also be thought of as chasing rainbows," she reminded him. Like the dream she had years ago that one day she and Alek would be married. Dreaming that *was* like chasing a rainbow—only there was no pot of gold at the end of it for her. No, maybe bright rainbow colors wasn't the way to go, after all. "I have another idea.''

"Which is?''

"We're both in midnight-blue costumes, with small gold suns, moons and stars. You know, going after your dreams can also be called reaching for the stars. That way, the costumes would be much more dramatic—and as I recall, one of the playrooms at the All-Children's Hospital has a dark blue ceiling with tiny stars scattered all over it, so it looks like a midnight sky.''

"You know, I think you're right about that. I like that idea. Midnight blue it is, then.''

Before they could talk further, one of the waitresses appeared at their booth. She was plainly frazzled from her busy morning, tendrils of dusky-brown hair escaping from beneath the cap of her uniform and her apron slightly askew around her waist. Still, she was young and bubbly enough to make light of her day so far, blowing her fringe of too-long bangs up out of her eyes and then wrinkling the pert nose on her Pollyanna face as she smiled at Mariah and Alek. Mariah could not refrain from smiling back when she noted that, ironically, the name tag on the waitress's blouse actually read Polly.

"What a day! I swear, my poor feet are swollen up like a couple of fat old toads this morning!" the girl announced artlessly. "What'll you have, folks?"

"Two Top of the Morning breakfasts, and lots of hot black coffee," Alek told her.

"Coming right up." True to her word, Polly reappeared moments later with their coffee.

Mariah also noticed how, from beneath her lashes, the waitress eyed Alek admiringly. As she poured the coffee, she stole glances at Alek and smiled openly at him. Women were seldom immune to Alek's good looks and charm, and Polly's flirting really didn't bother Mariah. She knew that, since her breakup with him, there had been no one to speak of in his life. Like her, he had had the occasional casual date, but there was nobody about whom he was serious. Mostly he had thrown himself into his work, as she had her own. Only now, this morning, was Mariah willing to admit for the first time that, as much as she loved ice dancing, her total dedication to it for the past two years had been as much to try to forget Alek as it had been to hone her craft. And, to some extent, her devotion had worked. There had been long blocks of time during her days when she had not thought about Alek Khazan at all.

It had been during her nights that he haunted her. Although, during her practice sessions, she had driven herself to the point of exhaustion to ensure that she would fall asleep the moment her head hit her pillow, the attempt had proved futile. No matter how tired, she had lain awake at night instead, tossing and turning, thinking of him, missing him, and wondering just where and when their relationship had gone so wrong. Mariah had found no easy answers; she had known that, in some respects, she had been as much to blame as Alek for their breakup.

She sipped her black coffee gratefully. It was steaming-hot, and took the chill from her bones. Because she spent so much time on the ice, she did not seem to be as susceptible to the cold as most people. She had, she thought, somehow become acclimated to it. Still, winter had come early this year and threatened to be bitter. The wind outside, although not strong, was sharp and crisp. From the gray clouds in the sky, a drizzle had begun that promised sleet or snow in the hours to come.

"Well, now that we've got the costumes settled, what about ideas for the program itself?" Mariah asked, turning from the bleak, wintry view afforded by the wide windows to resume the conversation that had been interrupted by the waitress's arrival. "Lanie and Jules both seemed very keen on something dramatic."

"Yes, well, those always *were* the most effective routines for us, Mariah, the ones we skated best together," Alek pointed out. "And since this is a comeback for us, I think you'd also agree we want our first program to make the unmistakable statement that not only are we back together professionally, but we're better than ever. After all, it never hurts to shake the competition up a little, does it?" He grinned at her—the beautiful, familiar grin that had always made her heart turn over in her breast.

To Mariah's dismay, this morning was no exception. Her heart began to thud so loudly that she thought Alek must surely hear it. To hide her sudden consternation and confusion, she took another long swallow of her coffee before replying.

"Naturally, it always helps to have a psychological edge over the competition—especially those who have a tendency to crumble under pressure."

They both knew that, over the years, the sport had seen its fair share of skaters who gave way under the enormous strain of competition, skaters known for their erratic performances, skaters who excelled at the Olympics, only to fall apart at the World Championships, and vice versa. It took a special breed of athlete to compete successfully in any sport, to endure the rigors of training, of performing, and the harsh glare of the media's spotlights. Not every athlete, no matter how he or she excelled at his or her chosen sport, was cut out for all the things that accompanied it. Like any good team, Alek and Mariah knew that, and they had capitalized on it in the past, as they would again in the future. It was one of the things that helped to set the best apart from all the rest, and the competition Alek and Mariah faced as ice dancers was stiff.

"So it would appear we have a consensus," Alek noted, nudging Mariah from her reverie. "We'll want to make the two routines totally different, while retaining their drama. Since 'Mariah' is going to be about a man attempting to tame a wild wind and will have an underlying western flavor, I vote we go with a much more classical routine for 'One Moment in Time,' something spiritual and uplifting, to suit the music's lyrics."

"Yes, that's what I think, too." Mariah was surprised to discover how easily she and Alek were reaching agreements this morning. In the past, it had been common for the two of them to argue about just about everything, from costumes to the interpretation of their music. Maybe Alek had indeed changed; equally as startling was the thought that maybe *she* had changed, too.

A few minutes later, Polly appeared with their breakfasts.

"I feel so stupid," she announced as she set their plates in front of them. "I thought the two of you looked familiar. But it took me a while to figure it out. You're Alek Khazan and Mariah Nichols, the ice dancers, aren't you?'' At their nods of confirmation, she rushed on. ''Wow! Is my mom ever going to be impressed when she finds out I waited on you two this morning! She's been a big fan of skating for years, long before the Tonya Harding–Nancy Kerrigan fiasco.'' The waitress pulled her order pad from the pocket of her apron and tore off a sheet. ''Would it be a terrible imposition to get your autographs for her? Her name's Helen . . . Helen Edwards.''

''We'd be happy to sign an autograph for her,'' Mariah said, taking the pen Polly handed her. After addressing a little note to Polly's mother, Mariah signed her name with a flourish before passing the pen and paper to Alek. ''It's always nice to hear the public enjoys figure skating as much as we do. It didn't used to be such a popular and well-known sport. In fact, it never ceases to amaze me that, despite all the great skaters in the past—skaters like Peggy Fleming and Dorothy Hamill, for example—it was the Tonya Harding–Nancy Kerrigan feud that really focused a spotlight on the world of figure skating. Unfortunately, that did more to bolster our ratings than all the brilliant spins and fabulous jumps in history.''

"Well, you certainly do see a lot more of figure skating on TV these days,'' Polly declared. "My mom's glued to her set every other week, it seems. Why, I honestly believe she'd run off with that Philippe Candeloro!''

"So would a lot of other women.'' Mariah smiled. Philippe was quite handsome, and extremely popular with the female fans of the sport. "Instead of bouquets and stuffed animals, I always half expect to see undergarments and hotel keys tossed out onto the ice following one of Philippe's performances.''

Polly grinned. "Wow! That must be something, knowing all those other skaters! Are you friends with any of them? I mean...how *can* you be, when they're your competition and all?''

"Well, we don't compete against *all* of them.'' Alek spoke up as he handed Polly her pen and paper back. "Only the other ice dancers. And some of those we used to compete against have turned professional in recent years, although it's possible these days to have your amateur status reinstated, even so. But really, despite the fact that they're competitors, many skaters are good friends. It's such a consuming sport that you don't have a whole lot of time for a social life beyond it, so you tend to be drawn to other skaters who know what it's like on the circuit.''

''Yeah, that makes sense, I guess.'' Polly nodded her understanding. ''Well, I guess I've taken up enough of your time. Thank you so much for the autographs! Mom'll just be thrilled! You two enjoy your breakfast now, and give me a holler if you need anything else.''

When Polly had gone, Alek picked up a slice of toast and, after opening a small plastic container of grape jelly, began to spread it with a knife on the buttery toast. ''I never before realized you found Philippe Candeloro so attractive.'' His tone was casual, but Mariah was not deceived.

She knew him so well that her pulse leaped with sudden excitement. Why, he was jealous! Of course, with both Alek and Philippe being so good-looking, there had always been something of a rivalry between them. But, surely, for Alek to express interest in her thoughts about Philippe could only mean he still had feelings for her. For a moment, although she knew Philippe only to speak to at competitions, she was tempted to insinuate that the two of them were more than just friends. But she couldn't.

"I hardly know him, actually. I was just stating my observations about him. Why?"

"Oh, no real reason." Alek shrugged nonchalantly as he concentrated on his breakfast. "Just curious, I guess."

But, of course, he would not have been curious if he had no interest in her, Mariah told herself again. Still, she would be foolish to get her hopes up, based on an offhand question. Foolish to become involved with him again at all, she reminded herself stringently.

So what if, despite everything, she still found Alek Khazan one of the handsomest, sexiest, most masculine men alive, and all her old feelings for him had rushed up to engulf her this morning? There was no future in loving him. She had already learned that the hard way. She did not want or need a second lesson.

Chapter Five

Do You Remember When?

In the days and then weeks that passed, Mariah was to remind herself more than once of her conviction that morning at the Irish Coffeehouse. Because, despite all her determination, it was not easy for her to avoid being drawn to Alek again. No matter how hard she fought her feelings for him, it seemed that, at every turn, her resolve weakened. He watched her every move with a fierce, hungry intensity that both frightened and excited her. In the past, such glances had led eventually to his impassioned lovemaking, which had left her breathless, exhausted and exhilarated. Especially difficult were practice sessions at the dance studio, at which Lanie was not always present to defuse tensions. At those times, Mariah was acutely aware of Alek's strong hands moving on her body, of his and her reflections in the mirrors that lined the dance studio's walls. The two of them were tall, black-haired, elegant, and striking together. They danced together as though they were performing some elaborate mating ritual—chassés, mohawks, lifts and spins all a prelude to something much more sensuous and serious, something that made Mariah's heart beat fast and Alek's voice grow hoarse as he called out the moves.

"Lay back," he uttered huskily now, his hands beneath her body, holding her as she bent deeply backward.

Once in position, performing what Lanie referred to as "snake arms," Mariah brought her hands up, only to bring them rippling slowly, sinuously, downward. The movement was made even more exquisite by the fact that, while she did it, she brought the thumbs and middle fingers of her hands together lightly, a small trick Lanie had taught her for giving the hands a more graceful appearance.

"Very good, Mariah," Alek uttered softly.

He was bent over her, his powerful legs spread, his hands holding her waist firmly. In this particular pose, his dark, handsome face was almost pressed against her breasts, which swelled above the V neckline of her black leotard. Mariah could feel his breath, warm and harsh against her skin, which was glistening with sweat from their practice session, and gradually she became conscious of the fact that her nipples had hardened, of their own accord, at the erotic sensation. They strained so rigidly against the fabric of her leotard that Alek could not help but be aware of them.

In the next moment, she knew it was so, as her midnight-blue eyes met his brilliant green ones, the intensity of his gaze taking away her breath. She had seen that look on his hard, lean visage in the past, a look that said he wanted her, had to have her—now. Both she and he froze in place. Silence seemed to stretch interminably between them, fraught with tension and expectation. Mariah could hear her heart beating so loudly in her ears that the sound deafened her. A small gasp escaped from her lips as, without warning, Alek's eyes darkened with desire. Then he abruptly buried his face between her breasts, his hands sliding roughly, urgently, up her body, tightening on her rib cage, his thumbs circling and caressing her nipples lightly.

"Mariah," he groaned, low against her skin. "Mariah."

She was vividly conscious of his swift, sudden arousal—and of her own response, the abrupt rush of heat that flooded her entire being. Her common sense told her to pull away from him before it was too late. But her heart cried out otherwise, and of their own volition, her arms wound around Alek's neck as his mouth descended to claim hers. In that instant, it was as though more than two years had not passed since he had last kissed her—while, at the same time, those years of separation imbued the kiss with a fierceness, passion and longing that spoke more eloquently than words could have of his desire for her. His lips moved on hers, devouring her hungrily, as he clasped her to him, pulling her upright and spinning her around to press her against the mirrored wall. His tongue outlined her mouth, then boldly insinuated itself inside, tasting, savoring, setting Mariah's heart to pounding even harder and faster than before. The chemistry between them was as hot and explosive as it had ever been, as though, during their time apart, it had not died, but instead had smoldered like embers, waiting for this moment, when it would again be fanned to flame.

Fingers tense and splayed, her hands framed Alek's face, combed back the strands of his hair that had come loose from his ponytail and that now, glossy and damp with sweat, tangled around his dark visage. Mariah could feel his hands roaming over her body ardently as he kissed her. The rough stubble of his beard grazed her skin, arousing her wildly. She opened her lips to his, sighing into his mouth as he swallowed her breath. Her tongue darted forth to tease and twine with his. All the old familiar feelings she had tried so hard to keep at bay now broke down the walls she had erected around her heart. In some dark corner of her mind, Mariah knew she had never stopped loving Alek Khazan. He had only to take her in his arms again and she melted like ice beneath a spring sun, her bones dissolving, leaving her weak and pliant against him, wanting him.

She was only dimly aware of his hands at her shoulders, sensuously sliding the sleeves of her leotard down to bare her braless breasts. His palms cupped them possessively. "Champagne breasts," he had always called them, insisting they would fill a champagne glass to perfection. Circles of delight radiated from their centers as he touched and stroked them eagerly, tearing his lips from hers to envelop one firm, flushed nipple. His mouth was hot, greedy, as he suckled her, his tongue licking and laving the stiff peak, before moving to its twin. Mariah's fingers burrowed convulsively through his hair, drawing him even nearer to her.

"Mariah . . . oh, Mariah . . ." Alek murmured against her breasts, his breath brushing her nipples enticingly. "How I've missed you . . . ached for you . . ."

Fervidly his lips seared their way up her slender throat, back to her mouth, his tongue plunging deep. Mariah moaned low against his lips as he kissed her, his hands continuing to caress her breasts, to stimulate their rosy crests. No one had ever stirred her as Alek did, made her feel as though her entire body were being consumed by flames, growing molten, becoming a mass of liquid fire and sensation. She burned at the very core of her being, ached for him to lay her down upon the hardwood floor and make love to her. Still, realistically, she knew that if he did, she would once more be swept away by him, would lose herself to him—only to have her heart broken again. And so, now, at last, reason prevailed, and she wrenched her mouth from his.

"Stop, Alek. Please . . . stop . . ." she whispered breathlessly, pressing one trembling hand to her lips and the other against his chest, holding him at bay.

"Mariah . . . why? You want this as much as I do. I can feel that in every fiber of your being, in the way you respond to me. And it's not as though this is something new for us. We were lovers before."

"Yes, but we're not now, and I—I don't know where this will lead, what it is you want from me. I don't want to sleep with you just because there are still . . . feelings of attraction between us, Alek. I *won't* do that. I'm just not the one-night-stand type. I never have been."

"Don't you think I know that?" He stared down at her sharply for a minute. Then, muttering an imprecation, he turned away from her, running one hand raggedly through his hair. A muscle flexed in his set jaw, visible evidence of the emotions that roiled within him. "I promised myself I wouldn't start anything like this. I don't know what I was thinking just now—except that I wanted you. There's been no one since you, Mariah. I've missed you. Sometimes I think I was the world's biggest fool ever to let you get away from me."

"What . . . what is it you're saying, Alek?" she asked, drawing her leotard up to cover her nakedness, not daring to hope he wished to renew their engagement, not knowing how she would answer if he did—because how could she risk her heart again?

"That I want you back in my life, Mariah." Alek paused for a moment, considering, gathering his thoughts. Then he continued. "Look, maybe I was only fooling myself, but I believed we could work together professionally without becoming involved together personally once more. But these passing weeks have made it clear to me that's not what I want—and I don't think you want that, either. We belong together, Mariah. I feel that so strongly inside, and I believe you feel it, too. We made a mistake before. But it's not too late for us."

"Yet you were willing enough before to call off our marriage, Alek," she replied defensively, playing for time. "At least, you didn't protest when I returned the engagement ring you bought for me. Now it seems you would have us pick up exactly where we left off—as though more than two years haven't come and gone. I just don't know if I can do that, Alek. In all honesty, I don't know if I'm strong enough to go through all that pain again, if things don't work out between us. And why should this time be any different from before?"

"Because we've both changed?" he suggested. "Because we're both older, wiser, more experienced, better equipped to handle the stress and strain of our careers combined with our personal lives?"

"That's not exactly what you said that first day of our reunion, on our way to the Irish Coffeehouse. You said then that marriages between celebrities are apt to fail—and you implied that would have been the fate of our own marriage, had we gone through with it."

"Yes, well, maybe I've decided I was wrong about that."

"Maybe so," Mariah agreed slowly. "But you see, Alek, I can't be certain whether it was your heart or your hormones that led you to this new conclusion, and neither can you. And I'm afraid that, when it comes to my own heart, I'm not nearly as strong as I claimed that first day, but . . . terribly vulnerable."

"I know I hurt you before. But you must believe me when I say I would never hurt you again, Mariah," Alek insisted softly. "I'm not a fool who can't—or won't—learn from his mistakes. I know you've been through a lot these past few years. And despite how I've tried to fight my feelings for you, I also know—and *you* must know—that I still love you."

"Do you, Alek?" she asked quietly, her heart at once soaring with joy and clenching with pain at his words. It seemed she had waited forever to hear him speak those words once more. Yet, now that he had, she was not sure she could set aside the past, commit herself to him again. "Do you really?"

"Yes, I do. I never stopped loving you. Our breakup was as painful for me as it was for you, Mariah. Why do you think there's been no one else in my life since then?" He fell silent once more, allowing her to absorb his words. Then he spoke. "If I give you back the engagement ring you returned to me, will you wear it again?"

"You mean you still have it?" She was surprised and touched by the admission. She would have guessed he had thrown the ring away in a fit of temper and hurt. The fact that he had kept it, instead, spoke volumes.

"Oh, Mariah." Alek's voice was low and contained an underlying note of anguish. "Of course I still have it. How could you think otherwise? What can I do to prove myself to you?"

"Be my friend, as you used to be. That was one of the things that hurt the most about our breakup, you know. I not only lost my lover, but also my best friend. There were so many times when I wanted to call you, to cry on your shoulder. But I couldn't—because *you* were the man I wanted to talk about, to be consoled about." She gave a small, wry, tremulous laugh at the irony of it, blinking back tears at the memory. "So, please don't press me for a decision right now. Give me some time to think about all this, Alek."

"I understand, and it's all right, Mariah. Really, it is. If that's the way you want it, then that's the way it will be. I'm willing to give our personal relationship the time you're asking for, however long it may take, and to go slowly, to get it right this time." After a moment, he gave her a crooked smile. "So, back to the old grindstone, then. Where were we?"

"Ah...at the layback," Mariah reminded him, even though she knew from the sudden deviltry that danced in his eyes, the manner in which his grin widened on his face, that he remembered as well as she. "But perhaps we should just forget that part and go on from there."

"Too bad. It would have been nice to practice that move all afternoon. But...so much for that idea. Do you want to run the tape back, or shall I?''

''I'll do it.'' Glad of an excuse to move away from him for a minute, Mariah walked over to the boom box that sat on the floor and punched the rewind button.

If she was honest with herself, she'd admit that, ever since consenting to their reunion, she'd harbored the hope that she and Alek would get back together not only professionally, but also personally. Still, she had never expected him to make the first move in that direction, to declare himself so openly, to confess he still loved her. *He still loved her!* Her heart thrilled at that knowledge. It was only her doubts and fear that caused her to tread cautiously, to hang back, when she yearned to fling herself into his arms.

The music started again, its powerful, soaring strains filling the dance studio. Despite herself, the beautiful notes were like wings beneath Mariah's heart as she laid her hand in Alek's own and they began to move together as one, turning, twining, oblivious of all but each other as they danced.

Chapter Six

On This Wintry Night

Mariah had a fear of flying, but in her profession, airplane travel was a prerequisite of the job. So over the years she had managed to grow accustomed to it, even if she had never truly conquered her fright. Upon disembarking from a flight, she never failed to feel as though she had barely escaped from the jaws of death, and now was no exception. Alek knew this, and he patted Mariah's hand reassuringly before they unfastened their seat belts, now that the airplane that had flown them from their hometown to the city that was home to the All-Children's Hospital had landed. Both of them stood, Alek ducking to avoid hitting the cargo space. Flipping open the hatch, he dragged forth their coats and carryons, slinging the straps of the garment and duffel bags over his shoulders.

"Here. I can take my stuff." Mariah pulled on the bright down ski jacket he had handed her.

"No, that's okay. I've got it." Alek motioned her forward, his hand at her elbow to steady her as, trying not to bump into other people in the crowded airplane, Mariah started down the narrow aisle, he, Lanie and Jules following close behind.

Presently, they were through the chilly jetway and into the warmer terminal. At the baggage claim, they collected the rest of their luggage, then proceeded to a rental agency to pick up the car Jules had hired. Armed with a city map, Jules drove them to the hotel, Lanie up front, beside him. Alek and Mariah rode in the back, she settling gratefully into the curve of the strong arm he wrapped around her. Besides her fear about flying, she found airplane travel dehydrating and exhausting. Physically, she felt as though she had been on a grueling three-month tour, and she yearned for a long, hot bath and bed. She would be glad when they reached the hotel.

Winter's early dusk had already fallen. The streetlamps shone with a soft glow along the highways that led from the airport into the heart of the city, illuminating the powdery snow that fell from the dark sky, making it glitter like diamond dust. Downtown, the bright lights of holiday decorations were ablaze in a multitude of colors. Angels, snowmen, Santa Clauses, sleighs and reindeer, Christmas trees and candy canes gleamed like a kaleidoscope. The bare branches of the trees in front of the buildings sparkled with tiny white lights, so the entire city appeared like some wondrous fairyland.

As Jules at last pulled the car to a stop before the hotel and they all stepped out into the cold night air, Mariah smelled the crisp wintry scent of smoke from burning fireplaces. When the hotel doors were opened by the doorman and bellboy, the fragrance of evergreens and holly wafted from the lobby. In its opulent center stood a towering pine tree, beautifully decorated and surrounded by a huge pile of gaily wrapped boxes.

To Mariah's relief, Jules and Lanie always handled the business details, so there was nothing for her to do but trail along after the bellboy hauling their luggage toward the bank of elevators. Soon she was installed in her suite, where a hospitality basket filled with local goodies sat upon a table.

"Do you need anything else, Mariah? Do you want some ice or something?" Alek inquired as he turned from speaking to the bellboy, who had finished pointing out the suite's amenities.

"Yes, please. I'm very thirsty from the flight."

"We'd like a couple of buckets of ice, too." Alek handed the bellboy a generous tip. Then he turned back to Mariah. "I know you're probably too tired to go out for dinner, so why don't I order room service for us?"

"That would be wonderful, Alek," Mariah replied, touched by his thoughtfulness.

"Great. I'll leave you to get unpacked, then, and call you when supper is served. I'll have them set it up in my suite. Meanwhile, if there's anything else I can do, just knock." He indicated the twin doors that joined his suite to hers.

"I will—and, Alek, thanks. I appreciate... well, everything, actually. Your caring, your patience, your understanding, your willingness just to be there for me, to give me the time I've needed. Despite the pressures of putting together the two new routines, these past several weeks have been some of the very best of my life. Almost like old times—but without all the bitter arguments that spoiled it all before. To be honest, I didn't think you could change, Alek. But you have."

"Yes, I have," he agreed, his face sober. "I lost something, some*one,* very important to me before. And I don't want to lose you again,

Mariah. Whatever it takes, I mean to hang on to you forever this time around. See you at supper—and be sure to lock this door behind me,'' he reminded her as he left the suite.

He was very conscious of her safety, not just because she was a woman, but also because, these days, any kind of celebrity was a potential target of stalkers and other crazies. From past experience, Mariah knew Alek would stand in the hallway until he heard her turning the dead bolt and fastening the extra security latch in place, so she did both. Then she began to unpack her clothes, hanging some in the closet, putting others away in the dresser. All the while, her mind dwelled on Alek. What she had told him was true: The past several weeks with him *had* been heavenly, despite all the long, hard hours the two of them had worked.

Even when they were not training, there had been reams of videotape for them to watch, cassettes not only of their competitors' previous performances, but also of pairs' and individual skaters' programs. They'd studied Scott Hamilton's footwork and the innovative routines of the top ice dancers.

Still, to her surprise, Alek not only had insisted they take at least some evenings off here and there, but Jules and Lanie had also agreed. It was almost as though the older couple were conspiring with Alek, Mariah had thought. Because on those nights, Alek had proceeded to court her. The word seemed old-fashioned in this day and age, but she could think of no other term that suited. He had taken her to supper, to the movies, dancing, even to an arcade once or twice. And during these romantic evenings out together, he had made it clear to her that he both loved and desired her. Even so, he had not pressed her for more than a few kisses and caresses, which had left her aching, unsatisfied, and wondering why she continued to hold him at arm's length, when she wanted nothing more than to surrender to him.

She loved him. Only her fear of having her heart broken again caused her to hang back. But surely Alek had done everything in his power to convince her he had changed, that he wanted her back—this time forever—that he would not hurt her a second time, driving her to break off their engagement again.

When her ice arrived, Mariah poured a cold glass of fruit juice from the small refrigerator in her suite. Sipping her drink, she drew herself a bath.

Sooner or later, she was going to have to come to grips with her tumultuous emotions toward Alek, she thought as she stepped into the fragranced water. She could not keep putting him off. She had to make a decision. She must either trust him—or not. She sighed, feeling torn. It would all have been so simple—if only this were the first time around for them.

She had just stepped out from the bathtub and was pulling on a fluffy, terry-cloth robe emblazoned with the hotel's crest when she heard Alek knocking on the adjoining door.

"Just a minute," she called, tying the robe tightly as she left the bathroom. There was a moment's delay while she fumbled at the latch on the door. Then she pulled it back to find Alek lounging against the doorjamb. "I'm sorry I took so long. I just finished my bath."

"So I see." Alek's intense green eyes roamed over her slowly, taking in the loose, damp tendrils of hair that had escaped from her French comb and now curled about her nape, his glance continuing to her bare legs and feet. Beneath his smoldering gaze, Mariah flushed as she became abruptly conscious of her nakedness beneath the robe. Despite her having tugged it around her body as closely as she could, the robe had still loosened, gaping open to reveal the valley between her breasts. Reaching out in the sudden, taut silence, Alek slid his fingers beneath the garment's wide lapel, drawing the back of his hand lingeringly down her soft, nude skin. "Supper is served," he noted huskily, nodding toward the table that had been rolled into his suite, which was covered with dishes. "However, I'd be amenable to skipping it and going straight to dessert."

As he stroked her bare skin, Alek moved in very close, invading her personal space. Now, she was backed up against her open door, with no place left to retreat. She was acutely aware of his size, his strength. He seemed to tower over her, magnetic, dangerously masculine, potent and predatory. Instinctively she felt a woman's age-old desire to submit to a superior male. Her heart hammered with both fright and anticipation. Her breath came quickly, shallowly. Reason urged her to protest against him, but somehow, the words stuck in her throat, and before she could force them past her lips, Alek's mouth captured hers. Mariah moaned low in her throat at the contact, at the feel of his lips moving upon her own, his tongue parting them, shooting deep, stabbing her with its heat.

His hands had spread open her robe, slipped beneath the thick terry cloth to cup her breasts. His palms glided erotically over her sensitive nipples, teasing them to taut, hard peaks. Waves of pleasurable sensation rippled from their centers, coursed through her entire body. She trembled against him, wanting him to stop, wanting him to continue. In some dark corner of her mind, she wondered if she had subconsciously wished to incite him by appearing before him dressed only in her robe, obviously naked beneath it. Perhaps she had. But in her heart, she knew she was still not certain she was emotionally ready for this, no matter how her body responded to him, burned for him.

"Alek, no," she murmured as his mouth scalded her throat, her breasts, his beard stubble grazing her skin. His lips closed over her nipple. He sucked it into his mouth, laved it with his tongue, sending a rapturous thrill through her. His fingers were at the knot of the belt that bound her robe, untying it. "No, Alek," she whispered again. "I'm—I'm not ready."

Her robe fell completely open, exposing the length of her nude body to his hungry eyes. His hand slipped between her quivering thighs, caressed her warm, wet mound.

"You're ready," he muttered thickly, pressing against her so that she could feel the hard evidence of his desire for her, feel his harsh, labored breath upon her skin.

"Yes...no... I mean, I'm—I'm still not sure. I—I need more time. Please, Alek."

"Go." He jerked back from her, his hands in the air. "Go get dressed before I forget I'm a gentleman and do something we might both regret."

Her heart pounding fiercely, Mariah fled. She snatched her clothes, then ran into the bathroom to dress. They'd come too close this time. She was playing with fire to think she could kiss Alek without wanting to make love to him. Once she was in his arms, self-control took a back seat to passion. And she knew it was the same for him, too.

When she finally worked up enough nerve she entered Alek's suite. He was seated at the supper table, waiting for her. To the casual eye, he would have appeared relaxed and composed. But Mariah was not deceived. He was as tightly coiled as the proverbial spring. The muscle still worked in his jaw. His brilliant green eyes glittered like a panther's. She felt guilty and ashamed. Her subconscious longing for him had driven her into subtly provoking him, and then she had drawn back, afraid, still uncertain. She would not blame him if he were angry with her.

Instead, with a low, rueful, mocking laugh, he observed, "Good thing we spend so much time on the ice. Otherwise, I'd be taking a lot of long, cold showers."

"If it's any consolation, I *am* sorry, Alek," Mariah replied softly as she sat down across from him at the table. "I just . . . got cold feet. Maybe if we can just get through the benefit, my emotions won't be in such a turmoil afterward. . . ."

"Hey, no problem. I promised not to rush you, and perhaps I was out of line. It was just that . . . seeing you standing there, in that robe, brought back so many memories that I guess I got a little carried away." Taking up the wine bottle, he poured them each a glass. "So, what do you say we eat before our dinner gets totally stone cold? Then I thought we'd go over the itinerary together, make sure we have enough practice time. There's also the tour of the All-Children's Hospital. That's tomorrow morning, as I recall."

"Yes." Mariah's voice was solemn, because her emotions toward the forthcoming tour were mixed. It wrenched her heart to visit the hospital, even though she knew how much the children enjoyed meeting all the figure skaters. "We don't want to forget our new publicity photos. The kids love getting autographed pictures."

"I'll make a note to myself. How's your wine?"

"Good." She sipped the fine Chablis appreciatively.

"And the food?"

"A little cold—but then, that's not the hotel's fault."

"No." Alek's eyes met hers meaningfully, causing Mariah to blush and lower her gaze.

Butterflies churned in her stomach, making her feel more nervous than she ever had before any performance. She could barely choke down her supper—and she drank far too much wine, wondering all the while if Alek hoped to get her drunk and seduce her. That image, too, held great, if unsettling, appeal. But after they had finished their supper and he had walked her to the doors that adjoined their suites, he only kissed her lightly on the forehead and bade her good-night. Mariah closed her door and latched it, but she heard no corresponding sounds from the opposite side, so she knew Alek had left his own door standing invitingly open. After undressing and pulling on her negligee, she slipped into bed, vividly conscious of the fact that only a thin wall—and her own insecurities—lay between her and him.

Chapter Seven

And Sometimes, Dreams

The All-Children's Hospital was a huge, sprawling redbrick complex several stories high and comprised of a number of different buildings and wings. It had begun life in the late 1800s as an orphanage. Since, in those days, many of the children who wound up in its wards had been from poor backgrounds, suffering from malnutrition and the effects of laboring in sweatshops, it had gradually evolved into a small hospital. Eventually, over the years, it grew into the vast structure it was today. The original edifice still stood, now serving as the lobby and general information and admissions areas. It was through this building that Mr. Fielding, the director of the Letters to Angels program, led Mariah and Alek and the other skaters when they stepped down from the bus that had brought them here.

Having skated in a previous Letters to Angels program to benefit the hospital, Mariah had been on this tour before. So she knew what to expect, and it was therefore with a mixture of gladness, hopefulness and sadness that she passed through the wide glass doors of the All-Children's Hospital and into the entrance lobby. Inside, a large gilt-framed painting of the hospital's founder hung on one wall, beneath which was prominently displayed a gold plaque engraved with the hospital's motto: Caring For Children Today, Because They Are The Hope Of Tomorrow. Unfortunately, as Mariah knew, despite the research that continued to be done, the advances that continued to be made, for many of the children at the hospital, there was no hope. There would be no tomorrow for them. The thought brought tears to her eyes, tears she knew were but the first of many she would experience before the tour ended.

"Mariah, are you sure you want to do this?" Alek took her hand. "If you don't feel up to it, I—"

"No." She shook her head. "I'll be all right. It's just that the children... When you see them, you just wish you could do more to help. You feel so guilty at giving nothing more than a few hours of your time to skate a couple of numbers you were probably going to use in competition anyway.''

"I know exactly what you mean, Mariah. But the money we'll raise by our skating will do some real good. Who knows, maybe it'll make one child's dream come true.''

"I know you're right. But in my heart, I still feel I could do more, that I *should* do more!''

It was a feeling that only increased as Mr. Fielding led the group of skaters through the various wings, his voice pleasant but passionate.

Through it all, what tore at Mariah more than anything was how brave and cheerful the children were. Those who could, greeted their visitors with a bold brightness or a shy gaiety that made her long to find a private place where she could cry her eyes out. She felt deeply ashamed of how she had lain in her hospitable bed morosely, turning away visitors and pitying herself after the accident. Instead of feeling sorry for themselves, these indomitable youngsters talked and laughed and cracked jokes with the skaters, who signed endless autographs on publicity pictures and in scrapbooks, on plaster casts and even on hospital gowns.

In yet another unit, Mariah approached the bed of a beautiful little girl who, before the group's appearance in the hallway beyond her ward, had been bent over a coloring book lying on the hospital table before her, her soft blond hair falling carelessly over one eye, an expression of intense concentration on her piquant face. The child looked to be about seven years old, and although Mariah could not have explained why, she felt strangely, irresistibly drawn to the little girl.

"Hello, there," Mariah said quietly as she entered the ward and neared the child's bed. "I'm Mariah Nichols. I'm with the group that's touring the hospital today."

"I know," the little girl replied, politely, only her big brown eyes speaking of her excitement. "You're an ice dancer, and you skate with Alek Khazan. He's been your partner twice now."

Mariah was genuinely surprised by the child's statements, because unlike the more popular sports, such as football and basketball, figure skating did not really have any stars the caliber of a Joe Montana or a Michael Jordan, the type of sports heroes with whom most children tended to identify and whose pictures were regularly featured on trading cards. And while the youngsters at the hospital were aware that the skaters were celebrities in their own right and begged them for pictures and autographs, Mariah knew most of the kids would not have known Oksana Bayul from Nancy Kerrigan. Further, ice dancers tended to be the least well-known of figure skaters; it was usually the individual skaters who received the lion's share of publicity and the spotlight.

"Now, how do you know all that?" Mariah asked lightly, genuinely puzzled.

"I know because you and Mr. Khazan are two of my heroes," the little girl confided, a trifle breathlessly. "When I grow up, I want to be an ice dancer just like you!"

"You do? Well, I'm extremely flattered, Miss...?" Mariah's voice trailed off as she realized she did not know the child's name. "You know, you haven't told me your name, so even though you know mine, we haven't really been properly introduced yet."

"I'm Bethany. Bethany Thacker."

"Well, as I was saying, Miss Thacker, I'm quite flattered to be numbered among your heroes. Would you like to have an autographed picture of me and Mr. Khazan?"

Bethany nodded shyly, her eyes shining with pleasure. Even so, for the first time, Mariah noticed the shadows of grief in their depths, the same shadows she had seen in her own eyes for months after Worth and Richard were killed. It was a different darkness from that in the eyes of the other youngsters—the ones who were burn victims and terminal cases. Bethany was not going to die or be scarred for life; this was the wing for crippled children. At that realization, Mariah glanced down involuntarily at the little girl's legs, but they were concealed beneath the sheets and blanket on the bed. Was it possible that this child who longed so fervently to become an ice dancer couldn't walk...would never walk? Mariah's heart went out to the little girl. Mariah knew what it was like to lie in a hospital bed, longing to ice dance—and wondering if she would ever even be able to walk again.

"You know what? I seem to have run out of pictures," she lied as she opened her leather portfolio a crack. "Wait right here. I'll be back in a jiffy, I promise—and I'll bring Mr. Khazan with me. Okay?"

"Okay," Bethany agreed, trying her best to conceal her disappointment and fear that Mariah might not really return.

But it was not in search of Alek that Mariah went—at least not initially. Instead, she made her way to the nurses' station down the hall.

She greeted the three nurses on duty as they glanced up at her inquiringly. "I'm Mariah Nichols. I'm with the figure skaters who are doing the Letters to Angels benefit, and I was wondering if you could tell me about one of your patients in this unit. Her name's Bethany Thacker. She's in a ward just down the hall."

"Oh, yes," the head nurse responded. "Such a sweet little girl. She's here for an operation."

"Can you tell me what for? I mean . . . I realize I'm not a relative or anything, and so it's probably against hospital regulations or something to give me any information about her condition. But, well, the thing is, she actually recognized me. I mean, she knew who I was, even before I told her. She's seen me and my partner, Alek Khazan, skate, and she told me she wants to be an ice dancer just like us when she grows up. I was . . . I was just wondering what her chances of that really are. Because if she's truly serious, there are classes for children at most ice rinks, and I could help her get started. But I . . . I don't want to say the wrong thing, to give her any false hope. . . ."

"That was very considerate of you, Ms. Nichols." The head nurse's voice was kind but sober. "Because the odds for the success of Bethany's operation aren't too good, I'm afraid. In all probability, she'll be in a wheelchair for the rest of her life."

"Oh, no," Mariah murmured. "Is it at all possible there's—there's been some terrible mistake? I mean . . . I know the staff here is excellent, but doctors are human, after all. Even the best of them sometimes make mistakes." Mariah remembered herself again, lying in a hospital bed—her legs paralyzed from the sheer trauma of the automobile accident and Worth's and Richard's deaths, and her fear that her career, her life's ambition, had ended in one fell swoop.

Although they had not found any evidence to support their theory, the physicians who examined her initially had believed there must be some as-yet-undiscovered injury to her spine . . . which had resulted in the paralysis of her legs. The horrifying misdiagnosis—however understandable under the circumstances—had compounded her shock and terror, so her hysterical paralysis had continued until a specialist was called in for consultation and finally recognized that her mind was playing tricks on her body, that there was, in reality, nothing truly wrong with her legs at all, other than some traumatized muscles and ligaments.

"We'd all like to think every youngster here has been misdiagnosed, Ms. Nichols," the head nurse declared, with both sympathy and understanding. "Unfortunately, for Bethany that's not the case. Her injuries are the result of an automobile accident in which she also lost both her parents. Their car was struck by a drunk driver. She hadn't any other relatives, so she's an orphan now, too, poor little kid. And since adoptive parents who want an older child rather than an infant—particularly a crippled child—are very few and far between, I'm afraid it's quite likely Bethany will wind up growing up in a series of foster homes."

"Oh, no," Mariah uttered softly again, instantly grasping the parallels between her own case and Bethany's—and the terrible differences, as well. "How sad, how horrible for her. She's such a lovely child and seems so bright, so intelligent...."

"She is, Ms. Nichols—and she really *does* love ice skating, especially the ice dancers, like you and Mr. Khazan," the head nurse said. "She's been so excited ever since she learned all of you were coming here to visit. It's the first time she's really shown any interest in anything since her parents were killed. That's part of the reason the doctors have held off on the surgery. They'd like to see her emotionally stable first, before doing the surgery. But just meeting you has done wonders for her, I'm sure.''

A thoughtful expression knitted Mariah's brow as she walked back toward Bethany's room. She ran into Alek in the hall and explained to him about Bethany, then led him to the little girl. Bethany's face lit up at the sight of them.

''Hello, Bethany.'' Alek withdrew a publicity picture and set it next to the coloring book on the table before her. ''I understand you're a big fan.''

''Oh, yes . . . yes, I am!'' Bethany cried softly, her enthusiasm obvious. Then she turned to Mariah. ''I was afraid you weren't really going to come back, but you did—and you really *did* bring Mr. Khazan with you!''

''Of course, I did. How could you doubt I would?'' Mariah forced herself to adopt a teasing, lighthearted tone. ''I'll have you know I always keep my promises, young lady.''

''Always?'' Bethany queried.

''Always.''

Mariah and Alek both signed their photograph for Bethany, chatting with her for several more minutes, during which time Mariah again observed how very good Alek was with children. He would make a wonderful father, she realized, feeling her heart fill suddenly with tenderness and yearning at the thought. Why had she ever held him at arm's length? she wondered. Why had she let her doubts and fear overshadow her love for him? He *had* changed. Could she not find the courage within herself to believe that?

Mr. Fielding appeared in the doorway, interrupting her reverie. "Skaters, could I have your attention, please. I hate to break up your visits, but it really *is* time we were moving on," Mr. Fielding announced, causing the youngsters to groan and boo him loudly. "I'm sorry, children. But we need to complete our tour."

"Yes, of course, Mr. Fielding. We'll be right with you," Alek called to him. Then he turned back to Bethany. "Well, Bethany, it looks as though duty calls, so I'm afraid Mariah and I have to go now. But I'll tell you what— We'll come back to visit you again, if you'd like."

"Do you mean it? Really and truly?"

"Cross my heart." Alek made the age-old childhood gesture that accompanied a sworn promise.

"Me too." Mariah did the same.

As she waved goodbye to Bethany, she couldn't help but wonder what would become of the little girl. Would her future really be as bleak as the nurse had painted it?

During the days that followed, that question haunted and tormented Mariah endlessly. True to their word, she and Alek visited Bethany faithfully. In fact, they were encouraged by Bethany's doctors, who insisted their visits were doing wonders for the child's spirits. While Mariah herself could see that this was indeed the case, she still could not help but worry whether she and Alek were doing more harm than good. In just a short time, they had grown inordinately attached to Bethany and she to them. And, although they did their best not to give her any false hope that she would eventually walk and ice-dance, the thought occupied Bethany's mind constantly. When she wrote her "letter to an angel," in which she described what she wanted most in all the world, she wished simply for a pair of ice skates.

"Oh, Alek," Mariah murmured as they left the hospital. "I just can't bear the thought that Bethany's operation might fail, that she might never walk again, much less be able to learn to skate."

"I know."

As he escorted her through the garage to their rental car, Alek slipped his arm comfortingly around her slender waist, as he had in the days when they were lovers and engaged. Strangely, it felt so natural and right for him to do this that it did not even occur to Mariah to pull away from him, that she was once more lowering her defenses against him, letting him get too close to her. In fact, she unconsciously laid her head against his shoulder, grateful for the warmth of his body and how he shielded her against the winter wind. His arm tightened around her, and there was a peculiar expression on his dark visage when he glanced down at her.

He *did* love her, Alek thought, not for the first time since their reunion. He had never stopped loving her. And he knew suddenly that if someone was to hand him a pen and paper and tell him to write a "letter to an angel" so that his dream of a lifetime might come true, he would wish for Mariah, as his lover...as his bride. She was everything he had ever wanted in a woman, in a wife. Seeing her with Bethany these past several days had only emphasized that fact. He did not know how he could ever have permitted Mariah to get away from him, to walk out of his life. And now that she was back in it on a full-time professional and a more limited personal basis, he knew with certainty that that was not enough for him, that he wanted her in the most personal, intimate ways...forever.

He wanted to awaken every morning for the rest of his life and see her lying in bed beside him. He wanted to share her dreams, her successes, her fears, her failures. He wanted to sit with her before the fire on a winter's eve, sipping wine and talking, to have the right to touch her, hold her and make love to her whenever he wished. Still, Mariah held him at bay, unsure of herself, of him. Nevertheless, Alek refused to give up hope that he could win her back in time.

"Somehow, I have faith that everything will turn out well for Bethany." Much as he longed to, Alek did not add, "And for us."

"What makes you say that?" Mariah wanted his reassurance, and yet was afraid to believe him, for fear her hopes would be dashed in the end.

"It's the holiday season." Alek told her. "It's a time of miracles—if only you believe."

Chapter Eight

Dance Forever with Me

The rehearsals had ended. Tonight was the big show and the arena was packed from floor to ceiling with spectators, whose ticket money would go to the Letters to Angels program to benefit the All-Children's Hospital. The media were present, too, along with the camera crew that would be recording the show for the national broadcast scheduled for Christmas Eve.

Backstage, Mariah was keyed up more than was usual for her before a performance. This would be her first time before a live audience since Worth and Richard had been killed. Even though this was not a competition and there were no judges present to hand out scores, she paced restlessly, her fists jammed into the pockets of her warm-up jacket.

"Relax, Mariah. It's wearing me out just to watch you," Alek declared from the stairstepper machine he was working out on, off to one side of the backstage corridor that led from the dressing rooms to the rink.

"I told her! I told her that myself, not more than two minutes ago!" Jules gestured volatilely with his hands to emphasize his words. "But did she listen to me? No, she did not!"

"Hush, Jules! None of us wants to hear one of your tirades right now." Lanie grimaced at him sternly. "The way you're behaving, a body'd think this was the Olympics or the World Championships."

"Oh, for heaven's sake! It's the debut of the reunion of Nichols and Khazan, woman! The entire figure-skating world—not to mention the media—is watching!" Jules insisted fiercely, practically shouting. "I just—" At the sight of Lanie's raised eyebrows, he broke off abruptly. Then, lowering his voice, he continued. "I just want everything to go well, that's all," he ended gruffly.

"It will," Lanie assured him. "Now, come away, Jules." She tugged firmly on his arm. "Unless I miss my guess, you're making Mariah even more nervous than she already is!" Over his protests, she led him away, casting a sympathetic smile over her shoulder at Mariah.

"Thanks, Lanie." Mariah mouthed the words behind Jules's back.

Alek vacated the stairstepper machine and grabbed his towel. He wiped off his face, then slid his arm around Mariah's waist.

"Time to get suited up and warmed up on the ice."

"Finally!" she said with relief. "It's the waiting, you know, that unsettles me."

"It always was."

Presently, all the skaters were flying over the ice, the individual and pairs skaters practicing their jumps, the ice dancers reviewing lifts and spins. Mariah and Alek had numbers in both the first and second halves of the show. They had chosen to perform their "Mariah" program first, so Alek was dressed in his black gunslinger costume, his flowing-sleeved satin shirt open at the collar, revealing a sexy portion of his broad chest dusted with fine black hair. His long black hair was loose, damp and tangling about his face emphasizing his dark attraction. Every time he neared the boards emblazoned with the names of the commercial sponsors for the Letters to Angels show, which walled the rink, the women in the audience went crazy, shouting and screaming, calling out his name and waving bouquets in his direction. Now and then, he paused to sign autographs. And once, when Philippe Candeloro, handsomely decked out in his *Godfather* costume, skated past, performing a triple toe-loop in the process, Alek glided into a jump of his own—a triple axel.

"You been practicing that move long?" Mariah asked, unable to repress her smile as she remembered that morning at the Irish Coffeehouse, and Alek's jealousy when he had thought she might be attracted to Philippe. It was obvious to her that Alek had been showing off for her benefit, a display of male rivalry that both flattered and amused her.

"Long enough to get it right," he replied smugly. "Just because I'm an ice dancer doesn't mean I can't do the jumps. I just happen to like to dance."

"You'll get no argument from me. Oh, look! There's Bethany!" Spotting the little girl, Mariah smiled and waved. "Come on, Alek. Let's go see her!" Her hand in his, Alek's arm around her waist, they skated across the rink to where the excited child was seated with a group of other youngsters from the hospital. "Bethany, I hoped you were going to be here tonight," Mariah said. "I'm so glad you were able to come."

"So am I," the little girl announced shyly, her face beaming. "Dr. Parkinson said it was all right, though. He even carried me inside here to my seat. I hoped I'd see you. I brought you both something." She held out a bouquet, along with a stuffed teddy bear that was dressed up to resemble a martial artist. "The flowers are for you, Mariah, and the bear is for Alek."

"Why, thank you, Bethany." Mariah was genuinely touched. "You know what, this white rose goes beautifully with the costume I'm wearing, and that amber mum will match the blue-and-gold outfit I'll be dressed in for our second number. So I'll put those flowers in my hair, I promise."

"And this little guy will make a perfect good-luck charm for my spot in the dressing rooms," Alek asserted, making the bear appear as though it were ice dancing, much to Bethany's delight. "The show's going to start, so Mariah and I have to go now. But we'll be back to see you again later."

"All right. Break a leg!" the child called after them enthusiastically as they skated away.

Their "Mariah" number was midway through the first half of the show. Still, all too soon, it seemed to Mariah, she heard the announcer introducing them to the applauding crowd. Then she and Alek were actually on the ice, beneath the bright spotlights that always made skaters' programs more difficult than usual, since it was, among other things, harder to gauge distances in the semidarkness. Her heart pounding, adrenaline rushing furiously through her body, she assumed her pose in Alek's arms, waiting tensely for the music to start.

The initial eerie, solitary notes of their bluesy version of "Mariah" drifted over the ice, followed by the fuller opening strains. At those, Mariah and Alek began to dance. Earlier, she had attempted to steel herself against her nerves, even while she had prepared herself to be a little shaky at first. But right from the start, as she began to move, Mariah suddenly knew that this was going to be one of those rare and fabulous nights when she was wonderfully, incredibly "on." Equally elating was the fact that she could sense the same in Alek.

Heated chemistry—sexual and exciting—seemed without warning to explode between them, an almost tangible thing the audience also felt. The arena, except for the music and the scrape of Mariah's and Alek's sharp blades on the ice, had been silent, as though the crowd were holding its collecting breath, waiting to see if Nichols and Khazan still were magic together. Now, the spectators went mad, hollering, whistling and clapping as Alek set out determinedly to conquer the wind that was Mariah. And she herself danced and spun as though she had wings instead of blades upon her feet, teasing and taunting him tantalizingly, alternately as shy as a gentle breeze and then as bold as an unbridled storm.

Her cloud of long blue-black hair and the diaphanous folds of her ethereal white costume floated and flew about her face and body as the saxophone wailed like the wind she had become, and the lead guitar moaned and keened in intricate counterpoint. Alek's own black hair was a sheeny, unkempt mane. His green eyes held a predatory glitter in the spotlights as he moved with her, the subtle swagger of his hips and the provocative thrust of his pelvis sinuous, sensual, like some lethal animal on the prowl, in search of a mate. He tossed his proud, dark head arrogantly, challengingly. His powerful arm snaked out as though he were cracking a whip. Then he abruptly caught hold of her wrist and yanked her to him, his hands forcefully propelling her up-

ward in a beautiful, complex lift that had taken
them hours and hours of training to perfect.

Mariah twined and twisted, wrapping herself
lithely around his hard, lean body as he lowered
her back to the ice. His strong hands were now at
her waist, supporting her as he spun her while she
lay back, arms imploring, beckoning, then
holding him at bay. The throbbing beat of the
drums had grown progressively louder, wilder,
and more savage. Now, in keeping with the music, she and Alek executed a serious of compli-
cated steps and moves, followed by another
stunningly involved lift. They ended their performance precisely on the music's final note,
with a triumphant Alek standing with his corded
legs spread, his right fist skyward, his left hand
snarled in Mariah's hair as she, now tamed, half
lay at his feet, her face upturned to him breathlessly.

The arena rang deafeningly with applause, the
audience on its collective feet in a thunderous
standing ovation that seemed to continue interminably. His sensual mouth curved in a smile of
satisfaction and appreciation at the crowd's response, Alek drew Mariah to her feet so that they
could take their bows. Then they skated around
the rink together, collecting as many of the bou-

quets and stuffed animals as they could. They made a special point of halting to speak to Bethany, whose eyes were huge with wonder and shining with excitement.

"Mariah, you *did* wear my rose!" the little girl cried, gazing raptly at the white flower Mariah had earlier stripped of thorns, threading the stem through a black French comb she had fastened in her hair, over one ear.

"I promised I would, didn't I?"

After that, Mariah did not think the night could get any better. But whereas the "Mariah" number had been wild, fierce and passionate, the routine to Whitney Houston's "One Moment in Time" was beautifully, unbelievably dramatic and spiritually uplifting. It was as though, before when they had danced, Mariah and Alek had been raw, earthy, primeval creatures, and now, transcended, they were become eternally exalted, heavenly beings. This time, when the music ended, Alek held Mariah herself skyward. Her head was thrown back joyfully; her arms were spread wide like the wings of an angel, her fingers tense and splayed, as though she were reaching out to grasp the very stars in the firmament.

For a full minute after the program was finished, the stadium was silent with awe. Then, suddenly, people everywhere began leaping to their feet, cheering and applauding furiously, causing the entire arena to reverberate. After he had slowly lowered her back down to the ice, Alek tilted Mariah's face up to his and kissed her tenderly and deeply, full on the lips, before he released her so that the two of them could take their bows.

Later, when she watched the videotape of the show, Mariah would hear the commentators declaring to one another that she and Alek had fallen in love again that night, right there on the ice, in front of thousands of wildly shouting and clapping spectators. And she would know it was not so, that she had given her heart away to him long ago and somehow had never gotten it back. But she would also know it was in that one moment of time that she had admitted to herself, finally and forever, that she did not, after all, want her heart back, that she intended to leave it safe in Alek's keeping for always.

"I love you," she whispered to him just before they turned to face the audience.

"And I love you, Mariah," Alek answered quietly, seriously, his eyes kissing hers. "I always have, and I always will."

Afterward, not only at the cast party that followed the performance, but also for years to come, people who had witnessed the Letters to

Angels show insisted something special had happened on the ice that night. But it was young Bethany who summed it up best of all. When asked by one of the commentators what she had thought of the program, she said simply, "It was magic."

Chapter Nine

Urgently in Silence

"Would you—would you...like to come in for a nightcap, Alek?" Mariah inquired, her heart thudding, as she glanced up at him in the hallway just beyond her hotel suite, to which they had now returned following the Letters to Angels show and cast party.

"Is it just a nightcap you're inviting me in for, Mariah—or something more?" Alek's voice was low, seductive. His green eyes gleamed speculatively, expectantly, as they locked on her blue ones mesmerizingly. Slowly he reached out, smoothing her hair back from her face before he cupped her chin, drawing the pad of his thumb lingeringly across her moist lower lip. "I mean, I'd just kind of like to know the ground rules before I agree to come inside. You see, as much as I'd like to, I don't want to...start anything again that you aren't willing to finish. I'm afraid my self-control where you're concerned has grown volatilely, perilously thin, especially after tonight."

There was no misunderstanding him. He wanted her. She had seen this side of him before, knew how tightly wound he was—especially after a performance—how it was only with the greatest of difficulty that he restrained himself, continued to play the part of a gentleman. He stood very close to her, so close that she could actually feel the heat that emanated from his tall, lean, powerful body. Without warning, a wild, atavistic tremor shot through her, setting her aquiver, aflame. A blush crept up to color her cheeks, and she found she could no longer go on meeting his eyes. She swallowed hard.

"Come inside, Alek." Was that really her own voice, so soft, so husky with emotion and desire? "I'm not going to ask you to leave, not this time, not tonight."

His sudden, sharply indrawn breath made Mariah shake so badly that she could not insert the electronic key into the door's lock. She did not have to look at him to know his eyes had darkened, now smoldered with passion. Wordlessly he wrapped his hand around hers, guided the plastic card into the slot, then quickly withdrew it, turning the knob as the green light flashed to admit them.

Inside, he flicked on the light switch beside the door. A single lamp flared to life, dimly illuminating the darkness, which was fragrant with the lush perfume of the flowers he had had delivered to her suite earlier, to wish her good luck in the show. The gorgeous bouquet sat in a heavy crystal vase on the table; beneath, a tiny shower of fallen petals strewed the carpet, like stars across the night sky. In the silence, Mariah felt Alek's strong hands at her shoulders, tugging off her fur-trimmed wool cape before he pressed his mouth to the curve of her bare nape, causing her breath to catch in her throat as an uncontrollable shudder of longing and need ran through her. Then, turning away, opening the closet, he draped the cape carefully around a hanger before he shrugged off his long topcoat and hung it up, too.

"What would you like to drink, Mariah?" he asked.

"A—a brandy, please."

As Alek prepared her drink, Mariah was unable to watch him. She was too nervous. After all, it had been more than two years since she and Alek had made love together. Rubbing her arms as though she were cold, she moved to the bank of windows on the far side of the suite. The curtains were drawn back, revealing the snowy city that seemed to spread out infinitely below, aglow with streetlamps haloed with mist in the darkness, amber beacons amid the bright colored lights of the holiday decorations. The scene was beautiful, magical, like something in a movie.

From behind her, she could hear the sounds of Alek pouring the brandy into glasses. Even without turning to gaze at him, she could see him, she realized. His image was reflected by the inky windows she faced. Somehow, he had always reminded her of a panther, with his brilliant green eyes, his mane of glossy black hair and his long, supple, muscular body. His every movement was cool and elegant, yet tinged with some intangible thing that invariably made her think of animal magnetism and menace. Perhaps it was his training in the martial arts, specifically Kung Fu, which drew much of its style from the animal kingdom, from tigers and other wild creatures. It gave him a dangerous edge, made him exciting.

But Alek had never scared her, nor would he. It was her own agitation and anticipation that had her so keyed up, Mariah knew. Despite how much she loved him, he *had* broken her heart once before. It was so difficult for her to trust him a second time, even though he had done everything possible to reassure her that he had changed, that their relationship would be different this time around. Still, she had made her decision at last, and now she would stick by it. After tonight, she just could no longer believe he would hurt her again.

Behind her, Alek switched on the radio. Briefly the suite was filled with the strains of Christmas music. Then he adjusted the dial, and a slow, sensuous blues song began to play. Somehow, strangely, it suited the wintry night. If the suite had contained a fireplace, a crackling hearth would have made the setting perfect. But the powdery snow that swirled outside, beyond the windows, reflecting the amber glow of the streetlamps, was perhaps not a bad substitute.

"Here's your brandy." Alek handed her one of the glasses. Then he lifted his own in a toast. "To us, Mariah," he murmured.

"To us," she echoed, raising her own glass.

Together they drank, in a silence broken only by the strains of low music. The amber liquor was warm and mellow. It seemed to melt upon Mariah's tongue, as she felt herself melting inside, to burn down her throat, as she burned at the core of her being. She trembled with expectancy and rising passion as, after a long moment, Alek gently but deliberately took her glass away, setting it and his own aside.

"You are so beautiful." He reached out, pulling the French combs from her upswept hair, so that the glorious blue-black mass tumbled down in shimmering waves about her. His fingers ensnared the strands at her temples, turning her face up to his own. For a fleeting eternity, he gazed down at her, in his intense eyes the certain knowledge that, soon, very soon now, she would be lying naked beneath him, that he would be a part of her, as he had been before. Mariah's breath caught in her throat at the sight. Her eyes fell beneath Alek's as his thumbs traced tiny, erotic circles on her cheeks. "You know I'm going to make love to you, don't you?" His voice held a hoarse, thick note that made her shiver as she nodded. "Tell me you're sure, Mariah," he demanded softly. "Tell me it's what you want."

"I'm sure, Alek. It *is* what I want," she whispered.

Between them, then, there was an interminable moment, as highly charged as the atmosphere before a wild, winter storm. Alek inhaled sharply, his eyes glittering with triumph, before his mouth descended to seize possession of Mariah's own. He kissed her once, twice, lightly and tenderly, before he gave way to his blind hunger for her, his lips growing urgent, insistent, against hers. His tongue parted her lips, drove hotly between them as she yielded pliantly to his fierce onslaught, her hands creeping up to twine about his neck, her fingers burrowing through his own loose hair.

He seemed to kiss her forever, his mouth devouring her, before at last, with a low groan, he swept her up in his powerful arms. Striding to the bed, he laid her down, bending over her, his lips and hands moving on her feverishly. He slipped off her shoes, dropping them heedlessly to the floor. He kissed her ankle, the back of her knee, the inside of her thigh, as his palms slid lingeringly, electrifyingly, up one black-stockinged leg.

"Did you wear this for me?" he asked as he tugged with satisfaction and pleasure at one strap of her lacy garter belt.

"Yes," she breathed.

"You'd better have," he growled, his eyes dancing devilishly as he glanced up at her, "because I warn you, Mariah—I am a very jealous man where you are concerned."

He took her mouth again, his tongue plunging deep, wreathing her own until she gasped for breath against him. She was only dimly aware of the fact that he had somehow unzipped the back of the black cocktail dress she had worn to the cast party, and that its bodice now tangled around her waist, baring her braless breasts to him. His lips left hers, scorched their way across her cheek to her temple, her ear. He nibbled her earlobe, his harsh breath warm and enticing against her skin, sending a wild thrill coursing through her.

In response, her rosy nipples puckered, hardened, straining eagerly against Alek's palms as he cupped her breasts. Her fingers shook as she pulled and fumbled impatiently at his shirt, wanting, *needing,* to feel his naked flesh against her own. He raised up to help her, sitting back on his haunches, his thighs imprisoning hers. His eyes were riveted on her face as he swiftly unbuttoned his shirt and cast it aside to reveal his dark, broad chest, heavily layered with muscle, and his strong, corded arms. Sweat sheened the fine black hair that matted his chest and trailed invitingly down his firm, flat belly to disappear into his trousers.

He looked like some pagan warrior as he knelt over her, drawing her dress down languidly over her hips, so that the silken material rubbed sensuously along her stockings, before he tossed it to the floor as carelessly as he had her shoes minutes ago. He unhooked her garter belt, which went the way of its predecessors. Then he slowly peeled away her stockings and lacy French-cut panties, so that she lay naked beneath him. And all the while he undressed her, he kissed and caressed her, honing her desire for him to a keen edge. Then, at last, his hand moved to his leather belt, unbuckling it, and presently, his bare skin, slick with sweat, covered her own.

"Oh, Mariah," Alek muttered in her ear, his teeth nipping her earlobe once more, his mouth and tongue wreaking havoc upon her senses. "You don't know how good it feels to hold you again like this. I've missed you. God, how I've missed you!"

He found her lips once more, kissed her deeply, ardently, before his mouth scalded her throat. His tongue flicked out to tease the sensitive place on her nape, causing a jolt of excitement to shoot through her body. Mariah gasped aloud, her breath catching raggedly in her throat. Her hands on his back spurred him on as his lips fastened upon her nipple. His tongue rasped across the stiff, flushed peak, teasing, taunting, making her moan and writhe helplessly against him. She could feel his powerful muscles rippling and bunching in his back as he clasped her to him, his hard sex nudging her belly, speaking wordlessly of his desire for her. At the heart of her womanhood, a hollow, burning ache seized her savagely, so that she longed instinctively, desperately, for assuagement.

"Alek, please. I need you inside me."

"No." He denied her maddeningly, his voice a long, low sigh. "Not yet." Still, his knees pushed her pale white thighs wide. His palm cupped her dark, moist, downy mound, exploring the soft, burgeoning folds that trembled and opened to him like an unfurling bud bursting into bloom. Slowly, torturously, he slid two fingers into her deeply, momentarily easing her frantic yearning as she arched her hips imploringly against his hand. He murmured her name huskily as he stroked her, spreading musky heat, flicking the tiny, throbbing nub at the heart of her, bringing her to the brink of climax again and yet again, only to stop. He was driving her wild.

Mariah whimpered with passion and need, her head thrashing as she bucked against him.

"Please, Alek," she begged again. "Please."

Unable to restrain himself any longer, he took her then, his body moving exigently to claim her own, his hands ensnaring her hair roughly as she arched her hips to meet the swift, forceful thrust that pierced her to the very core. Gripping his wrists tightly, she cried out softly, a low moan of surrender, of gratitude, of rapture. It had been so long since he had possessed her. Too long.

"Does it feel good, love?" Alek held himself poised above her, deliberately prolonging the moment of his entry, gazing down at her intently in the semidarkness, his eyes like twin flames.

"Yes . . . yes . . ."

"There's been no one else but me, has there?"

"No."

Triumph and satisfaction flared in his eyes at that. Then, groaning her name, his mouth abruptly seizing hers again, he began at last to move inside her, plunging hard and deep, faster and faster, as he lost what little control he had somehow managed to retain. Mariah's blood roared in her ears as she strained against him, wrapped her long, graceful legs around him and lifted her hips to meet each strong thrust. Her climax was so powerful that it took her breath away, leaving her gasping and shaking in his embrace as the tremors exploded within her, seeming to go on forever. Alek rapidly followed her. His hands tightened on her body fiercely, as though he would never let her go. He threw his head back, his breathing harsh and labored, as his primal release came. Shuddering long and hard against her, he spilled himself inside her.

After a while, he slowly withdrew, pulling her into his arms, kissing her deeply and cradling her head against his shoulder. Beneath her palm, his heart thudded as furiously as her own. The rasp of their breathing filled the air. In the quiet afterglow, his hand stroked her damp, hair, her silky skin, glistening with sweat from their lovemaking.

"I have something for you," Alek said finally in the stillness, which was broken only by the low strains of bluesy music that still drifted from the radio.

"I thought you just gave it to me," Mariah teased gently, smiling up at him lovingly, her heart in her eyes.

"Besides that, I mean." He smiled back at her sexily, his eyes appraising her lazily, appreciatively, from beneath drowsy lids. "*That* I plan to give you again and yet again before this night is through. No, this is something else." Bending to reach the floor, he picked up the trousers he had discarded earlier, searching one pocket, from which he withdrew a small velvet box. Then, after tossing aside his pants, he snapped open the lid to remove the diamond engagement ring nestled inside. Grasping Mariah's left hand in his, he slid the ring onto her finger. "Don't ever take that off again. Because if you do, I'm warning you right now that, this time, I will protest so long and violently that the media will be showing film at eleven of my holding you hostage until you agree to marry me."

At the sight of the engagement ring she had worn once before, Mariah's heart filled to overflowing with love for him.

"I promise you I'll never take it off again, Alek," she replied quietly, soberly, tears of deep emotion stinging her eyes. "Never. I *do* love you, you know—with all my heart."

"And I you. Now, there is one thing more."

"What's that?"

"There's a beautiful little girl at the All-Children's Hospital who's become very precious to us both, and who could very much use a couple of loving parents. I know that, before, we hadn't planned on having a family anytime soon.

But I was wondering if perhaps you'd changed your mind about that, if you'd like for us to adopt Bethany?''

"Are you—are you serious, Alek?" Mariah was both touched and stunned. "Do you mean it? Regardless of the outcome of her surgery?" The child's operation was scheduled for the day after tomorrow, and the results would be known by Christmas Day.

"Yes and yes and yes. So, what do you say? Shall we have her come live with us?"

"Oh, Alek. Yes . . . yes! Oh, I can't wait to see Bethany's face when we tell her! Do you think she'll be happy at this news, that she'll *want* us to adopt her?"

"I believe so, or I would never have suggested it. I'll check into all the details first thing tomorrow morning, I promise you. But now, the night is young . . ."

"The night is late—"

"The night is young," Alek reiterated firmly, aroused again, intoxicated by her very nearness. He pressed her down upon the bed, his body moving determinedly to cover hers once more, his leg riding between her thighs, opening her. His hand tugged gently at her moist, fleecy curls; his fingers slid slowly, provocatively, down the delicate seam of her. "And we have more than two years of lost time to make up, so we're going to have to practice endlessly."

"Somehow, I don't think this qualifies as an Olympic sport," Mariah insisted with false solemnity, her eyes dancing, laughter bubbling in her throat as he kissed the corner of her lips.

"Too bad. I would have awarded you a gold medal," he declared huskily, before, his eyes darkening again with renewed passion, he silenced her with his mouth, once more taking her to the heights of ecstasy and back.

Chapter Ten

If Only You Believe

"Well, go on. It's yours. Open it, sweetie," Mariah urged as she smiled at Bethany tenderly. It was Christmas morning, and the little girl sat in her bed at the All-Children's Hospital, a big, gaily wrapped box on the hospital table in front of her. It was her present from Mariah and Alek, who stood to one side, both of them nearly as expectant and excited as the child herself.

"What is it?" Bethany asked, her eyes shining, her cheeks flushed.

"I don't know. Open it and find out." Alek added his own words of encouragement to Mariah's.

Slowly, holding her breath, as though scarcely daring to believe something wonderful might be inside the box, Bethany untied the huge red bow and carefully lifted the lid. At the sight of what lay within, she gasped with amazement and incredulity, tears of joy filling her eyes.

"Ice skates," she whispered worshipfully. "A pair of ice skates all my own! Oh, Mariah, does this—does this mean my operation was a success? Will I walk again?"

"Walk!" Mariah exclaimed, her own tears of happiness spilling down her cheeks as she hugged the child tightly. "Oh, Bethany, honey, you're not only going to walk! You're going to skip and run and play just like other kids. You're going to ice-dance, if that's what you want."

"And what's more—" Alek spoke again "—Mariah and I are going to be married. Very soon." From beneath hooded eyes, he shot his bride-to-be a heated glance that made her heart leap in her breast and that informed her wordlessly just how impatient he was for their wedding day—and night. "And while we know no one can ever take the place of your parents, we'd like very much to adopt you, for you to come and live with us after you get out of the hospital."

"You mean . . . forever? That I wouldn't ever be alone anymore? That I'd be—I'd be *your* little girl always, and never have to go live in a foster home?" On Bethany's face was such a mixture of hope, longing and disbelief that it wrenched Mariah's heart.

"No, never," she responded quietly, fiercely. "You'd be ours for always, and we would love you very much, Bethany. I promise."

"And you always *do* keep your promises, just like you said. Oh, Mariah, my angel really *did* answer my letter! It is a miracle!" the child cried, her delight and agreement plain.

"Yes." A hard lump of emotion rising in his throat, Alek reached out to take one each of Mariah's and Bethany's hands in his, squeezing them tightly. "Sometimes they *do* happen—if only you believe."

"*I* believe," Bethany announced firmly.

"And so do I," Mariah declared softly as Alek kissed the little girl lightly on the forehead before drawing his bride-to-be into his arms and kissing her on the mouth—deeply, passionately, with all the love he felt in his heart for her.

The Ice Man had melted.

From outside, the joyful ringing of church bells somewhere in the distance reached Mariah's ears. And just as she and Alek had earlier that morning, on the solidly frozen pond in the park beyond the All-Children's Hospital, lovers and other skaters danced and dreamed in the falling snow.

*   *   *   *   *

Anne Stuart

Kissing Frosty

Dear Reader,

As far as I'm concerned, New Year's resolutions are bound to fail (how many of us are skinny?) and a waste of time. If your life needs a major change, a jump start, or even a gentle push, then it's much better to do it now, rather than wait for a mandated holiday.

Nevertheless, I believe in celebrating everything, from Summer Solstice to the Feast of the Immaculate Conception to Brad Pitt's birthday, so if the New Year has rolled around, go for it.

Just don't make the mistake of resolving to find a husband. You'll end up in trouble like my heroine in *Kissing Frosty*. Love never works if you go looking for it—you have to wait until it shows up. That doesn't mean you can sit back and forget about it. Love has a habit of showing up when you least expect it, but if you aren't alert you might not notice.

Be wary of kissing snowmen, or wishing for what's bad for you. Strange things might happen. Trust that you'll get the answer to your dreams. It might not always be the answer you expect, or the answer you think you want, but it will be the *right* answer.

My personal resolution is to write lots of books and not worry about things beyond my control.

Oh, and to lose weight, of course.

Happy New Year to all!

Love and kisses,

Anne Stuart

Prologue

The Winter Solstice
Watson Hole, Wyoming

"All right, what are we going to do now?" Megan McGraw demanded, staring out over the frosty, moonlit scene in front of them.

Nadja Commorski blinked owlishly through her oversize glasses. "What do you mean?"

Meggie shrugged. "We've eaten too much pizza and ice cream, drunk too much wine, cried over that stupid movie, lusted over Brandon Scott, and it's still not even midnight. I thought we were going to celebrate our latest disaster. All we've done is make ourselves sick."

"Maybe Roebuck will change his mind?" Nadja suggested, in her soft, timid voice.

"I doubt it. My natural-foods restaurant and your new-age store don't bring in the kind of money he'd make if he bulldozed our building and put up condos. Which is exactly what he'll do, as soon as we depart."

"He can't make us leave."

"Sure he can," Meggie said bitterly. "We had a gentleman's agreement with him, not a lease. Unfortunately, none of us are gentlemen. Which leaves us up an icy creek without a paddle. And at the advanced age of thirty-two, I'm getting tired of wandering around. It's time I settled down."

"I thought you had."

Meggie glanced fondly at her young friend. "My biological clock is ticking, Nadja. I want a baby. I want a docile, nonthreatening, handsome husband to pay the bills and keep me in style. Is that so much to expect from life?"

"Not for most people," Nadja said. "I wouldn't have thought you'd settle for something so tame."

"I can do tame," Meggie said in a meditative voice. "So what have you got in your bag of tricks?"

Nadja looked faintly guilty. She was almost ten years younger than Meggie, with a skinny, sparrowlike body, a small, pointy face, frizzy hair, and an air of gentle anxiety. "What makes you think—?"

"Come on, Nadja, we've been sharing business quarters for a year and a half now, struggling together. I know that somewhere among your crystals and potions you have a magic spell or two. You've already told me that tonight's the night of the winter solstice, a night when magic happens. Let's make some magic.''

"Meggie, I sell these things, I don't use them. At least, not most of them," she added, endearingly honest.

"You must have something to summon forth a man. A love potion?"

"There are dozens of them in the shop," Nadja said wryly. "They're my biggest sellers, though they've never worked for me. Besides, you've kept away from romantic entanglements for as long as I've known you. Who did you want to summon?"

It was a cold, frosty night in the tiny ski town of Watson Hole. The town was decorated for the Christmas season, and each shop had lights, ice sculptures, wreaths and trees galore. Even Nadja's and Meggie's. Meggie sauntered across the snow-packed street to the corner of the alleyway, where a huge, somewhat disreputable-looking snowman she'd helped build early that afternoon sat. He was suitably rotund, but there was something about the composition of his coal eyes and his carrot nose that suggested a certain cynicism. "How about we find a magic hat and turn old Frosty into the perfect mate?" she suggested, slinging her arms around his icy middle.

It took her a moment to realize that Nadja hadn't responded. She turned, one arm still around the snowman, to see her friend's speculative expression.

"There is an incantation," Nadja said slowly.

Meggie pulled away. "I'm kidding, Nadja. He'd melt in bed."

"No, I mean he could be used as an oversize poppet. Something to transfer energy. It wouldn't do any harm to try."

"What are you talking about?"

"We can use Frosty to summon your true love. If you've got something belonging to him."

"Nadja, I don't have a true love. Maybe Brandon Scott, if he weren't five years younger than I am, and much too pretty..." she added with a laugh.

"I don't think you really want to marry a movie star, Meggie," Nadja said disapprovingly.

"Probably not. Still, he is awfully nice to look at. And there are plenty of pictures in that old *People* magazine you have under the counter.

Where they call him the sexiest man in the world. Let's use that."

"I don't want to rip up my magazine," Nadja protested. Her face screwed up as she thought about it. "Oh, what the hell . . . it won't do any harm to try."

"That's the spirit," Meggie said. "Shouldn't we do it by midnight? That only gives us fifteen minutes."

Nadja sighed. "You get the picture, I'll get the stuff. Just promise me you'll invite me to Hollywood and introduce me to Tom Cruise."

"He's married."

"Well, find someone who isn't," Nadja said. "Or I'll take Brandon, if you get tired of him."

"Who could get tired of someone who looked like him?" Meggie said soulfully.

It took them less than ten minutes to get what they needed. They searched through Nadja's new-age shop, giggling like naughty children, and when they were finished, Nadja was loaded down with candles, herbs and unguents and Meggie had a photograph torn from a magazine. "I didn't have to defile your *People* magazine," she assured Nadja. "I found a picture of him in an article about the Oscars."

"Pin it to his chest," Nadja said, lighting a dark blue candle. The flame shivered in the cold night air, but, fortunately, there was no wind.

Meggie did as she was told, vaguely hoping that the police wouldn't choose this moment to patrol the narrow Swiss-style streets for mischief-makers. Not that they'd be arrested—they'd lived in Watson Hole long enough to be known. But Meggie didn't relish the thought of explaining exactly what fool thing they were doing.

"Okay," Nadja said, setting the candles in the snow at various points around the rotund snowman. "Now step inside the pentagram and put your arms around Frosty."

"Brandon," Meggie told her, doing as she was told. "He's cold, Nadja. Maybe you better hurry this up."

"Hey, I'm not experienced at this sort of thing. If you'd thought of it earlier, we could have called one of my customers..."

"I have some dignity," Meggie said, resting her head against Frosty's. The packed snow was icy beneath her cheek, and the chill soaked through her clothes. "Go ahead."

Nadja sighed. "Close your eyes and kiss him," she said, lighting a tiny pile of leaves that smelled like sausage. "I'll take care of the rest."

Meggie closed her eyes. Frosty was too fat for her to reach all the way around, and the chill of his packed form, instead of numbing her, felt oddly burning. She pressed her lips against the icy face, and for a strange moment it felt as if she were kissing real lips. A man's mouth, firm and hard. She tried to summon forth the celluloid features of the world's sexiest man, with his mane of streaked blond hair, his pouting lips, his gloriously sorrowful eyes. But someone else kept interfering, a shadowy figure, dark and disrupting.

"It's done," Nadja said abruptly.

Meggie opened her eyes and released her grip on Frosty. She glanced up at him speculatively, but he didn't move. "I don't think it worked, Naddie," she said doubtfully. "He hasn't turned into a movie star."

"These things take time," Nadja said reprovingly. "You can't expect instant results."

"We don't have a hell of a lot of time, Nadja. We're supposed to be out of here by New Year's Day."

"This isn't Federal Express, Meggie. Things happen in their own time," Nadja intoned.

"Oh, God, don't go all new-age on me, Naddie," Meggie begged. "Tell you what—let's go back home. At least I can dream about Brandon Scott carrying me away to Hollywood. It's probably all for the best. I don't have the highest opinion of men in the first place, and even perfection, in the form of Brandon Scott, would probably have its drawbacks."

"I could learn to live with them," Nadja said wryly. "Don't confuse me by talking about reality, Meggie."

"Reality is the pits," Meggie said in a mournful voice. "What about the picture? Do we leave it stapled to Frosty's heart?"

"Tuck it in your bra."

"I don't sleep in my bra, Nadja," Meggie said severely.

"Well, tuck it under your pillow, then."

"That's part of the spell?"

"I'm making it up as I go along. It can't hurt," Nadja added.

"No, it can't hurt." She pulled off the ice-crusted page from the magazine, folded into a tiny square and tucked it inside her bra. It burned against her skin. "Night, Nadja. See you in the morning."

Chapter One

Frosty had developed a decided tendency to smirk at her, Meggie thought days later, as she was cleaning the counter of her café. It was past closing time, dark outside, and only the remaining holiday lights illuminated his hefty shape. She'd stared at him for the past few days, some small, foolish part of her half hoping he'd disappear, and that Brandon Scott, the hottest thing of the nineties, would set foot in her store. But so far, the damned fat snowman had stayed put, smirking at her.

Nadja was back in the kitchen, finishing up the pots and pans. It had been a busy day, but then, most of their business was between Christmas and New Year's. Three more days till that old skinflint Roebuck closed them down, and Meggie still didn't have the faintest idea what she'd do.

There were other natural-foods restaurants in the small, trendy village, and she was a good cook. But she'd lost the taste for working for someone else. Besides, she'd done cooking. Just as she'd done her stints as a paramedic, rodeo clown, country singer, executive secretary, hospice worker, carpenter, journalist, bartender and chambermaid. Hell, she'd even done a stint as a litter-bearer at Lourdes. She'd packed enough careers, enough lives, into her thirty-two years to keep her memories busy for the next fifty. Always moving on, ever since she'd left college, midway through her junior year. Her dependent, widowed mother had died, the money had been gone, and Meggie had been free for the first time in her life. Free to walk away from entanglements and other people's smothering needs, free to walk away from the demands of her possessive, unimaginative boyfriend. Free as she'd been ever since. And she'd never been bored.

That freedom was beginning to pall. It was time to decide whether to try stability again. Relationships. Or spend the rest of her life alone.

Doubtless she'd find the answer if she just relaxed and waited for something to happen. If she was just patient enough, an opportunity would present itself.

"Someone just drove up," Nadja called from the kitchen.

"Didn't you put the Closed sign up?"

"I did."

Meggie quickly snapped off the lights. She wasn't in the mood for stragglers looking for a bean-sprout sandwich. If money wasn't so tight, she'd be sorely tempted to sneak into the only place in town that served red meat and get herself the biggest, rarest steak in the world. But Saucy Jack's astronomical prices didn't include a professional discount for his fellow restaurateurs, and Meggie needed to hoard every penny.

The car lights outside flicked off, and she heard the slamming of two car doors. "Whoever they are," she said, "they don't take a hint."

Nadja appeared in the kitchen door, her thin face anxious. "You want me to send them away?"

"I can do it," Meggie said wearily, crossing the small dining room. Someone was pounding at her door, a fact that didn't particularly please her, and if the noise wasn't so irritating she'd have been tempted to ignore them.

But she couldn't ignore the rattling of the doorknob. She switched on the outside light and yanked open the door, fully prepared to send her unwanted customers on their way.

She took one look at the two men who were standing there and began to scream.

* * *

"What the hell's wrong with you, lady?" O'Leary demanded, shoving the door open all the way. The idiot creature just stood there, screeching, and he reacted instinctively, shoving her against the wall and clapping his hand over her mouth, shutting off that infernal yowling. "You got a problem?"

She'd stopped making any kind of noise. She had gorgeous eyes, staring at him above the hand he'd clamped over her mouth. There was no way he could have missed them, even though they were glaring at him with a mixture of fear and shock. "That's better," he muttered, dropping his hand, releasing her. Though, for some reason, he didn't really want to. "Aren't you a little old to be acting like a groupie?"

The eyes were a golden brown, and they slid over him with only a brief glance, going instead to the man behind him. O'Leary was used to it. Traveling with Brandon Scott got a man used to feeling invisible.

"Oh, my God!" There was another woman in the dimly lit restaurant, younger, plainer, just as horrified. For a moment, John James O'Leary wondered whether they'd wandered into a mental colony. "It worked!"

The woman close to him opened her mouth, and he half expected her to start shrieking again, but she seemed to have pulled herself together. She kept looking at Brandon in disbelief, but that was normal enough. Brandon, as usual, didn't even seem to notice the reaction he was causing.

"The restaurant's closed," she said in a hoarse voice. And it was no wonder she was hoarse, O'Leary thought cynically.

"Don't be ridiculous, Meggie!" the young one said, flicking on the lights, illuminating the small, cozy place.

"Yeah, Meggie," O'Leary said, getting his first good look at her. "You got a couple of hungry customers here."

She was quite a luscious handful, though he hated to admit it. She was taller than average, rounded in all the right places, with a mane of wild, honey-streaked hair that tumbled around her shoulders. Strong shoulders—he liked that in a woman. She had a big, stubborn mouth to go with her gorgeous eyes, and an air of wariness that didn't even hint at vulnerability. She was a scrapper, a fighter, a survivor. Like he was.

She was also fool enough to be smitten by America's sweetheart, Brandon Scott, the darling of just about everyone missing a Y chromosome and a hell of a lot who weren't. The prettiest, sweetest, dumbest male on the face of this earth, and for the past three days he'd been O'Leary's constant companion. It was enough to make him want to scream as loud as the transfixed Meggie.

The plain one scurried from behind the counter, blinking through her thick glasses. "What can we get you, Mr. Scott?" she asked, practically wringing her thin hands.

Brandon gave her his usual smile, and O'Leary half expected her to swoon. She managed to keep upright, by sheer effort, but O'Leary had played a variation on this scene almost every place they stopped, and it had gotten old, fast.

"Look, lady," O'Leary said, "we've been driving for five hours, we're tired, and we're hungry. Just give us something to eat, some directions, and we'll be out of here."

"Of course," the skinny one said, ushering Scott to a table. O'Leary followed, vaguely aware that the voluptuous Meggie was still standing there in blessedly silent shock. He glanced back at her, expecting her to be staring at Brandon with a besotted expression on her face. Oddly enough, she looked more horrified than entranced.

"Ginseng tea," Brandon murmured, in the soft, rich voice that made millions swoon. "And a sprout-and-tofu sandwich on whole-grain bread."

"And I'll just have a cup of coffee," O'Leary said, leaning against the counter. He'd been sitting for too long—he wasn't in the mood to fold his long frame into one of those delicate-looking chairs. He glanced over at Meggie. "You wanna get it for me, sweetheart?"

He knew that would galvanize her. She came to with a jerk, glaring at him. "We don't have coffee," she said. "This is a natural-foods restaurant.

"You telling me coffee's not natural? It's grown in the mountains of Colombia, picked by Juan Valdez, and brought here just for my delectation. Don't tell me you don't have any."

"We carry several grain beverages—"

"Coffee," he insisted. "Loaded with caffeine."

She had a magnificent glare, one that went well with her generous, heaving bosom. He was old-fashioned in many ways—he liked a woman with curves and breasts. "I'll see what I can find," she said, stalking through the swinging doorway.

"I'll bet you will," he muttered under his breath. She'd probably come back with rat poison. If he was real lucky, she might find an old jar of instant coffee with enough powder left to make a weak cup. He might prefer the rat poison.

She was back suspiciously quickly, and the hand-thrown earthenware mug she slammed down in front of him was filled with a dark, delicious-smelling liquid.

"Goat's milk or soy?" she said with spurious sweetness.

"Black," he said, bracing himself for a huge swallow.

She'd already turned away from him when he set the half-empty mug down on the counter again. "Hey, Meggie," he said.

She glanced back at him, her long hair swinging. "You have a problem with the coffee?" she said frostily.

"You know damned well I don't. This isn't just coffee."

"I couldn't find any rat poison."

Since he'd just been thinking the very thing, the phrase startled him. "Are you some kind of witch?" he demanded.

She looked momentarily guilty. And then it passed. "Do you believe in witches, Mr. — ?"

"O'Leary," he said. "And you made it quite clear you know who my friend is. No, I don't believe in witches. I just wondered how a place that claims not to have coffee manages to serve a truly great cup of it. These are freshly ground beans, probably fresh-roasted, as well."

"Life is full of little mysteries," she said.

"Yeah, well one of those mysteries is how we find a place called Madame Rose's Palace."

He'd managed to surprise her again. "You're staying there?"

She was relaxing, just a tiny bit, and he decided to take advantage of it. He slid onto one of the stools, taking another sip of the finest damned coffee he'd had in months. "That was the best the studio could arrange for us on such short notice," he said.

"This was an unexpected trip?" The question was innocent enough, but he couldn't rid himself of the feeling she had a hidden agenda in asking it.

"America's sweetheart and I were supposed to be at a film festival up in Montana. For some reason, we both had this stupid need to take a detour to Watson Hole, so we decided to go to-gether.''

"You mean you're not his bodyguard?" she asked incredulously.

She was one of the most annoying women he'd ever met, he thought. Even if she did make great coffee. "Do I look like a muscleman? I'm not his bodyguard, his publicity agent or his keeper. As a matter of fact, I'm a screenwriter. Since we've worked on several pictures together and we were headed in the same direction, I decided to give him a ride." And regretted it every living mo-ment of the way, he added silently.

"Why didn't he want to drive?" she asked.

"He can't. He lost his license last year for speeding. So he's forced to rely on the kindness of strangers. Fortunately, all he has to do is smile and bat his lashes over those baby blues and people will lie down and die for him.''

"And you resent that?"

His head jerked up at that caustic remark. "Hell, no, Meggie," he said lazily. "It keeps them off my back." He reached into his pocket absently, looking for the cigarettes he'd given up two weeks, three days and thirteen hours ago. Empty, of course. He reached for his coffee in-stead, draining it. "So, where's Madame Rose's

Palace? And what the hell is it, for that matter?"

"It's a historical landmark, just up the street," the woman said, a wicked smile curving her full lips, which he found a hell of a lot more enticing than Brandon Scott's famous pouty smile. "It's redbrick, with red lights in the window. You can't miss it."

"Why is it a historical landmark?"

"It's the oldest building in town, and it's been renovated so that it looks exactly the way it did in the late 1800s. Without the women, of course."

"The women?"

"It's a whorehouse, Mr. O'Leary. I imagine you'll feel right at home."

Damn, he thought. He liked this woman. "You spend a lot of time there, do you?" he inquired in a silky voice.

He liked her laugh, as well. "Finish your coffee, and Nadja will show you where it is."

"Why not you?" He wasn't sure why he was asking. She'd probably just hang all over Brandon.

But then, she hadn't done more than glance at Brandon since he'd sat down. "I've got things to do," she said briskly. "Don't worry, if you stay here long enough you'll be bound to run into me. How long are you staying?"

"I don't know."

"Why are you here?"

"Beats me," he said lazily. "Got any ideas?"

And he watched, with utter fascination, as the color drained from her face.

Chapter Two

Megan was having a difficult time of it that late winter afternoon. Not only had Brandon Scott actually arrived on her doorstep, looking even more glorious in real life than he did on the screen, he'd been accompanied by an evil-tempered troll.

Not that O'Leary looked like a troll, she thought fairly, glancing at him. If Brandon hadn't been around, he might have seemed quite attractive. For one thing, he was tall, and rangy with a kind of muscly leanness that was a far cry from Brandon Scott's carefully bulked-up physique. His face wasn't pretty—at some point during his life, his impressive, beaky nose had been broken, and his high cheekbones, narrow, clever face and strongly marked eyebrows made him look faintly satanic. Clever men irritated her. She preferred them cute and passive.

He had hair so dark she wondered whether he might have some Native American blood in him. His wide mouth might have been considered sexy if it wasn't twisted in a mocking smile, but there was no denying he had extremely fine eyes. They were very dark, almost black, and yet there was something about them that drew one in.

All in all, it was a lucky thing the sexiest man in the world was sitting in her restaurant, or she might be spending far too much time watching this mocking stranger in the rough cotton sweater and the faded black jeans that hugged his long legs, and not concentrating on Brandon Scott, who was wearing . . .

She didn't know what he was wearing. The realization horrified her. She had summoned him through supernatural forces, he had arrived just for her, and all she could do was argue with his friend.

"I have no idea why you'd want to show up here," she finally said, shrugging, turning to look at her heart's desire.

Brandon Scott was eating his sprout sandwich with single-minded concentration. Meggie should have been pleased that he liked her cooking, but there was something about sprouts that gave her the willies. She would have to expand his culinary choices.

Nadja was hovering over him, like a doting mother, but when she felt Meggie's eyes on her, she looked up, flashing her a look of excitement.

"You finished with your sandwich, Brandon?" O'Leary asked, in the patient voice one usually reserves for children.

Brandon immediately pushed back his chair, touching his perfect, pouty mouth with his cloth napkin. Meggie made a mental note to save the napkin. If things didn't work out, she could always sell it to some deranged fan for a fistful of money.

"Nadja, would you show them where Madame Rose's Palace is?" Meggie moved forward to clear the table. For some reason, she wanted to move away from O'Leary, and his dark, observant eyes.

Nadja's expression would have been comical if it wasn't so blatant. "No," she said flatly. "I can't."

Meggie wanted to throw the dishes at her. If she pushed it, Nadja might just come right out with the reason Meggie should take them to Madame Rose's. After all, Brandon Scott had come for her, not Nadja.

"All right," she said in her most annoyed voice, dumping the dishes back down on the table. "Wait a moment while I get my boots and coat."

"I hate to put you to any trouble." It was Brandon Scott's famous rich, deep voice, directed at her for the first time. It came accompanied by a slow, sexy smile and those incredible blue eyes. Meggie stood motionless for a moment, waiting to melt in delicious response.

Nothing happened. Except for O'Leary, moving between them. "Come on, sweetheart," he drawled. "You can moon over him later."

It took no effort at all to pull her attention away from Brandon's dazzling smile. "You know, O'Leary, I think you've been watching too many Humphrey Bogart movies," she said sweetly. And as she disappeared into the back room, she heard the unsettling sound of his laughter.

He had a damned sports car. A two-seater, and O'Leary was already behind the wheel, looking at her out of his wicked eyes, when she joined them outside. "I'm afraid you're going to have to force yourself to cuddle up with Brandon for the ride," he said.

"It's not that far. I can walk."

"You can sit on my lap," Brandon murmured.

Yeah, sure, Meggie thought. He'd probably never had one hundred and thirty-five pounds of mature female flesh on his lap, and she wasn't about to introduce him to the experience. There was a limit to just how effective Nadja's brand of magic was. "I don't think so," she said.

"Let him sit on your lap, then," O'Leary growled.

Her immediate thought was obscene enough to still even her runaway mouth. Brandon just smiled sweetly and held the door for her. "There's plenty of room for both of us, if we squeeze," he said. "I know I'm kind of beefy, but I'll try not to crowd you too much."

Since Meggie knew perfectly well that her hips were at the very least six inches bigger than Brandon's, she started to melt, only to be brought up short by O'Leary's derisive snort. "Get in the damned car, will you?"

It was clear that Brandon wasn't going to get in first and let Meggie cuddle up to the door handle. Gritting her teeth, she scrambled inside, glaring at O'Leary, who watched her with impassive malice as she tried to make herself as tiny as possible in the leather bucket seat before Brandon climbed in.

She had no choice. Brandon might have skinny hips, but the car was minuscule, and she found herself with her butt on the emergency brake, her thigh up against the gearshift.

"This is a damned stupid car for a grown man," she informed O'Leary bitterly as Brandon settled himself next to her.

O'Leary put the car into Reverse, his hand sliding along Meggie's thigh. "Tell it to Brandon," he said cheerfully. "It's his car. I drive a Jeep."

He had long fingers, and she'd have sworn he was letting them linger against her thigh, just to try to disturb her. She tried to move, then realized she couldn't. Brandon was pressed up against her other side, quite solidly. And it was with another start of horror that Meggie realized she'd barely noticed him. He was warm, solid and male. He was the sexiest man in the world. And she'd been too busy paying attention to the irritating man in the driver's seat.

Fortunately, the drive to Madame Rose's Palace was brief. Unfortunately, Meggie couldn't manage to drum up too much enthusiasm for her first cuddle with her intended. She blamed it on O'Leary's dampening presence.

The place was dark and deserted, only the framed red lights glowing from several of the upper-story windows, when O'Leary pulled the ridiculous car in front of it. "You're lucky they're letting you stay here," Meggie said as he cut the engine. "They usually only let CEOs, and the like, use the apartments."

"You don't think I qualify, Meggie?" he murmured. "I think we'll feel right at home in a bordello."

"I imagine you will," she said sourly. "The two guest apartments on the third floor come with all the amenities, even if they are decorated in period style."

"All the amenities? I thought you said it didn't include ladies of the night."

"I'm sure we can find someone willing to put up with you. For a price," she said sweetly.

"And what's yours?"

It was just another of his gibes, one that Meggie should have responded to in kind. Except that suddenly there was a strange, underlying heat to his words. A heat that reached out and curled inside her....

Until she realized the door was open. Brandon had already disappeared into the house, and she hadn't even noticed.

"More than you could afford," she snapped, scrambling out of the car and slamming the door behind her. That was another problem with sports cars, she thought bitterly. The doors didn't make a satisfying crash when you slammed them. Just a piddling sort of thunk.

O'Leary was standing beside her in the frosty night air, looking up at the place. "Why'd you get out of the car? Don't you want a ride back to your restaurant?"

"No thanks. I can walk. And I won't bother showing you around Madame Rose's Palace. It's easy enough to figure out where to go. Just don't be too shocked at some of the pictures on the walls."

"Naked ladies?" O'Leary murmured. "I can't wait. Which reminds me. I wouldn't set your sights on America's sweetheart in there."

"What are you talking about?"

"Brandon. The sexiest man alive, remember?"

"You aren't going to tell me he's gay?"

"Nope. But I know from experience, he likes his ladies just past the age of consent, bordering on the anorexic, and not a brain in their heads. Sorry, sweetheart, you fail on all three counts."

"I beg your pardon?" She could be as frosty as the night air. "I'd like to know what business it is of yours?"

"Just doing my neighborly duty," he said with spurious concern.

This day had not gone well, and the sudden appearance of the man of her dreams was turning out to be less than enthralling. She looked at the man looming over her, and said, in her sweetest, calmest voice, "The bottom line is, I'm too long in the tooth and too broad in the beam for him. Is that what you're so tactfully trying to tell me?"

"In a nutshell."

There was an icy snowbank behind him, on the left. There were thick shrubs decorated with tiny white lights behind him on the right. She opted for the shrubs, taking him off guard. She was halfway down the snow-packed street by the time he'd struggled out of them, and she could hear his curses floating after her.

And she found she could smile after all.

Madame Rose's Palace was like something out of a movie set, O'Leary thought as he followed Brandon up to the third floor. The studio had had to pull strings to get them a place to stay there, and since neither Brandon nor O'Leary could come up with a reason why they suddenly had this overwhelming need to go to Watson Hole, it had made things a little more difficult.

But they were here now.

"This place is cool," Brandon said, stretching the syllables of the word. O'Leary controlled his instinctive wince. It wasn't that Brandon wasn't a perfectly nice kid, it was simply that he was about fifteen years younger than O'Leary and about ten bricks shy of a full load. It only made sense—the boy was blessed with extraordinary good looks, a beautiful voice, an undeniable acting talent and a sweet nature. There was no reason he should have brains, as well.

"Very nice," O'Leary grumbled. Actually, he kind of liked the gilded tawdriness of his room. The fat, cavorting cupids on the brass bedstead. The red flocked wallpaper and velvet bed hangings, the erotic paintings on the walls that were an odd mixture of quaint and arousing. But the bed was too big, even for a man as tall as he was. It needed someone soft and luscious sliding between the sheets.

"What did you think of her?" he asked abruptly, leaning against Brandon's doorjamb.

Brandon's room was similar, though done in shades of dark blue velvet.

"Who?" Brandon pulled off his sweater and shook his long blond hair with the casual abandon of a fashion model.

"The woman at the restaurant."

Brandon's perfect face scrunched in thought. "She wasn't very pretty, was she?" he said after a moment.

For some reason, that offhand dismissal infuriated O'Leary. It made no sense, but then, not much had made sense during the past few days. "It's a question of taste," he growled. "Some people might prefer their women to have curves."

"Yes," said Brandon. "She had very kind eyes, didn't she?"

O'Leary thought back to Meggie's eyes. They were a rich brown, shrewd and challenging. "I wouldn't say so. Anyway, she's not your type."

"I didn't know that I had a type," Brandon said.

"Maybe not. But if you do, she wasn't it," he said firmly. He wasn't quite sure why he was so determined to warn Brandon away from her. But he was.

Brandon smiled. "I didn't think you even noticed her. You were too busy arguing with the other one."

It took O'Leary a moment to comprehend. "I thought we were talking about the other one. Meggie."

"I was talking about Nadja. The skinny one, with the frizzy hair and the glasses."

"Oh," said O'Leary, suddenly deflated. "Well, what did you think of Meggie?"

Brandon Scott's smiles were as famous as his long blond hair. He had several versions—the slow, sexy one, the gentle one, the male-bonding grin. It was that last one he gave O'Leary. "I think you'll be very happy together, Jay." And he closed the door between them, quite gently.

Meggie's mood had done a nosedive by the time she returned to the restaurant. Nadja had already closed up and gone, and Meggie was half tempted to drive over to the tiny apartment she shared with two other girls on the top floor of an old Victorian house on the edge of town.

She didn't. She went straight upstairs to her own rooms, dropped her rented video on top of the VCR and headed into the kitchen. She kept her stash of diet Coke behind the bottles of organic carrot and raspberry juice. She kept her bags of taco chips hidden behind the dried banana flakes. She assembled a junk-food feast, complete with guacamole, hot dogs, cinnamon buns for dessert—enough cholesterol to choke a horse—plunked herself down on the mattress in front of her TV and started the video.

Winter of the Heart was Brandon Scott's most famous movie so far. Nadja and Meggie had seen it three times in the movie theater and twice on tape, and it never failed to transport the two of them into a state of weak-willed adoration. She was counting on its having its usual salubrious effect.

The opening frames weren't much of a help. For the first time, she noticed the writing credits. Screenplay by John James O'Leary, based on a novel by Nathaniel Harris. She shoved a chipful of guacamole in her mouth, snarling.

By the time she was halfway through, she knew she should turn the tape off, but she couldn't help herself. Brandon Scott in glorious buffed Technicolor had lost his magical effect. Meggie watched the familiar scenes unfold, and all she could think about was the annoying predictability of the plot.

By the end, when all the women and half the men lay dead amid the gorgeous scenery, her mood hadn't improved. She snapped off the TV and went in search of ice cream.

She must have dreamed about him, of course. When she woke the next morning, she was covered with a fine film of sweat, her body tingled, and she knew her dream had encompassed one of the finest sexual encounters of her life, far better than anything she'd ever actually experienced. The problem was, she couldn't remember anything about it.

The first thing she saw when she came downstairs was John James O'Leary, sitting at her counter. She almost turned around and walked out again, but she steeled herself. She'd never been a coward, and she wasn't about to start now.

"We're not open for breakfast," she said.

It was amazing to her, how a grin could be condescending, infuriating, mocking—and utterly charming, despite it all. "And a good morning to you too, Meggie. Yes, I slept well, thank you for asking, and I'd love a cup of coffee."

"Did Nadja let you in?"

"She did. I sent her up to Madame Rose's with a sack of nuts and twigs for Brandon. She seemed to think you should be the one to deliver his breakfast, but since she said she couldn't make coffee, I didn't give her any choice."

"We don't do take-out service."

"Not even for the sexiest man in the world?" O'Leary taunted.

If there was any way she could possibly survive without coffee, she would have done so, but some things were simply beyond her. "You're really starting to annoy me, O'Leary," she muttered, heading back out into the kitchen.

She should have known he'd follow her, looming over her as she ground the beans, lounging against her refrigerator. "There are other places to get coffee, O'Leary."

"Yeah, but none of them with such charming company," he shot back. "By the way, where do I buy a pack of cigarettes in this place?"

"You smoke?"

"I'm trying to quit."

The day was looking up. She couldn't keep the wicked smile from her face. "The problem has been taken out of your hands, O'Leary, at least for now. Cigarettes are outlawed in Watson Hole. You can't buy 'em, you can't smoke 'em."

He stared at her in shock. "You're kidding."

"Nope. This is the most politically correct town in the entire United States. You can't wear fur within the city limits, you can't smoke cigarettes, you can't use foam cup or paper napkins or wood heat. You can only buy nonalcoholic wine and beer, you get fined if you use more than a certain amount of gasoline per month, and you get free condoms everywhere you go. They were trying to outlaw red meat, as well, and they've almost succeeded."

"Oh, God," O'Leary said.

"She's allowed, but She has to be multicultural and multigendered."

"What the hell am I doing here?" he murmured to himself.

"You tell me."

They stood in contemplative silence, watching the coffee drip. "I watched *Winter of the Heart* again last night," she said casually. "I noticed that you wrote it."

He looked at her warily, clearly not duped into expecting lavish praise. "So?"

"So how come all the women die in the movie? And how come they have all the personality of a flyswatter, and how come they're just on screen to give Brandon a chance to take off his shirt or look depressed?"

"Didn't you appreciate Brandon taking off his shirt?" he countered.

"I didn't think a woman had to die for it."

"I gather militant feminism isn't outlawed in Watson Hole. Listen, sweetheart, I didn't write the book, just the adaptation. For which, I might mention, I received a Golden Globe and an Academy Award."

"You must be very proud," she said with spurious sweetness.

He glared at her. "You're very annoying, you know that? If it weren't for your coffee, I'd be half tempted to take you outside and dump you in a snowbank."

"You and what army?"

He let his eyes run down the length of her, slowly, and it was all she could do not to react. She was wearing black sweatpants and a T-shirt that said The More I Know Of Men, The More I Love My Dog, and her long hair was screwed up in a knot on the top of her head. She seldom bothered with makeup, and today was no exception. He could hardly be impressed.

"I might enjoy trying to give you a taste of your own medicine," he murmured.

Sudden, unexpected sexual heat was in his voice. A heat that curled between her breasts and traveled downward. She took an instinctive step away from him, unsettled. "Yeah, but I make great coffee," she said, pouring him a mug. Hoping he didn't notice that her hand was shaking. "So when are you leaving?"

He took the mug, his hand brushing hers. Hands that were long-fingered, elegant. She cursed inwardly. She'd always been a sucker for beautiful hands. "In a hurry to get rid of us, Meggie? You haven't had a chance to fling yourself at America's sweetheart yet."

"Who says I want to?"

"Everyone wants to, Meggie," he said flatly.

She smiled at him over her own mug of strong, wonderful coffee. "Oh, poor O'Leary. I'm sure there are some women in this world who would settle for you. Don't give up hope."

She was hoping to infuriate him. Instead, he merely gave her a measured look. "I won't, sweetheart."

He set his mug of coffee down on the counter. He took her coffee away from her, as well, setting it down beside his. And then, to her absolute astonishment, he kissed her.

Chapter Three

He tasted like coffee. He tasted like winter, and toothpaste, and an icy heat that was like nothing she'd ever felt before. Somehow, her body had gotten pressed up against his, his hands were around her waist, holding her, and he was using his mouth like an instrument of the devil, seducing her into a brainless mass of bean sprouts marching toward destruction.

Oh, Lord, and she wanted to go! She wanted to sink into that dizzying mass of need and elusive fulfillment, she wanted to let her brain go flying free and concentrate only on her body and the powerful, churning reaction he was coaxing from her. He'd pushed her up against the counter, he was using his tongue, and she was just about ready to put her arms around his neck and kiss him back with all the fierce, burning need that had been banked inside her for too long when she heard the front door of the restaurant open.

The shock of it made it easy to shove him away. "It's too early in the morning, O'Leary," she said. Summoning her last ounce of self-control and taking her coffee, she strode past him into the dining room of the restaurant. Before he could see just how badly he'd shaken her.

Nadja was busy hanging her parka on the row of wooden pegs across the back wall, and for some reason her gaze slid away from Meggie's with an almost guilty furtiveness. She knows, Meggie thought.

"How's Brandon?"

Nadja threw back her head and smiled brightly. "Gorgeous, of course. If you'd only woken up in time, you would have been the one to see him. God, Meggie, he's enough to make your teeth ache."

"Too many sweets tend to have that effect," O'Leary drawled, sauntering out of the kitchen.

Nadja's pale skin turned a bright red. "I didn't realize you were still here."

"I'm on my way out," he said. He didn't touch Meggie as he moved past her, and she could almost sense the faint stirring of air currents against her body as he walked by. It felt like a caress.

She said nothing, waiting until he'd left. She could see the street from her vantage point, and she stared after him until he was almost out of sight, halfway up the hill to Madame Rose's. And then she turned to Nadja.

"Something is very wrong," she said in a doleful voice.

"What do you mean?"

"We screwed up. Did the spell backward, summoned an evil twin. I don't know—it's just wrong!"

"Don't be ridiculous. I followed the directions. We used the snowman as our poppet, we cut out a picture of Brandon Scott and stuck it to his chest, I lit the candles, burned the sage and did the incantations. You pictured him in your mind, didn't you, while you were kissing Frosty?"

"I tried," Meggie said.

"And here he is. Five days later, the man of your dreams arrives in town for no discernible reason, he doesn't even know why he's here, and you think something's wrong?" Nadja said with a trace of irritation. "Sometimes you don't know how lucky you are."

"I just wish he hadn't brought O'Leary with him," Meggie said in a small voice, perching on one of the wooden stools and dropping her chin into her hands.

"Why not? I've never known a man to get the better of you, and while O'Leary might come close, I'd still put my money on you anytime." Nadja joined her at the counter, shoving a hand through her frizzy hair. "Besides, he didn't happen to just show up here, any more than Brandon did. There must be some reason why he chose this time to come here. Some destiny he has to fulfill."

"That's what I'm afraid of," Meggie muttered.

"You think he'll come between you and Brandon?"

"Sort of."

"Well, don't let him," Nadja said in a bracing voice. "If you want Brandon Scott, you fight for him, with every fiber of your being. Don't let anything get in your way—not friendship, not second thoughts. Just do it. And don't waste your time with regrets."

There was an odd note in Nadja's voice, one that pulled Meggie out of her self-absorption to stare at her oddly. "You're ten years younger than me—how come you're sounding like Obi Wan Kenobi?"

Nadja's pale mouth curved in a ghost of a grin. "Age doesn't necessarily equal wisdom, young Skywalker."

"Too true."

"So what are you worried about? Besides O'Leary trying to throw a monkey wrench into your future?"

She couldn't bring herself to confess the truth. That she was having a hard time even noticing her heart's desire when O'Leary was anywhere around. And O'Leary's unexpected kiss hadn't helped her equilibrium one tiny bit. It was nothing more than hormones run amok—she hadn't been kissed in years, and it was only natural she'd react to it. If it had been Brandon Scott kissing her, with that rich, pouty mouth of his, she probably would have climaxed on the spot. Instead of simply coming perilously close to it.

"I just want to make sure we did it right," she said stubbornly.

Nadja sighed. "Okay, we'll check tonight."

"Why not now?"

"If you want to draw another pentagram in the snow, light candles and have you wrap yourself around Frosty in broad daylight..."

"Tonight will be soon enough," Meggie said hastily. She glanced around the empty restaurant. "I suppose I should start getting ready for the lunch crowd. We've only got two more days of this."

"Maybe we'd be better off closing the place now and concentrating on packing up."

"Then what in God's name would I do with all that leftover tofu and bean sprouts?" Meggie asked.

"Eat it?"

"You're sick, Nadja," she replied, insulted, pushing away from the counter and heading back into the kitchen. The scent of coffee was rich in the air, and O'Leary had left his coffee cup on the counter, where he'd kissed her. She scooped it up, ready to dump it in the sink, but something stopped her. She stared at it for a moment, meditatively. And then, almost without realizing what she was doing, she put her mouth against the rim, where his mouth had pressed.

The realization of what she was doing hit her with a shock, and she dropped the mug on the floor, watching it shatter at her feet. Once again the knowledge hit her, certain and sure. They'd screwed up that incantation. They might have summoned Brandon Scott, but all she could think about was John James O'Leary.

O'Leary was everything she didn't want in a man. Strong, demanding, bad-tempered, forcing himself into her consciousness when she'd rather be dreaming about Brandon Scott. She'd spent almost ten years of her life ignoring men, but O'Leary wasn't a man to be ignored.

And it scared the living hell out of her.

O'Leary would have been all right if he hadn't made the mistake of taking a nap. He'd brought his laptop with him, and once he'd managed a decent breakfast and a gallon of coffee that was far inferior to Meggie's brew, he concentrated on getting some work done. He missed his cigarettes, damn it. Almost as much as he missed seeing Meggie McGraw snarl at him.

Speaking of snarling, he'd had to stay in the kitchen long enough to pull himself together. If her plain little friend hadn't come in, he would have gotten her to open her mouth to him. He would have lifted her up on the counter, moved in tight between her legs and worked her into the same mindless, lustful, irritated state he was in.

He'd just felt her begin to respond when she pulled away, and he'd kept his reaction to himself as she escaped—there was no other word for it—from the kitchen. He didn't want her knowing what she did to him. Not when even he couldn't figure out why.

Two flights beneath, tourists were trooping through the bordello, giggling at the naughty oil paintings, fascinated by the rough-and-tumble life of times gone by. Up here, all was peaceful, with only the painting of the voluptuous creature over the desk disturbing his thoughts.

He wondered if he could talk the Watson Hole Historical Society into parting with that painting. He doubted it. According to the guidebook, the lush creature reclining on the red velvet sofa was thought to be none other than Madame Rose herself. No one could tell for certain, because her face was hidden, turned away from the artist.

He stretched out on the bed, only planning to rest for a moment or two before he went in search of something decent for lunch. He stared up at Madame Rose, at her creamy white flesh, her thick tumble of honey-streaked hair, and he wished he could see her face. For some reason, she reminded him of Meggie. Though, on second thought, that wasn't so odd. Anything sexual made him think of Meggie.

She came to him in a dream of gaslight and whiskey and the rich, seductive smell of cigarette smoke. Her face was still hidden, her body draped in diaphanous silk, and she looked like an erotic dream come to life. She moved out of the shadows and knelt on the bed beside him.

"Nothing but the best for Madame Rose's private customers," she murmured, reaching for the brass buckle on his jeans. And as her hand trailed over him, he looked up into Meggie McGraw's wickedly gorgeous face.

He woke up with a start, alone on the bed. The darkness of early winter had settled down around the place, and the reconstructed gas lamps outside the front of the building glowed beneath the lightly drifting snowflakes.

There were no cars on the streets, and no electric lights, and for an odd moment he had the sense that he'd traveled through time. That if he stepped outside of his bedroom he'd be stepping into the past, into the time of Madame Rose. He stood leaning on the windowsill, letting his imagination drift. Until he saw Brandon pull up in that car he shouldn't be driving.

He had someone with him, and O'Leary peered down, trying to see who the blonde du jour was. He recognized Meggie's skinny little friend with a sense of shock. There was no mistaking the frizzy hair beneath the scarf, the thick glasses. No mistaking Brandon's effortless charm, even from this distance.

O'Leary pushed away from the window. Brandon always insisted he adored women, all women, but up until now his taste had still seemed to run to perfectly proportioned goddesses.

He went back to his computer, switched it on and stared at the screen in brooding silence, his fingers tapping on the cherrywood table. It was none of his business if Brandon wanted to seduce and abandon Meggie's innocent little friend. As a matter of fact, he ought to be grateful Brandon had set his sights on Nadja, rather than Meggie. O'Leary had yet to meet a woman who was immune to the world's sexiest man.

Though why gratitude should have anything to do with matters was beyond him. Why should it matter whether Brandon slept with Nadja and Meggie?

Because he wanted to sleep with Meggie, he admitted to himself. And the thought of Brandon Scott putting his perfect hands on her gave O'Leary a tension headache.

He switched off the computer and rose. He needed to warn Meggie, he decided. Her best friend was in danger of getting her heart broken, and Meggie would want to know about it. Yes, that was what he would do, he thought. And then maybe he'd look a little harder for a place that sold cigarettes.

He met Brandon walking up the snow-packed street, snowflakes speckling his blond mane. "I don't think you want to go down there, Jay," he said. "You won't be welcome."

"What have you done this time, Brandon?" O'Leary demanded wearily.

"Had a wonderful day with Naddie," he said sweetly. "It doesn't have anything to do with me, or with you, either, I expect. They're doing some sort of Wiccan incantation, and testosterone would upset the balance of nature."

O'Leary just stared at him. "Oh, my God," he said in disbelief.

"Actually, it's probably 'Oh, my Goddess,'" Brandon said. "They should be finished soon enough. Nadja and I are going out for dinner at the natural-foods restaurant up the mountain. You're welcome to join us."

O'Leary didn't bother to hide his shudder. "What about Meggie?"

"She can come, too, but Nadja says she hates health foods."

"Then what's she doing running a health-food restaurant?"

"You hate Hollywood. What are you doing writing screenplays?" Brandon replied with maddening, unanswerable logic.

O'Leary snarled, then started past him down the snow-packed road.

"I really think you ought to leave them alone," Brandon called after him.

"I'm not going to bother them. I'm looking for cigarettes." It wasn't an actual lie. He *was* looking for cigarettes. And he had no intention of bothering Meggie and her little friend as they danced naked around a campfire, or whatever it was they were doing. He simply wanted to watch.

It took him a while to find them. They were out in back of the restaurant, in a small side street, and the light from the candles surrounded the odd tableau. O'Leary ducked into the shadows, watching, and forgot all about cigarettes for the first time since he'd quit.

"Don't you think we should have waited until after midnight?" Meggie demanded, looking over her shoulder uneasily. The alley was deserted, as usual, and overhead a sliver of moon hung crooked in the sky. A witch's moon, Meggie thought, shivering in the icy breeze.

"I need to find out what went wrong." Nadja's fierce quiet was uncharacteristic. She moved around the pentagram, lighting the candles as she sprinkled sage over each one. "I'm not willing to wait."

"Why not?" Meggie was more than willing to wait for an answer she wasn't sure she was ready to have. She didn't want to know that they had screwed up somehow. Strangely enough, she was even more unwilling to find out that everything was as it should be. That Brandon Scott was here for her, and it was just taking both of them a ridiculously long time to realize it.

Nadja shrugged her skinny shoulders. She had a hat pulled down close to her hair, and her brown hair frizzed out the sides. She squinted at the candle, and though Meggie couldn't see behind the thick lenses of Nadja's glasses, she almost suspected that Nadja was crying.

But Nadja was sane, grounded, and had no earthly reason to cry. Whereas Meggie was feeling as if she had a bad case of PMS, when logic and her calendar assured her she didn't.

"All right," she muttered, reaching into her bra for the crumpled page from the magazine. "Let's get it over with." She unfolded it and pressed it against the snowman's bulbous chest, securing it with a tack. "How do we do it this time?"

"The same way," Nadja said. "Put your arms around the snowman, press your breast against the picture, and picture him in your mind. The way he looks in the picture. And then kiss him."

Meggie smoothed the crumpled sheet against Frosty's icy chest. "I'll try," she muttered. "I didn't have too easy a time visualizing him..." Her voice trailed off.

"What's wrong, Meggie?" She heard Nadja's voice coming to her from a distant place, and for a moment she wondered whether she'd fainted. She stepped back from the snowman, bringing the magazine page with her.

She wasn't sure whether to laugh, to curse, or to cry. She looked at the piece of paper clutched in her fist. It was a picture of Brandon Scott, all right, looking tanned and gorgeous at last year's Academy Awards. When she ripped the page out of the magazine, she'd barely noticed the couple standing with him. The Oscar-winning screenwriter John James O'Leary, and his far-too-gorgeous date for the evening.

"I think I found our problem," she said in a dull voice. She passed the damp, wrinkled paper over to her friend. Nadja squinted at it for a moment, then carried it over to one of the candles that were stuck in the snowbank, squatting down to get a better look at the picture. And then her eyes met Meggie's.

"You didn't notice this before?" she asked in a quiet voice.

"It was darker that night. Midnight, in case you'd forgotten, and I think we'd had too much wine. We must have, otherwise we never would have done anything so incredibly stupid in the first place."

"How did you know? How did you guess?" Nadja demanded.

She sounded upset, and Meggie knew she should rouse herself, comfort her best friend over the failure of her first attempt at spell-casting. But right then she was too busy feeling sorry for herself. "I knew," she said in a small, bitter voice. "Blow out the candles, Naddie. We have our answers. Unless you know how to undo it?"

"Meggie, it was a joke. A parlor trick. Don't you remember what it says on everything I sell— 'These items are for entertainment purposes solely'? It was nothing but a coincidence that he showed up here."

"There are no coincidences—isn't that what you're always telling me?"

"Well, this time there are." Nadja bent over and blew out the candles, scurrying around the deserted alleyway. "There's a perfectly logical explanation. And the fact that there's another man in the picture shouldn't have any bearing on the matter. You know what you want. Go for it."

"Go for it," Meggie echoed dully. Except she didn't know what she wanted. Her hormones, her heart, were at war with her brain. And she'd made it a policy never to be unduly swayed by common sense.

"I'll take this stuff back to the shop. Brandon's asked us to go up to Zach's for dinner. I told him we'd be ready by seven."

"Zach's?" Meggie echoed. "He'll feed us seaweed for dinner."

"It's entirely natural and full of nutrients."

"It's entirely horrible and full of sand," Meggie shot back. "I'll stay home."

"Meggie, you wanted him..." Nadja said, and there was no missing the sound of desperation in her voice.

"Past tense, Nadja. The spell backfired, and right now I don't give a damn about Brandon Scott, gorgeous as he is. You go and eat seaweed with him. He won't even notice I'm not there."

For a moment, Nadja didn't move. "Are you really certain, Meggie?" she asked, an odd expression on her face. "You really don't want him?"

"After all your hard work? I'm afraid not, kid." Meggie ran a hand through her thick hair. "You go ahead and have a good time. I have to do something about exorcising my particular demon."

Nadja hesitated a moment longer. And then she was gone, disappearing into the starry night with a swirl of her handwoven poncho, leaving Meggie alone in the darkness.

She'd called both of them. And when she put her arms around Frosty, closed her eyes and summoned him, it hadn't been the perfect California beach bum who arrived. It had been someone darker, leaner, meaner.

"O'Leary," she said in a bitter voice, "why in God's name did it have to be you?"

"Just lucky." His voice floated out over the still night air, and for a moment Meggie thought she'd dreamed it. She turned to look at Frosty for one long, uneasy moment, but the great white monolith didn't move. She wondered just how much O'Leary had heard. When the shadows shifted, he stepped forward into the murky moonlight and Meggie's heart stopped beating. "You want to tell me what the hell's going on here, Meggie?"

And for one brief moment, Meggie considered ripping Frosty's head off and heaving it at her unwanted eavesdropper.

Chapter Four

Meggie looked furious, which was no surprise. She was always looking pissed as hell when she looked at him, and O'Leary had grown used to it. This time, however, she looked oddly stricken, as well. As if she'd been told her dog had died.

"Eavesdropping, O'Leary?" she said in a deceptively even voice, kicking out the traces of the pentagram from the snow. "Don't you have any other way to get your jollies?"

"Not in the land of the politically correct," he said.

"You come from L.A. You should be used to political correctness."

"Actually, I live on an old ranch in Montana. The kind of place where you can find a good steak and a pack of cigarettes when you need them. The kind of place where men are men and women are glad of it."

"The kind of place where half of Hollywood has descended and bought up the land at inflated prices from people who've been there for generations. Just who did you rip your place off from, O'Leary?''

"My father. And his father and grandfather before him."

He'd finally managed to shut her up, though he knew it wouldn't last long. There was a meditative expression on her face that he could recognize even in the darkness, as if she was considering whether he might not be the devil incarnate, after all. "What's it like?" she asked in a marginally nicer voice.

"Five hundred acres of hills, rocks and the sweetest little waterfall you've ever seen. My parents sold it to me when my father retired. The two of them drive around the country in an RV the size of Rhode Island, and they told me they weren't coming back to Montana till they had some grandchildren."

He could have sworn she'd turned pale, but it was really too dark to tell. "I didn't know you were married," she said.

"Haven't been for eight years."

"She couldn't put up with you, eh? I can't say I'm surprised."

That was the Meggie he knew and loved. "Yeah, but I've mellowed over the last few years," he said.

"You're a regular pussycat."

He considered crossing the packed snow and kissing her again, and then thought better of it. If he kissed her now, he wasn't going to stop, and he really didn't feel like dropping his jeans in the snow. He'd been hard-pressed to think of anything but her mouth since he'd kissed her that morning, and the longer he waited, the more overpowering the very thought became.

He could wait a few more hours. Until he got her someplace warm, dry and secluded. And he could see whether he'd really flipped out and he was imagining the hot thread of longing in her belligerent eyes whenever she looked at him.

"So where do we find a truly great steak in this crunchy-granola town?" he drawled.

"Saucy Jack's, just up the road from Madame Rose's. And what's this *we*, white man?"

"You aren't going to make me eat alone, are you? With only my dubious self for company?"

"Why would I want to do you any favors?" she said warily.

"You wouldn't. You'd want to pick on me and fight with me some more, and I wouldn't be surprised if you wanted to do it over a good steak." He waited. She was wavering, and he had absolutely no intention of letting her say no. He couldn't rid himself of the feeling that time was running out, and if he didn't move soon, it would be too late, and she'd be gone.

She wasn't in any particular hurry to put him out of his misery. He stood there in the chilly moonlight, waiting, and he had a sudden, strange notion. He could see himself down the years, waiting for her while she tried to figure out the best way to annoy him. And for some reason, that bizarre vision was strangely enticing.

"Are you by any chance asking me out on a date, O'Leary?" she said, her voice laced with suspicion.

"Lord, sweetheart, what if I am? It's not much of a commitment, is it? I'm not asking you to bear my children."

Now he'd really managed to startle her, and he couldn't figure out why. For some reason, she was treating this as if the fate of the world, or at the very least, the rest of her life, rested on the answer. If she tried to say no, he'd just start kissing her.

"Okay," she said, in such a small voice that for a moment he doubted he'd heard her correctly.

There was something odd going on. The cool night air was dry and sparkling with electricity, and for some strange reason he glanced over at the snowman, wishing he'd heard more of Meggie's conversation with Nadja. Frosty just squatted there impassively enough, but for some reason O'Leary could almost imagine an expression on that bulbous face. One of sly amusement.

"Okay you'll go to dinner with me?" he asked. "Or okay you'll have my babies?"

He wanted to see if he could push her far enough to find out why she'd panicked, but she'd already gotten past whatever was troubling her. "For a great steak, I'd go out with Newt Gingrich," she said. "And Saucy Jack's has great steaks. As for the kids, if you want your parents to visit that badly, then maybe you'd better rent some."

"Don't you want kids?"

For some reason, she glanced at the snowman. "All in good time, O'Leary," she said. "All in good time."

This was a major mistake, Meggie thought as she walked beside him up the hilly street. Behind her she could just imagine Frosty, watching them as they headed toward the steak house.

None of this made any sense. She didn't believe in magic spells, she didn't believe in snowmen, she didn't believe in summoning people or love at first sight. And most of all, she couldn't believe how much she wanted O'Leary, the bad-tempered swine, to kiss her again.

She'd been presented with a choice back there, a simple enough choice. She'd wanted Brandon Scott, who was rich, famous, gorgeous and sweet. She'd summoned him, and ever since he'd arrived all she could think of was his traveling companion, who wasn't nearly as pretty, rich or famous. Not to mention the fact that he was singularly devoid of sweetness.

There was no use reasoning with herself, berating herself, or hiding in her apartment over the store any longer. The moment she kissed the snowman, she'd put these events into motion, and she couldn't fight them anymore. It was time to give in and see what happened.

Saucy Jack's was packed. It was December 30, the night before New Year's Eve, and like most ski resorts, the town was crowded to capacity. O'Leary made no effort to help her with her coat, which was a good thing. She probably would have smacked him. The bar and anteroom were jammed with people. "Looks like we're in for a long wait," he said.

"Not necessarily." She started back toward the kitchen, and he followed.

"Meggie, darling!" the burly, bearded chef called out to her from across the madhouse of a kitchen. "You've been a stranger!"

"Not tonight, Jack," she called back. "Anyone in the Vegetarian Room?"

"It's yours, Meggie. Who's your friend? Do I smell love in the air?"

Saucy Jack was well named. Fortunately, Meggie had her back to O'Leary, so he couldn't see her uncharacteristic blush. "You smell burning steak, Jack," she said severely, as she started up the winding metal stairs.

She was oddly breathless by the time she got to the private dining room, and she told herself it was the steep climb, rather than the man who followed close behind her. The first floor of the restaurant held the public rooms, and the second held a series of smaller private dining rooms. Most of them were filled, as well—she could tell from the noise of muted conversation. She opened the door to the Vegetarian Room and then almost closed it again.

It was too late to back out. "Here we are," she said brightly, strolling in.

She'd forgotten that the room looked like something out of Madame Rose's Palace—forgotten the huge overstuffed sofas, the candlelight, the decadent Victorian lushness of the place.

But O'Leary was already closing the door behind them. "I hope this doesn't mean we eat vegetables tonight?" he murmured, leaning against it. Barring her escape.

She didn't want to escape, did she? "The Vegetarian Room is the most private of all Jack's private dining rooms. It's for those clean-living souls in town who don't want to be seen when they eat red meat and drink whiskey."

He glanced at the overstuffed sofa. "Are those the only sins people indulge in around here?"

She knew what he was thinking. She knew, because she was thinking the same thing. "Most people have their own bedrooms, O'Leary," she said sharply.

He moved away from the door, starting toward her, and she took a deep breath, waiting. She liked his face. It wasn't pretty, like Brandon's. It was narrow and clever and dangerously intelligent, and his dark eyes held secrets that enticed her. She didn't even dare look at his mouth, for fear that she'd fling herself against him.

She liked his body, too. She liked tall men, men who were lean and strong, rather than bulky. And his hands made her hot and cold at the same time.

She wanted his hands, and his mouth, on her. And she wasn't used to this feeling, this wanting. She took a tiny step backward, coming up against the table. Then the door opened and the waiter appeared.

She didn't realize her sigh of relief was audible until she saw the faint, ironic grin on O'Leary's face. O'Leary's mouth. "It's only delayed," he murmured under his breath, holding her chair for her with mocking politeness.

They ate red meat and drank wine. They had coffee and cognac and sinfully wonderful cheesecake. They talked, and they laughed. And Meggie could feel herself fall deeper and deeper under Frosty's spell. Or was it O'Leary's spell? She could no longer tell.

They'd ended up on the sofa. A dangerous move, but so far he'd kept his distance, lounging in one corner while she curled up in the opposite, her hands cradling the glass of cognac. "So are you going to tell me what was going on with the snowman?'' he asked lazily, and she was too warm and too comfortable to be wary.

"I suppose so. Do you believe in magic?"

"No."

She smiled into her cognac snifter. "Spells? Crystals? Incantations?"

"I don't even believe in destiny," O'Leary said.

"Then it would be a waste of time trying to explain to you what happened."

"Try me," he murmured. And she told herself there was no double meaning.

"It was the night of the winter solstice. A night of great magical power," she began.

"If you say so."

"Don't interrupt me if you want to hear this." Her voice was stern.

"Sorry."

"Nadja and I decided to see if we could work a little magic. The restaurant was closing, I'd had enough of Watson Hole, and I decided I needed a handsome prince to rescue me."

"Oh, let me guess," he said. "Brandon Scott."

"It's half your fault," she protested, still feeling stupid. "If you hadn't made him so appealing in that sexist movie . . ."

"If *Winter of the Heart* was so sexist, why did you even bother to see it?"

"After the seventh time, it began to annoy me," she said with great dignity. "But you've got to admit, the boy is devastatingly pretty."

"He's not my type," O'Leary drawled, watching her.

"I don't think he's my type, either," Meggie admitted mournfully.

"You're getting sidetracked," he said, but she thought his dark, dark eyes looked vaguely pleased.

"We decided to see if we could summon Brandon to Watson Hole. Nadja works with me, but she also runs a new-age bookstore, you know. She has access to everything—crystals, incantations, herbs and candles. And I must admit we'd had a little too much wine with our pizza. So we decided to see if we could turn the snowman into Brandon Scott."

"You've been listening to too many Christmas songs," he said. "Obviously it didn't work. Frosty's still there."

"But so is Brandon. He showed up a week later, for no particular reason. He just arrived at my doorstep, as if he'd been summoned."

He stared at her. "That's why you screamed."

She nodded. "It was unnerving, to say the least. I hadn't really believed it would work. Even when I kissed Frosty..."

"You kissed the snowman?"

"It was part of the spell." She couldn't help the defensive note in her voice.

"And how do snowmen kiss?" He'd somehow moved closer. He'd finished his own cognac, and his tanned, beautiful hands were free. She clutched her own glass more tightly.

"Not as well as Brandon Scott."

He froze. "When did you kiss Brandon?"

"I haven't. But I've seen all his movies, even the bad ones. He's one of the all-time great kissers."

"And you're one of the all-time great idiots," he shot back. "Don't you know that screen kisses are all show? There's a technique to them, and it has nothing to do with real kissing."

Meggie shrugged. "I'll take your word for it."

"No, you won't." He took the glass of cognac out of her hand and set it on the table in front of the couch. She considered fighting him for it, but then she decided it would be undignified. If he was going to kiss her again, and she strongly suspected he intended to, then she was determined to be cool and unruffled.

He slid his hand along her neck, tilting her face up to his. "With a screen kiss," he said, "you put your mouth at a slant, alongside the partner's mouth. Depending on how passionate it's supposed to look, you grind your jaw up and down a lot."

"It sounds painful." Her voice was no more than a whisper.

"It's not very arousing." His voice was low, too, persuasive. Dignity, she reminded herself, staring at his mouth. "Whereas a real kiss is an erotic feast in itself." His thumb brushed across her lips, and they parted, trembling. "One open mouth against another," he whispered. "Tongue and teeth, heart and soul."

He still didn't move closer. Meggie felt hot and cold at the same time, and light-headed with longing. Her heart was beating so loud and so fast, she wondered that he didn't hear it. "It sounds very . . . pleasant," she whispered.

His smile was slow, and incredibly erotic. "Pleasant?" he echoed in a soft voice. "I could make you come just by kissing you."

She stared at him, transfixed, breathless, waiting. Only to have him move away from her, leaving her unkissed. "So you really believe you brought Brandon Scott here by kissing a snow-man?'' he said.

It took her only a moment to pull herself out of the trance. "There was more to it than that. We had to put a picture of Brandon on Frosty's chest. And that's where we screwed up."

"Oh, yeah?"

"You're beginning to annoy me, O'Leary," she said, reaching for her cognac and draining it.

"Beginning to? I thought it was hostility at first sight."

"Exactly."

"So how did you screw up?"

"I put the wrong picture on Frosty's chest. It was Brandon, all right. But you and some blond bimbo were in the picture, as well."

"Blond bimbo?"

"Someone with enormous breasts, clinging to your arm and looking at you like you hung the moon."

"Oh, Annabelle," he said, remembering. "Actually, it was the bra she was wearing. I don't think she's any better endowed than you are."

"I might hit you, O'Leary," she said in a meditative voice.

"You've had too much cognac." He reached for the empty glass, but she clung to it tightly. "So you ended up summoning both of us?"

"Obviously."

"Obviously," he echoed wryly. "And you expect me to believe that?"

"You're here, aren't you?"

She'd managed to startle him out of his obnoxious superiority. "A coincidence."

"There is no such thing as coincidence," she intoned.

"You've definitely had too much cognac." He rose, stretched, and she looked up at his lean body with confused, disgruntled longing. "Come on, Meggie, a little fresh air will do wonders. I'll walk you home and put you to bed so you can sleep it off."

He reached down, caught her hand and hauled her to her feet. She stumbled against him, and his arm came around her to steady her. Their faces were close, dangerously close.

Meggie knew exactly how much she'd had to drink. One glass of wine and a snifter of brandy. She could drink most ski bums under the table when she was in the mood, and it wasn't the alcohol that was making her dizzy and irrational.

She wasn't about to tell him that. "Such a perfect gentleman," she said coolly, pushing him away. "Let's go."

He caught up with her halfway down the snow-packed street. A light snow had begun to fall, but Meggie was ignoring it. Ignoring him, even though he had her jacket in his hand and it was probably in the low twenties. "You're going to freeze to death," he said as he caught up with her.

"It'll sober me up," she managed to say.

"You still haven't explained why you haven't flung yourself at Brandon since he arrived."

"I told you, we screwed up."

"So you got me, as well? What's the big deal? Just ignore me."

She stopped, glaring up at him in the moonlight. "Don't you think I haven't tried? You are amazingly obtuse, aren't you, O'Leary? I didn't get you, as well. I got you instead. Brandon is the one who came along for the ride."

He stared at her. Without a word, he put her coat around her, pulling it tight. Pulling her against him. She didn't fight him or pull back. She simply let him put his hands on her.

"You're telling me that Frosty didn't turn into Brandon Scott? He turned into me?"

"You got it," she said. "Though I think he kisses better."

"I doubt it," he said. And finally, finally, he put his mouth against hers.

Chapter Five

She was cold, so cold, but where her body pressed up against his, she was burning hot. His mouth against hers was cold, as well, tasting of snow and cognac and coffee. She was trapped against him, imprisoned by the coat flung over her shoulders, and she had no desire to escape. She tilted her head back, closed her eyes and let him kiss her, fighting the overwhelming urge to kiss him back.

If she kissed him back, she'd be lost, forever. She didn't believe in magic, in spells, in summoning forth spirits, and she certainly didn't believe in snowmen. O'Leary lifted his head, and when she opened her eyes she could see him looking down at her.

"I'm still in one piece," she said. But her voice shook slightly, and some of the grimness vanished from his eyes.

"Yeah," he said, "but you had to fight it."

She wanted him to kiss her again, but he didn't. He simply pulled the coat more closely around her, threaded his arm through hers and continued down the snowy street.

They stopped outside Madame Rose's Palace. There was no sign of Brandon Scott's sports car, and the building was almost dark. O'Leary glanced up at the place, making no effort to release Meggie's arm.

"I thought you were going to walk me home," she said in a deceptively even voice.

"This is as far as you're going tonight," he said.

"Says who?" As a response, it lacked a certain sophistication, but right then Meggie wasn't feeling sophisticated.

"Me," O'Leary said. "Come inside and I'll ply you with cognac."

"You told me I'd had too much."

"I lied."

"I'm not going to sleep with you, O'Leary," she warned him as she climbed up Madame Rose's front steps.

"Fine," he said. "I'll do my best to keep you awake."

She should turn and run. She wanted to. He wasn't holding her that tightly, and he certainly wasn't going to coerce her. If she wanted to leave, to run away, all she had to do was pull her arm away, wish him good-night and walk away.

She stepped inside the perfumed parlor of Madame Rose's bordello and let him close the door behind her. He locked it, barred it, but he didn't bother to turn on the lights. The tiny, decorative white lights from the shrubbery cast a pale glow inside, enough that she could see his face. She backed up, instinctively, not sure why she did so, coming up against the solid hard-wood door.

"If you put the chain on, how will Brandon get back in?" Her voice was low, hushed in the dim light.

"He's already found someplace else to spend the night."

Meggie made a little grimace. "I don't imagine Nadja will be too happy about that," she said. "She seems to be reacting to him the way I was supposed to."

"I think she'll be very happy. No one's ever said Brandon isn't good in bed, and he's sleeping with her."

She accepted that information calmly enough. "Good for her. I hope," she added, honestly enough. She glanced behind her at the barred door. "And how am I supposed to get out?"

"Just lift the chain, Meggie. No one's forcing you to stay here," he said, as he pushed the coat from her shoulders. It fell in a pile on the floor, and she shivered.

"I don't think this is a good idea." She couldn't keep from watching his big, beautiful hands as they stripped off his jacket.

"Why not? It's fate. You summoned me, you say, whether you wanted to or not. So here I am, primed and ready."

"You don't believe that."

"I'm here, aren't I? And I want you. I believe that much."

The flat honesty of his words shook her. "Listen, all you have to do is drive up to the ski resort, and you can have your pick of dozens of women who look just like . . . like that woman in the picture," she said, somewhat desperately. Why the hell had she come in with him? What had happened to all her carefully honed self-protective instincts?

"I don't want a woman like Annabelle. If I did, I would have stayed in Hollywood. I want you."

"Stop saying that!"

"Why not? It's true." He seemed more fascinated than offended by her protest.

"You don't even know me. You know nothing about who I am, my hopes, my fears, my dreams..."

"Sweetheart, just because I want to strip off your clothes and screw your brains out doesn't mean we need to get involved. I'm talking a one-night stand here, not a lifetime commitment."

Her outrage finally vanquished her nervousness. "You despicable cretin," she said furiously, pushing away from the door. "You slimy, sexist, brain-dead pig. You have the soul of a turnip and the moral standards of a water closet. You—"

He caught her, pulling her up against him, and she could see that he was laughing. "And you have a way with words, Meggie. I'd much rather have you pissed at me than scared."

She should have ripped herself out of his arms, but for some reason she couldn't. "I don't get scared."

"Bullshit, Meggie. You say I don't know you? Wrong, lady. I know you more intimately than people I've known for decades."

"I'm so glad I'm that easy to figure out," she said bitterly.

"You're not at all easy. You're a bundle of contradictions. It must be that your magic snowman is giving me a little help."

"I never should have told you," she muttered.

He threaded his long fingers through her tangled hair, the gesture unbearably intimate, as he tilted her face up to his. "Shall I tell you about yourself, Meggie? Prove how well I know you? I know you're impatient, too smart for your own good, trying damned hard to be a cynic and losing because you've got a dreamer's heart. You're loyal, generous, and self-sacrificing, and deep underneath your tough exterior you're scared to death."

"I'm not afraid of anything," she protested in a hoarse voice.

"You're afraid of everything, Meggie. You're afraid of commitment, of being alone. You're afraid of downhill skiing and tofu and bean sprouts, you're afraid of magic, and you're afraid of men. And most of all, you're afraid of me and what I might make you feel."

It was a good thing the hallway was dark. He wouldn't be able to see that her face had drained of color. She couldn't see it, either, but she could feel it. The stricken expression that no amount of defenses could keep from her face as he summed her up so damned accurately.

She made one last effort. "You're ridiculous. If I'm afraid of men, how come I tried to summon Brandon—?"

"Because he's a fantasy. A mindless, pretty little boy who wouldn't threaten or challenge you in any way. He's someone perfectly safe. And for some reason, you're looking for safety."

"Obviously I'm not going to get it with you," she managed to say.

"Obviously not. But I'm not convinced it's what you really want."

"You are egocentric, aren't you?" she said with a respectably cool tone, despite the fact that his long fingers still cradled her face. "Why don't you let go of me, and I'll take myself back home to my apartment? Alone."

"I can do that, Meggie," he said. "If you kiss me."

She rolled her eyes. "I've already kissed you, O'Leary. Twice. And, frankly, the earth didn't move."

He ran his thumb across her lower lip, and despite her best efforts, it trembled. "Meggie, Meggie," he whispered, bending toward her.

"You stood still, patient and well behaved, while I kissed you. That's not the same as you kissing me back, and if you haven't realized that by now, then you're even more innocent than I thought."

"I'm not innocent," she protested, deeply offended.

"Prove it, Meggie. Kiss me, and then walk away."

He knew her too well. How he'd managed to see right through her well-disguised fears was a mystery, but she wasn't going to give him the satisfaction of realizing he was right.

"Certainly," she said in a brisk voice, sliding her hand up the side of his neck and pressing her lips against him. Hard. And then she backed away, and he released her, his dark eyes watching her.

"There," she said, ready to leave.

"Surely you can kiss better than that, Meggie," he taunted her. "You're such a connoisseur of screen kisses, I'd think you'd had a little more practice."

"I've had plenty of practice."

"Prove it."

"O'Leary..." she protested.

"Kiss me again, Meggie. Do a thoroughly indecent job of it, and I promise never to taunt you again."

"Promises, promises." But she made the very foolish mistake of stepping up to him again, putting her hands up on his shoulders and tilting her mouth up to his. He didn't move, didn't do anything to help her, and she knew perfectly well that a fast, hard kiss wouldn't help her vanquish her fears and this annoying man.

"Kissing is a highly overrated activity," she said severely.

"You obviously haven't been kissing the right men."

She put her mouth against his, softer this time. His lips were firm, well-defined, and she allowed herself a tentative nibble with her own. He still didn't move, just stood there, patient, as she slowly explored the outside of his mouth.

She touched his lower lips with her tongue, and he opened his mouth to her, with far more patience than she would have thought O'Leary capable of. He waited for her, and she advanced, carefully, ready to retreat at the first sign of aggression. But he simply stood there, letting her learn the contours of his mouth.

She liked it. Oddly enough, it was almost as if she'd never kissed anyone in her life. Maybe kissing Frosty had opened up a whole new realm in the heretofore unappreciated world of kissing.

She grew a bit more enthusiastic, sliding her arms around his neck, pressing her body up against his. His hand stayed at his sides, not touching her, a fact that she found vaguely annoying and insulting, until she happened to rub against his groin and discovered just how aroused he was.

She broke the kiss, meaning to step back, but she couldn't. She simply took a deep breath and moved closer, pulling his head down so that she could kiss him again, and this time he kissed her back.

His hands slid up her thighs, bringing her loose skirt with him until he cupped her hips, pulling her tight against him. She shivered slightly in the cool night air, and when he broke the kiss she felt as if she were going to explode.

"Are you going to run away, Meggie?" he whispered. "Or are you going to come upstairs with me?"

"I'm coming upstairs with you," she said.

* * *

If he wasn't so damned turned on, he would have laughed. She sounded like someone facing her execution, and she put her ice-cold hand in his and let him draw her up the two flights of stairs so many couples had traveled, for exactly the same purpose, with all the enthusiasm of an early Christian martyr.

Who would have thought fierce, fiery Meggie would be shy and uncertain? Who would have thought someone who aroused such lusciously sexual feelings inside him would herself be sexually timid? It was all part of the enigma of Meggie McGraw, and before he'd even realized it, the stakes had risen tremendously. He had to go about making love to her with the dedication of an artist. One wrong move and he could cause irreparable harm.

He shouldn't feel uncertain. He was a sensual man, talented and creative in bed. He knew tricks, moves, ways to arouse the most stubborn woman. But tricks wouldn't do with Meggie. He refused to consider why, but the rest of his life depended on the next few hours. And if he wasn't so turned on, he'd be almost as scared as fearless Meggie McGraw.

He didn't bother to turn on the light. He closed the door, took her cool, limp hand in his and placed it against his chest. Against his pounding heart. "Tell me, Meggie," he whispered in a calming voice, "did someone do something to turn you off?"

"No." The word was almost inaudible. It was also a lie.

For some reason, he decided to push it as he began unfastening the tiny buttons of her sweater, starting at her throat. "No one hit you? Forced you? Raped you?"

She jerked her head up, staring at him, that heartbreaking mix of fear and courage in her eyes. "Life isn't always that simple, O'Leary," she said. "I'm sorry, but I just find all this a highly overrated activity."

Relief swept through him. "Not like in books or the movies, is that it? No waves crashing?"

"No."

"And exactly how many lovers have you had, Meggie?"

"Four hundred and thirty-seven," she snapped. "Is that enough?"

"Obviously not." He'd finished unbuttoning the sweater, though she didn't seem to have noticed. She was wearing a soft, lacy bra, God bless her, with a front clasp. He undid it, and for a moment she panicked, wrapping her arms around her chest.

"Change your mind, Meggie?"

For a moment, she didn't move. She glanced over at the huge, rumpled bed where he'd spent the afternoon napping, dreaming erotic dreams of her. And then she looked at him.

"No, I haven't changed my mind," she said in a small voice.

"Then let me see your breasts."

After a moment, she dropped her arms, still looking like a martyr. He moved closer to her, pushing the sweater off her shoulders, pushing the bra with it, so that she stood in front of him in her long, full skirt, her thick hair tangled around her shoulders, like a Pre-Raphaelite beauty.

Before he could touch her, she put her hands out, and he half expected her to push him away, to grab her discarded clothes and run. Instead, she reached out and began to unfasten the buttons on his soft denim shirt, staring at them with single-minded determination, as her beautiful breasts rose and fell with her labored breathing.

Her hands touched his skin, cool against his heated flesh, as she pushed the shirt from him.

And then her eyes met his, defiantly. "Next?" she said.

"Your smart mouth won't protect you, Meggie," he said.

"It won't?"

"You don't need protection from me." And he kissed her so softly on her mouth that he felt her soften and melt.

Never in his life had he had the faintest desire to carry a woman to bed. Without thinking, he scooped Meggie up, holding her tight against his chest, skin to skin, and moved across the room with her. He laid her down on the bed, covering her body with his, covering her breasts with his hands, pressing his groin against the cradle of her thighs, as he kissed her, slowly, letting her accustom herself to the feel of his mouth against hers, his chest against her breasts, his erection pressing against her belly.

She kissed him back, sooner than he could have hoped. He felt her fingers trace the muscles on his shoulders, down his arms, and he let his mouth descend the side of her neck, nibbling, tasting.

She stiffened when he put his mouth on her breast, then leaned back, determinedly patient. Something else she didn't like, as well as kissing.

Something else he'd have to teach her to appreciate.

She was a quick student, a fact that clearly surprised her. Her hands, which had lain passively against the sheets, reached up and caught in his hair. Within moments her back was arching and her hips were moving restlessly, as he moved his mouth to her other breast, feeling the nub harden against his tongue.

He was going to take it slow, spend the entire night carefully seducing her into a state of mindless oblivion, despite the cost to his own well-being, but she was already racing past him. He could feel her tension, her astonishment and her need, and he could only thank God he wouldn't have to risk insanity by waiting much longer.

He tore the button on her skirt, yanking it off her, taking her lacy panties with it. She'd closed her eyes, and he knew he could unfasten his jeans and take her like some Edwardian bride. And he could make her enjoy it.

But it would be cheating. He took her hand in his, and she opened her eyes, wary, some of the haze of bewildered desire fading. He put her hand on the stiff bulge beneath his zipper, half expecting her to pull away.

She didn't. She stared at him for a moment, and then her long fingers stroked down the length of swollen denim, so that it was he who closed his eyes with a groan of impossible longing, ready to explode.

But she deserved better than that. He pushed her onto her back, very gently, and used his mouth on her, nibbling at her breasts, kissing her navel, putting it between her legs until she was beating at his shoulders, gasping with frustrated need that he could fulfill so easily.

But he wasn't going to make her come that way. Not without him. He shoved off his pants, then moved up over her, filling her with one thick, sure thrust, holding very still as she convulsed around him.

He waited until the first wave passed, and then he began to move, pushing in deep, pulling out and then thrusting deeper still. At first she could barely respond. She simply lay beneath him, accepting, her body still shaken with the aftermath of her climax.

But she was capable of more, and he knew it, even if she had her doubts. He felt the rise of tension once more, the occasional soft cry. He buried his head against the side of her neck, lost in the scent and texture of her, of Meggie, learning her delight and his, and when he heard her cry out in choking need, he put his hand between them, touching her.

Her cry drained his soul, drained his body, and he poured himself into her, lost, his teeth on her shoulder, his heart in hers.

He wasn't sure who regained some portion of sanity first. It should have been him. He should have taken it all in stride—he was used to the transcendent pleasures of lovemaking.

Ah, but he wasn't used to the transcendent pleasures of making love with Meggie McGraw. The way she curled up against him, hiding her tear-damp face against his chest, oddly, endearingly shy, tore at his heart. Her faint, watery sigh made him long to tighten his gentle hold on her, and the feel of her smooth, warm skin made him hard again.

She slept, exhausted, against him, curled up trustingly. In the warm room, he cupped her breasts, and they hardened instantly against his skin. He stared down at her, at the salty streaks of tears that ran down her pale face, and he told himself to ignore the strange burst of joy and panic that battled inside him.

He could leave. He could always leave. Hadn't he told her it was a one-night stand?

And hadn't he known he was lying? The woman in his arms was his, whether they were joined by fate, by lust, or by the vagaries of a blank-faced snowman perched on the edge of the village.

Just as he belonged to her.

And outside, the icy snow began to fall.

Chapter Six

When Meggie awoke, she was alone in the rumpled bed. A murky twilight filtered in the window, and she burrowed deeper into the feather bed, deciding it had to be near dawn. She closed her eyes and breathed in the scent of him. Of them.

Her body tingled with the afterglow of all the things he'd done to her. All the things she'd done to him. He'd lied to her—he'd let her sleep, but not for long. She would drift off, sated, replete, and then awake, to find him wrapped around her, inside her, just as she was ready for him.

She hadn't been kissing the right men, he'd told her, and the truth of that was unavoidable. None of her options were particularly appealing. Either she was extremely difficult to please, or the magic she and Nadja had conjured on the winter solstice had been powerful indeed. Or the third, most terrifying possibility of all. That, by some twisted joke of fate, O'Leary was her destiny. A destiny he said he didn't believe in.

She didn't want O'Leary. She wanted someone safe and nonthreatening, someone who could give her children and freedom and leave her alone. She expected that making those children would be the same slightly uncomfortable, slightly ridiculous situation it had always been before, but it was one she was willing to put up with.

But not after O'Leary.

She could still feel his hands on her. His mouth covering her body. The feel of him, inside her. She could feel him, and she wanted him again, needed him.

She opened her eyes in the semidarkness, wondering where he'd disappeared to at the crack of dawn. And then she focused on the carriage clock by the bed in disbelief. It was half past nine in the morning.

She stumbled out of the bed, dragging the sheet with her, and headed for the window. She knew what she'd find before she got there.

A storm had blown up during the night, something very close to a blizzard. The visibility was so limited she couldn't even see the street outside Madame Rose's. But she knew what wouldn't be there. O'Leary's car.

Except that it wasn't O'Leary's, she reminded herself absently. It was Brandon's. And he was probably gone, as well.

She turned and looked over the room. He'd managed to pack everything without waking her, an amazing feat, considering how lightly she usually slept. But then, she'd had far more than her usual share of exercise the night before—she probably could have slept through a herd of elephants.

No note to be seen. O'Leary had left after his one-night stand, just as he'd warned her. If she'd had any sense at all, she'd be relieved.

After all, if she'd enjoyed sleeping with one man, she could probably find another who'd be as good, or better. Someone with a sweeter nature than O'Leary, which wouldn't be hard to find.

It took her almost half an hour to make the ten-minute walk back to the health-food restaurant, battling the weather. It was no surprise that the place was dark and deserted, with no sign of Nadja. After all, New Year's Eve was technically their last day of business, but their customers had already found new places to patronize, and the weather was hardly conducive to impulse shopping.

She headed straight upstairs to her apartment, to her shower, marveling at her wonderful calm. Nothing could touch her, she thought as she used up every bit of hot water, scrubbing her body. Her defenses were back in place, no one could hurt her. Her interlude with O'Leary had been . . . instructive, but it was a fortunate thing he'd up and disappeared without any embarrassing morning-after scene. Now she could get on with her life, without his annoying presence. She had plans to make, places to go.

She found the note lying on the counter when she wandered out into the dining room, a cup of coffee in one hand, and for a moment her heart leaped inside her, and the coffee trembled in her hand. She set the mug down carefully on the counter. Reaching for the paper, she told herself that Nadja's scrawling handwriting was a relief. And who else would have left her a note?

Meggie—I've gone to California with Brandon. Please don't be angry with me. You're right—we must have screwed up on the incantation. All I know is I can't help myself.

I couldn't find you to tell you we were leaving—we wanted to get out before the blizzard hit. Brandon says to tell O'Leary that he can keep the car for now. Don't be mad at me.

I'm sorry about the snowman. Nadja.

Meggie set the paper down again. It was past noon by now, and that strange, eerie light continued as the storm battered the village. It was going to be a hell of a New Year's Eve she thought. And then the last sentence registered.

She ran outside into the deep snow, with no coat and only her canvas sneakers on her feet. The storm was too thick for her to see more than a few feet ahead of her, but she didn't hesitate. She stumbled toward the side alleyway, searching for the rounded shape of the magic snowman.

He lay in a pile of snow, smashed to pieces, already covered with a thick layer of new snow. Someone had driven into him, most likely, or some teenage hooligan had taken a shovel to him. It didn't matter. He was gone, as surely as if he'd melted in the bright sun. For a moment, Meggie stood there, unmoving, as the snow coated her hair and eyebrows.

"What the hell you doing out here, Meggie?" The snowplow driver leaned out the window and shouted through the whirling snow. "This stuff's gonna keep up for another five or six hours. Best go get warm."

She shook herself, and the snow went flying. "Thanks, Danny," she said numbly, turning away from the ruins of her one brief bout of magic.

"Sorry about your snowman," he called as he rolled up the window. "You can always make another, if this snow keeps up."

She didn't even bother to give him a reassuring smile—he wouldn't have seen it through the whirling snow. Instead, she just waved at him.

The power went off just as she reached the restaurant. She'd left the door open in her mad dash outside, and already snow had drifted into the front entrance. She slammed the door shut against it, kicked off her shoes and walked barefoot on the cold, wet floor.

She sat down at the counter, picked up her coffee and burst into tears.

Life certainly was a pain in the butt when you least needed it to be, O'Leary thought furiously, reaching automatically for the cigarettes that were never there. It was always two steps forward and one step back. Sure, he'd gotten to spend the most earth-shattering night of his thirty-seven years with a woman who fascinated him almost to the point of obsession. But after that his mental processes had melted entirely.

It had made perfect sense to him at four-thirty in the morning. He'd throw all his stuff in the back of Brandon's stupid little car, make the four-hour drive north into Montana in three hours flat, pick up the Jeep, tell Marge to expect visitors, and be back before she even realized he'd left town.

Of course, he'd reckoned without a blizzard clamping down over the highway once he'd reached the halfway point. And top-of-the-line all-weather radials didn't do diddly-squat in deep, drifting snow. He made it to the ranch—or, more exactly, to a snowdrift half a mile away from the main house, in just over six hours. Only to find that the phone was out once he got there.

He kept telling himself that Meggie was a reasonable woman, and he knew he lied. Her very lack of reasonableness was part of her dubious charm.

He told himself she had to know him well enough to realize he wouldn't have just taken off. And he knew that was exactly what she'd believe.

He paced the old pine floors of the sprawling ranch house, staring out into the storm with mounting frustration and something oddly akin to panic. Three times he tried to leave, only to have the wind whip up the fallen snow into a cloud of zero visibility. The fourth time, just after five o'clock in the afternoon, he kept going, headlights piercing the swirling snow and the pitch-black night.

The snow turned to a mushy kind of sleet sometime in the middle of the afternoon. Meggie sat alone in the deserted café, listening to the most lugubrious country music she could find on the battery-powered radio, and stared out into the storm. She was drinking lukewarm diet Coke now, and eating everything in sight as she waited for the power to come back on. For the snow to stop. So she could get the hell out of there.

Not that her ancient Toyota was all that good in deep snow. It didn't matter. As long as she was out of Watson Hole by the New Year, she'd be all right, she promised herself. She could put the past behind her.

And never, ever, would she kiss a snowman again.

Oddly enough, she mourned Frosty. Instead of brooding over O'Leary's expectedly faithless ways, she concentrated on the tumbled pile of snow that had once embodied her romantic dreams. Of course, they'd been the wrong romantic dreams, summoning the wrong man to interfere with her carefully arranged life-style, but nevertheless, she mourned him.

The lightweight snow from the blizzard would have been worthless for packing. Once it warmed to a wet sleet, Meggie pulled on ski bibs that had never seen a ski slope, tucked her feet into her warmest pair of boots and headed out into the afternoon light. The wet snow plastered her face and hair, soaking through her down parka. She didn't care.

It took her almost an hour to finish building the new snowman, on the very spot where Frosty had stood. The new version was a sleeker one, taller, with a rakish tilt to his head that somehow reminded her of O'Leary in one of his baiting moods. As she worked, she hummed under her breath, a tuneless little hum that was part "Frosty the Snowman" and part "You Can't Get a Man with a Gun." When she finished, it was fully dark, the lights were still out around town, and the sleet had turned to a sullen rain.

Meggie looked up at her snowman with a jaundiced eye. "I'm going to keep away from cold climates, kid," she said aloud. "At the very least, I'm going to avoid snow." She leaned forward, putting her arms around his middle. "In the meantime, take care of yourself, Frosty. And thanks for O'Leary. Even if he is a son of a bitch."

She pressed her mouth against Frosty's freshly ice-packed face. And then she headed back to the café, determined to get the hell out of Dodge before she asked the snowman to bring O'Leary back to her.

It shouldn't have taken her long to pack. She was a woman who traveled light, and even if some inexplicable part of her had started longing for some kind of permanency, she hadn't yet started acquiring the things that made moving a royal pain.

Within an hour, working by candlelight, she'd managed to pack up her clothes, books and CDs and drag them downstairs to the front door. She glanced back at the kitchen, strongly tempted to walk away and never look at another bean sprout, but she couldn't do that to Nadja. Sooner or later she'd be back, once she realized that all men, Brandon Scott included, were pigs, and she wouldn't want to deal with a refrigerator full of moldy health food.

Meggie yanked open the refrigerator and stared inside in dismay. Blocks of tofu filled the second shelf, sitting in slimy bean water. On the shelf above, bean sprouts grew, their little tentacles stretching down toward the tofu as if they were separated lovers.

With a shudder, Meggie started hauling out the tofu, dumping it in the trash. A big block slipped out of its protective wrapper, landing on the butcher-block counter with an ominous splat, and Meggie just stared at it, wondering if she could steel herself to pick it up with her bare hands.

She was so engrossed in her battle of self-will that she didn't hear the front door open. She'd just managed to force herself to touch the gelatinous mass when O'Leary sauntered in the door, looking cold, ice-coated, and gorgeously smug.

If it wasn't for the smugness, she would have dropped the tofu and run to him, and the hell with good sense and self-preservation. If he'd said something apologetic, or sweet, she would have forgiven him anything.

Instead, he leaned against the doorjamb, his dark eyes bright and mocking, and drawled, "Miss me?"

She looked down at the glop of aging tofu in her hands, then looked up at him. A moment later, the mass was winging its way toward his head.

His reflexes were impressive. He ducked, and the stuff smacked against the doorway, then slid down into a gelatinous puddle on the floor.

"Yes," he said meditatively, staring down at the mess. "You missed me."

She dived for the refrigerator, searching for more ammunition, but he was too fast for her, pulling her away and slamming the door shut. She yanked her hand free, glaring at him as she backed away across the candlelit kitchen. "What were you expecting?"

"I've only been gone a total of fourteen hours, Meggie," he said, in a voice of perfect reason. "Don't you think you're overreacting?"

"It depends on what fourteen hours we're talking about. Why did you leave?"

"I had to get a couple of things."

"What?"

"My Jeep. I figured I couldn't fit all your stuff in the back of Brandon's toy car."

Her hands were sticky from the tofu. She rubbed them on her thighs, staring at him in disbelief. "Why would you want to put my stuff in your car?"

"I thought you could come back to Montana with me." He sounded almost casual about it, and she considered picking up the tofu from the floor and trying another shot.

"Why should I want to do that?" she said suspiciously.

"Beats me. Why should I have shown up here in the first place? No one ever said it made any sense."

She considered it. She considered him. There was no way she could look at him and not feel the pull, the need that twisted her insides. It wasn't as simple as lust or desire, as pure as liking, as easy as love. It was a tangled knot of angry, needy emotions, and whether she liked it or not, she was caught.

"How long would I be staying?" she asked him, her voice just as casual.

"Oh, it'd be up to you. I was thinking maybe fifty, sixty years."

She stared at him. "This is crazy."

"Yes."

"You think I'm going to do it?"

"Yes."

She scowled in frustration. "I can't be in love with you. I've only known you for three days, and I'm not someone who falls in love." She took a step closer to him, away from the tofu. "Are you in love with me?"

"Yes."

She shook her head. He was leaning against the refrigerator, seemingly at ease, staring at her out of dark, watchful eyes. "You're expecting me to throw common sense away, to just toss my stuff in your car and go with you without even considering the future? I suppose you expect me to marry you and have babies, as well?"

"Yes," he said.

She glanced back at the tofu longingly. "Can't you say anything but yes?" she snapped.

"Yes," he said. "Come here, woman, and take a chance."

"Oh, hell," Meggie said. And she flung herself against him, before wisdom and fear could prevail. His arms came around her, tight, and he was warm and strong and real, and she could feel the layers of ice melt around her. Outside, she could hear the church bells toll midnight, as the New Year broke around them. Inside, Meggie started to cry.

And she was home at last.

*   *   *   *   *

Carla Neggers

Husband for Hire

Dear Reader,

Most of us end up making New Year's resolutions we know, deep down, we'll never keep. I think it's a way of reminding ourselves what's truly important in our lives and what isn't. My sure losers go like this:

     1. I will finish my sister's wedding present, an intricate cross-stitched sampler. I'm late. She and Bill were married on Valentine's Day 1983.

     2. I will not let vegetables rot in the bottom of the refrigerator.

You see? Sure losers. But I don't beat myself up over this stuff. My sister hasn't asked about her sampler in several years. Won't she be surprised when I do finish it? I work on it a little every year. As for the fridge— well, really, who cares? It's not like there's *always* something growing in the veggie drawer. Just occasionally.

"Time takes fresh start again." It's one of my favorite Ralph Waldo Emerson quotes. For me, *that's* what New Year's is about. When I sit by the fire on a dark, cold Vermont New Year's Eve and reflect on the past year, I want to know I've done the important stuff. I've spent time with my family and friends. I've written the best books I could, I've given myself the breaks I need. When I imagine the next year, I want to know I'll keep doing the important stuff. The sampler and the fridge— hey, there's always *next* year!

Have a great '96!

Carla Neggers

Chapter One

"Look at it this way," Cady Dye said. "A week in New York—all expenses paid—has to be more exciting than watching the moose feed in the bog up here in the woods."

Cole Forrest tossed his shovel in the back of his truck, having just dug Cady Dye out after an overnight storm had dropped eight inches of snow on the lakes region of Maine. A picturesque sight for Christmas morning. He'd even shoveled off the roof of her borrowed cabin to keep the weight of the snow from caving in on her. After five days, he had discovered Cady Dye was one intense woman, fast-talking and very determined about getting her way—just as he'd expected.

But the cold Maine air was doing interesting things to her teal-colored eyes, and the backdrop of snow and ice set off her trademark rusty curls in a manner that had him imagining his fingers in them. Dangerous stuff. It was Christmas Day, and Cady Dye was alone on an isolated lake in northern New England. It could just mean she needed a breather from her high-pressure, nomadic life. It could also mean she didn't have many friends and there was a good reason for it.

Either way, Cady Dye wasn't Cole's type, her teal eyes and rusty curls notwithstanding.

He pulled off his canvas work gloves. In spite of the twenty-five-degree temperature, he was sweating. He'd gotten right on the job, while the snow was still light and fluffy and easy to shovel—not that Cady Dye showed any indication of going anywhere. She seemed content to sit by the wood stove and watch old movies on the VCR. Cole hadn't noticed a single human footprint in the snow that drifted across the frozen lake and into the woods of white birches and evergreens. Appreciating the gorgeous view from behind a window wasn't good enough for him. He had to get out in the countryside.

But when he finished shoveling, he'd found her standing behind him. She'd pulled on one of those parkas that could be three or four different coats, depending on what you zipped in or didn't zip in. Cole had on an old chamois shirt and his black-and-red checked wool hunting vest.

But thinking Cady Dye was out of her element and therefore vulnerable, he knew, would be a mistake.

Then she'd made her surprise proposition, and all his preconceived notions about her had immediately been set into a turmoil.

"A week in New York," he repeated. He kept his tone matter-of-fact. "And all I have to do is pose as your fiancé."

"Correct."

She was being very matter-of-fact herself. Maybe *too* matter-of-fact. It was as if she'd been thinking over this little scheme of hers for a while. It wasn't anything impulsive, born simply of being alone on Christmas Day.

"All expenses paid, plus a hundred dollars a day?"

She nodded. "We leave in the morning. You'll be back here January second, or possibly even late on New Year's Day."

"How many parties?"

"Angie's annual post–Christmas, pre–New Year's dinner on the twenty-eighth. She's a friend, so that will be easy. It should help with any jitters you might have."

Jitters?

"Then there's a dinner with two of my colleagues on the twenty-ninth," she went on, ticking off her week without hesitation. She'd worked this all out in advance. "We do a cocktail party the next evening, then a New Year's Eve party at Robin Cross's place on Park Avenue."

Robin Cross coanchored one of the morning news programs and owned the cabin Cady had borrowed for the week before Christmas. A long time ago, it had been Cole's father's getaway—except he'd seldom gotten away to it.

"The cocktail party on the thirtieth," Cole said. "Where's that?"

Cady Dye gave him a look that suggested it couldn't possibly make any difference to him, because he wouldn't know what she was talking about if she told him. It wasn't so much snooty as pragmatic. Not one to waste time, Cady Dye.

But she said, "It's at Billy Del Rio's place in Greenwich Village."

Billy Del Rio. Well, well . . . Cole knew Billy. He was a war correspondent of legendary proportions, addicted to the job, mentor and friend to Cady Dye—if not a bad influence, certainly not a good one.

"We're colleagues," she added, apparently just in case Cole might not know. "We just got off a tough assignment. He's at home for a few weeks."

"Then he's not the guy you're trying to scare off with this fiancé scenario?"

She sighed. Accustomed to being on camera, Cady Dye would know how not to show her emotions. But Cole still felt he'd struck a nerve. "I didn't say I was trying to scare off anyone," she said smoothly. "Part of our deal, Mr. Forrest, is for you to be satisfied with what I tell you, which won't include details of why I feel our little charade is necessary. So there'll be no reading between the lines or guessing or asking questions that I have no intention of answering. Okay?"

"In other words, I'm to take your money and keep my mouth shut."

"Yes. I'm paying you well, Mr. Forrest."

Indeed she was. But money played no role— zero—in why he hadn't stuffed her headfirst into a snowbank after she made her proposition. He had integrity. He had *principles*. He wouldn't pose as any woman's fiancé for mere money. But he might if she was in more trouble than she wanted to admit. He'd seen Cady Dye's reports from her last hellish posting. It had been a tough assignment, all right.

"You don't strike me as the manipulative type," he told her, keeping his tone mild and nonconfrontational.

She inhaled deeply, about as close to bristling as she was going to get when she was trying to close what she would regard as an up-front, if unusual, business deal. She wouldn't like thinking of herself as manipulative. She was straight-up, in-your-face Cady Dye, the reporter her television network stuck in whatever hot spot in the world happened to be hottest. She wasn't the sneaky, scheming newswoman of the old stereotype.

"I'm satisfied I'm doing the right thing," she said loftily, the cold air bringing a rosy glow to her cheeks. "That'll have to be good enough for you. If you don't want to do this, just say so."

"And you'll go somewhere else?" Cole was amused by the idea. He knew this corner of Maine, and its people, well. "Arnie down at the gas station's looking for extra cash. 'Course, he dropped out of school in the tenth grade and hasn't seen a dentist in years, but he's got a good heart—"

"Mr. Forrest, I've given you my offer. Yes or no."

He squinted at her, the sunlight bright off the fresh snow. Cady Dye, he realized, didn't want Arnie from the gas station, or anyone else. She wanted him.

He wanted to know why. She was from a world he'd rejected, and here she was, luring him back into it.

"Sleeping arrangements?" he asked.

She didn't blush. No, not Cady Dye. But she did avert her eyes, just a little. It was enough to tell Cole that the prospect of the two of them in bed had crossed her mind—a reasonable enough conclusion, since she was asking him to pretend they'd fallen madly, passionately, in love during her brief sojourn in Maine. "We'll—um—have separate rooms. A friend's loaning me her residential suite in a hotel on Central Park. She's skiing in Vermont for the holidays." Then she added, almost as an afterthought, "I don't have a place of my own."

A week in a New York City hotel suite. Not how Cole had planned to round out the old year and ring in the new. But Cady Dye had him hooked, and she knew it.

"Oh, I almost forgot," she went on quickly. "I'll be happy to provide you with proper clothes—"

The woman did have gall. She couldn't have gotten where she was—would never have survived—if she didn't. Cole eyed the snowbank he'd created when he plowed her dirt driveway. He might yet change his mind about popping her into it.

"I've got clothes," he said.

"Yes, I'm sure you do, but you'll need to have—"

He looked at her. "You're going to have to take me as I am, or not at all."

"This is a business arrangement. It's not as if you're *really* my fiancé. People have to believe we'd be—well, compatible, on more than a primitive level, that there's more than animal chemistry between us. Not that there *is* any, of course, but—" She faltered, practically choking on her words—a rarity, surely, for Cady Dye. She glared at him as if he were the one who'd tripped her up. "You know what I mean."

"I certainly do." Animal chemistry. Yeah, he knew what that meant. He could feel it. It wasn't something he'd have to fake.

Neither, he was certain, would Cady Dye, even if she wasn't about to admit it.

She narrowed her eyes suspiciously. "I'm only saying if we look too mismatched, this thing won't work. Nobody'll believe it."

Cole walked around to the cab of his truck and pulled open the creaking door. He'd seen Cady Dye on TV in a flak jacket, her rusty hair in dirty tangles, as she took millions of viewers with her into the world of whatever conflict she was covering, showing them the human side, with all its complexities and shadows. Yeah, the two of them were mismatched, all right. But it had nothing to do with how they dressed.

She'd followed him, her bare hands knotted into fists at her sides—whether against the cold or out of tension, he didn't know. In her bright teal eyes, Cole could see her famous determination, the scrappiness and guts and drive that had made her so good at what she did. And yet here she was trying to persuade him, a virtual stranger, to pose as her fiancé, a nutty idea if he'd ever heard one. What if all her friends and colleagues found out? What made her think she could trust him not to squeal on her? If he did, her reputation would suffer.

It didn't add up. Cole liked things that added up.

He climbed into his truck without giving her a reply.

"All right," she said, relenting. "You can choose your own wardrobe, but if it's totally unsuitable, I reserve the right to take you shopping in New York."

He'd thought she knew who he was. Now he wasn't so sure. Which could make their week together even more entertaining. "You're not exactly known for your stunning wardrobe, you know."

She cocked a brow. "I hardly need an assortment of sequins and heels in a combat zone."

He ignored her light sarcasm. She'd made all kinds of assumptions about him that weren't necessarily accurate. Of course, he'd made a few about her, too. "A man's cotton shirt in white or blue-and-white stripe, khaki pants, and that belt with the big gold buckle—America wouldn't recognize you in anything else."

"Well, America doesn't have to recognize me in New York, and I can hardly show up for a formal dinner in khakis. Anyway, it's *your* wardrobe that needs to pass muster, not mine."

"Relax," he said. "It'll pass."

"This means you've agreed? You'll pose as my fiancé?"

He grinned at her. "I don't know if it beats watching the moose feed in the bog, but yeah, I'll do it."

She smiled, ignoring *his* light sarcasm. It was, he thought, a dazzling smile. It made her eyes sparkle and a tiny dimple show up in her left cheek. He didn't think he'd ever seen her smile on television. Ducking bullets, interviewing rebel commanders, exposing human-rights violations—it wasn't the sort of work that brought smiles. Her reporting had always seemed painstakingly balanced, thorough, and utterly human.

Cady Dye, Cole knew, was his reason for agreeing to her little arrangement. Not money or boredom or adventure or even curiosity. Just Cady Dye.

It should have been enough, he knew, for him to get in his truck and drive out of there, up over the hill to where he had his log house and the life he wanted.

"Wonderful," she said. "I'll see you in the morning, then. Merry Christmas, Mr. Forrest."

"If you're to be my fiancée, you should call me Cole."

"Yes, I suppose that does make sense." Then she added, charmingly hesitant, "Cole."

It was a start. He gave her an encouraging wink. "Merry Christmas, Cady," he said, letting her name roll around on his tongue, the way a fiancé might.

Before he could see her reaction, she turned on her heel, slipping on the ice as she started back to the cabin. She recovered just before she landed on her fanny. Cady Dye, he suspected, would pride herself on recovering just in time, before disaster struck. And she'd pride herself on doing it in a direct and up-front manner.

It was out of character for her to resort to trickery and manipulation.

So why was she doing it? Why was she passing him off as a phony fiancé?

Cole started his truck. There wasn't much he could do right now except go home and pack. He was having Christmas dinner with his mother, brother, aunts and uncle. If Cady Dye had a problem she couldn't—or wouldn't—confront head-on, it wasn't going to affect her or him between now and tomorrow morning. Then it'd be off to New York, back into the whirlwind from which he'd extricated himself five long years ago.

But Cady Dye didn't seem to know that. Just who did she think he was?

For Christmas Day, Cady had rented two versions of Charles Dickens's *A Christmas Carol* and had a gourmet dinner delivered from a local inn, complete with turkey, apple-cranberry stuffing, winter squash and Indian pudding. She had a nice fire in the potbellied wood stove, and books to read, and even a pine-bough centerpiece that served as a stand-in for a Christmas tree. She was alone, but she wanted to be alone. She'd *chosen* to be alone. Her parents and sister and niece and nephew had all gathered in Hawaii for the holidays, but Cady had needed solitude.

So why on earth had she gone and hired a man straight out of *The Last of the Mohicans* to pose as her fiancé?

Cole Forrest had eyes the color of charred wood, and dark, shaggy hair, and his attire was old, scarred, frayed, functional. He was as much a part of the Maine wilderness as the moose who frequented the nearby bog. She had to acknowledge a basic physical attraction to him. It was one of those elemental things. Primitive. Probably had to do with biology and the days of cavemen and woolly mammoths and such. Nothing a modern, intelligent, independent woman couldn't overcome.

He would suit her purposes, and that was all that mattered. Hiring him had been expedient. The existence of a not-unanticipated physical attraction wouldn't get in the way. Being experienced with New York and the ways of the world, she would retain the upper hand. Cole Forrest shoveled snow off people's roofs. She had nothing to worry about.

That evening, when she was snuggled under her wool throw and had a fresh log on the fire and Scrooge was being escorted through the English countryside by the Ghost of Christmas Past, the cabin's ancient rotary telephone rang. Cady picked it up, assuming her parents were calling yet again to make sure she was having a wonderful Christmas and didn't need psychological help.

"Cady, Cady, Cady..."

Her heart lurched. How had he found her in Maine? "Billy—come on, you've got to stop this stuff."

"Billy who?"

She gritted her teeth. "Billy Del Rio, a moron who needs some sense knocked into him before he does something really stupid—"

"I've never heard of Billy Del Rio."

Cady snorted and slammed down the phone. It was far from the first such call, and she doubted it would be the last.

Scrooge's fiancée was telling him to go to blazes. Cady pictured her "fiancé." Cole *was* rather like a moose. Big, steady, methodical, potentially dangerous if provoked. But get him a trim, put him in a decent suit, give him a good watch and shoes, and he'd do fine. She'd certainly come up with worse dates in her day, even if no fiancés so far.

And the expense and indignity of it all would be worth it, she thought, if she and Cole Forrest could knock whatever had gotten into Billy Del Rio out again.

Chapter Two

Cole Forrest didn't look as out of place in their New York hotel suite as Cady would have expected.

That worried her.

She would have felt more reassured if he were a bit off-balance. He would look to her for direction and leadership, and she would have a better chance of keeping him under her control. She did *not* need another loose cannon in her life. Billy Del Rio was enough. *She* was enough. The entire trip down to New York, she'd tried to recreate the sense of urgency and logic that had prompted the brilliant idea of hiring herself a fiancé.

The residential suite was high up in an elegant hotel on Central Park South. It consisted of a living room with a dining alcove overlooking the park, and a tiny kitchenette. The decor was all chintzes and flowers, with big framed prints of peonies and roses. Cady doubted Cole looked any more out of place than she did. Given her work, her attitude toward her living quarters was strictly pragmatic. But she did appreciate the stunning view of the city.

Cole was unpacking his things, having assumed—correctly—that he would get the sofa bed in the living room. His leather luggage was old and battered, but of good quality. He had refused to let Cady inspect his wardrobe before leaving Maine. He'd traveled in dark canvas pants and a chambray work shirt with a black T-shirt underneath, which struck her as inordinately sexy. She reminded herself that she was supposed to be comfortable with his sexiness, not taken aback by it. They were supposedly to be married, after all.

She winced. This could be a tricky charade to pull off. On the one hand, she needed a man her friends and colleagues—and Billy Del Rio— would believe she might marry. On the other hand, she couldn't afford to let her physical attraction to Cole Forrest distract her from dealing with why she'd hired him in the first place, namely to refocus Billy's attention on his work and off her. He was in trouble, off the deep end, and they'd been through too much together for her not at least to give him a chance to mend his ways—and the push to do it. She didn't need to entertain any fantasies about herself and Cole Forrest.

But they did, to her distress, keep coming up.

He looked around at her from the closet, in the short hall between the bedroom and the living room. Across the hall from the closet was a spacious, elegant, well-equipped bathroom. "Having second thoughts?"

Was it so obvious? She cleared her throat. Confiding in Cole Forrest was out of the question. She couldn't allow herself to be lulled by the false intimacy of their situation. "I'm just getting my bearings. I haven't been in New York in a while."

"Not what you're used to, is it?"

She shook her head, slipping past him to put her small zippered toiletry kit in the bathroom. Over the years, she'd learned to make do with a few simple necessities. Being in New York didn't change her ways. They were ingrained in her. "I flew into Boston and headed straight up to Maine. I tried to use my week up there to readjust to being back in the country, and just to unwind."

And, she thought, to hide from Billy Del Rio, and to process what he was doing to her and why. In the end, he'd found her.

"Anyway, New York's not exactly what you're used to, either." She smiled as she emerged from the bathroom. "Not a moose to be had."

"More's the pity," he said, finishing up in the closet. She had no idea whether he was serious. She had assumed Cole Forrest would always be transparent, easy to figure out and predict. Not so.

The telephone rang, startling Cady more than it should have. She noticed Cole's dark eyes on her when she jumped. A week in the wilds of Maine hadn't quieted her nerves. She would need more time, even if Billy Del Rio stopped pestering her.

"I'll get it in the bedroom," she said.

But she made the mistake of leaving the door open, not imagining Billy could have tracked her down this fast. She knew when she picked up the phone that there was nothing she could do if Cole chose to eavesdrop. Maybe he wouldn't be that rude and devious. Never mind that in a similar situation she wouldn't have hesitated herself.

She recognized the raspy voice at once. "Cady, Cady... and I thought I was your only love."

Billy. *Damn* him. She swallowed, noticing Cole's suspicious look as he glanced at her from the closet. She couldn't tell him about Billy Del Rio. He wouldn't understand.

"Who's the new boyfriend, Cady?"

She hung up. How did he know already? *How?*

"Wrong number," she told Cole, sounding lame even to herself.

He leaned against the doorjamb, managing to look at once relaxed and ready to spring into action. "Cady, I think you should tell me what's going on."

"There's nothing—"

"If you're worried I might tell someone, don't. I have no one to tell." He pulled away from the doorjamb, moving toward her. She noticed his dark, shaggy hair; it seemed to work with his New York image as well as with his Maine-mountain-man look. "Seems you don't, either."

Cady sank onto the edge of the bed. Her friend who had rented the suite had put out a dish of potpourri; Cady could smell cinnamon and cranberry. She averted her eyes from Cole. "Okay." She breathed out, forcing herself to think. How much did she want to tell Cole Forrest? How much did he deserve to know—did she *need* him to know? And how much, she wondered, did she want him to know, because he was right about the fact that she had no one to tell?

"I'm being harassed," she said bluntly. "Some guy keeps tracking me down and calling me."

"You're sure it's a man?"

"Yes."

"Any idea who?"

She shrugged. But she knew *exactly* who. She just didn't intend to tell Cole. He was the type who'd take the bull by the horns, go find Billy Del Rio and slam him against the wall and tell him to shape up or else, which was maybe what Billy needed.

Lord, she was confused.

"I'm fairly certain it's someone who knows me, or at least has access to my schedule," she said, not too evasively. "He could know someone close to me and be using him—or her—to get to me."

"He could *be* someone close to you."

Billy was close to her. A colleague, a friend, a mentor. They'd been through a lot together. Maybe too much. Their network had its ideas about what to do with Cady Dye and Billy Del Rio, its ideas about their futures. Their *separate* futures.

"Well, if it's someone close to me, he'll see you and realize he hasn't got a chance and leave me alone."

"That's it? That's your plan? You hired me on the chance this guy'll back off because you're *engaged?*"

"Yep."

"Suppose his game's power, not romance? Suppose he's harassing you to rattle you, and he doesn't give a damn who you're sleeping with?"

She licked her lips, trying not to complicate her life by imagining actually sleeping with Cole. "Then I guess my plan will have failed, and I'll have to go back to the drawing board."

He narrowed his eyes at her. She could feel his unexpected intensity. In Maine, he'd seemed so easygoing. "You haven't told me everything," he said. "There's more."

She jumped to her feet, suddenly restless. She felt ridiculously trapped by her own desire to go ahead and tell Cole everything. Never mind her loyalty to Billy. The idiot was harassing her. What did she owe him?

"It doesn't matter if there's more or there isn't. I've already told you more than I'd intended. I assure you, I'm no one's willing victim here. Look, I'm hungry. You want to go get something to eat?"

She expected Cole to press his case, but he didn't. Biding his time, no doubt. "We can just eat here—or do you want to get out?"

In spite of her restlessness, Cady was tired. A dangerous combination. Add the confusion over Billy, being in New York, and a sudden sense of loneliness—and she didn't dare trust herself. "There's not much in the kitchen," she said, putting her problems out of her mind and focusing on her immediate needs. "I'll order room service—"

Cole waved her off, heading down the short hall into the living room. "No, you relax after that phone call. I'll do it."

"Thanks," she said, following him. "Robin Cross did assure me you were a decent sort—reliable, steady."

And not too bright, she'd also indicated. But Cady had seen no evidence of a lack of intelligence, and suspected Robin might have been stereotyping her property's caretaker.

Cole went to the phone on the chest next to the sofa. Cady was intensely aware of his presence in her space, but she reminded herself she was accustomed to sharing cramped quarters with others, men and women alike. She was comfortable around men. The suite was plenty big for her and Cole Forrest. Having him in close proximity with her for the next week wasn't a problem.

Ha! she thought.

But she realized he was scrutinizing her. "I've never met Robin Cross."

"What? But I thought she hired you."

He looked mystified. "Hired me?"

Cady felt a dull pain in her stomach at the prospect of having possibly made a huge mistake. "You're the caretaker for her cabin, aren't you?"

He laughed. It was a deep, raw, sexy sound that made Cady's mouth go unexpectedly—and disconcertingly—dry.

"You must be thinking of Tom," he said.

Tom. Tom who? She didn't speak.

"Wait'll I tell him someone confused the two of us. He'll get a big kick out of that." Cole's laughter continued as he picked up the phone and dialed. He glanced at Cady. "You want anything in particular?"

"Turkey sandwich, lettuce, tomato, no mayonnaise." Her heart was pounding. Somehow, she'd jumped to a terribly wrong conclusion about Cole Forrest. She, who prided herself on her thoroughness, on not jumping to conclusions. "Who's Tom?"

Cole held up a hand. He placed their order, succinctly and without hesitation, undaunted by any perceived complexities of room service in a big New York hotel.

When he hung up, he studied her a moment, his charred-wood eyes unwavering, amused. "Tom's the guy Robin Cross hired to look after her place. I filled in for him last week, and was supposed to this week, but I got a better offer and found another buddy to take my place. Tom and his wife packed up the kids and headed for Disney World. Drove. They've been saving for ages."

"You mean— But if—" Cady swallowed. She *hated* making mistakes, and this one was beyond comprehension. She was living with this man for the next week, and she had virtually no idea who he was. "If you're not Robin's caretaker, then who—then what—"

He sat in a pretty cushioned chair at the round table in the alcove overlooking the park. The New York skyline glittered against the night sky. He looked every inch the Maine mountain man. *Every inch.*

"I live in the log house across the cove from your cabin, up over the hill. My family's owned property on the lake for close to two hundred years. Longer, if you include my Abenaki ancestors, but they had a different idea about land."

Cady was stunned. "I had no idea. I thought—I assumed you were the regular caretaker. Robin didn't give me his name, but I never thought— It didn't occur to me—"

"Tom's a great guy," Cole Forrest said, clearly amused, as he folded his hands on his tight abdomen, "but you wouldn't want him as your fiancé."

"I don't want *you* as my fiancé. Lest you forget, our arrangement is strictly business. There's nothing personal about it. I'm paying you well for your time. I—" She was talking fast, pacing, veering out of control as she tried to put a respectable spin on her foul-up. She swung around toward Cole. "You do understand, don't you?"

Amusement still flickered in his dark eyes, the shadows of the night adding to the interesting angles of his face and adding to the sense that there was more to Cole Forrest than she'd found convenient to believe.

"I'm not going to pounce on you in the middle of the night, if that's what you're worried about," he said mildly. "I'm just saying you wouldn't have thought of hiring Tom to pose as your fiancé if you'd met him. It simply wouldn't have occurred to you."

"You've a high opinion of yourself, Mr. Forrest."

He just laughed. Catching her with her pants down didn't bother *him*.

She retreated to the bedroom to get her bearings. She wondered what Cole Forrest did for a living. Not, obviously, tend seasonal cabins and cottages in the Maine lakes region. She knew *nothing* about this man! The hardworking, dogged, decent caretaker and volunteer fire fighter Robin Cross had described *wasn't* Cole Forrest.

Now Cady was going to pass him off as her fiancé, tell her friends she was marrying him, *act* as if she were marrying him, all in a possibly doomed attempt to keep Billy Del Rio from self-destructing. For the past thirty years, people had predicted he would sooner or later. It was simply a matter of when and how.

Maybe she ought to let Billy go down in flames. Turn him in for what he was doing. Tell their producer. Tell *everyone.*

But she couldn't. They'd been through hell together, she and Billy Del Rio.

She would have to go through with her pretend engagement to Cole Forrest—whoever he was.

Cole stared out at the glittering lights of New York. It was well after midnight, but he hadn't yet slept. He needed to adjust to his surroundings first. He needed, he thought, to make his peace with being here, in the city.

At night, New York prompted a different kind of awe in him from the starlit sky on a winter night in Maine. There, he was constantly aware of how solitary life was, how much he needed that solitude. He would look out at the shadows on the moonlit lake and fail to imagine living anywhere else.

Yet here, in New York, he found the presence of so many millions of people—almost within his grasp—peculiarly reassuring, energizing, filling his imagination, infusing him with possibilities.

Or maybe it was just the one woman asleep in the next room.

Cady Dye. It was an easy name, a memorable name. Millions knew it. Millions had followed her reports from one tragic conflict to another over the years, relied on her professionalism and balance and grit—on her being there for them, getting the story.

She'd hired him to play her fiancé, thinking he was Robin Cross's caretaker. Mistaking him for Tom.

Didn't make much sense.

Her explanation of her mysterious phone call was, at best, incomplete. If she was being harassed and threatened, the Cady Dye of international fame would simply call the police. She wouldn't pussyfoot around with a phony engagement. She wouldn't risk the hit her reputation would take if word got out.

So what was going on?

Cady Dye, he suspected, was burned out, or damned close to it. He could see the signs. The restless energy. Spending Christmas alone. Turning what could be a straightforward case of harassment of a well-known reporter into a major intrigue, adding fuel to the fire by hiring him. She was used to drama, being in the center of a whirlwind. When there wasn't one, maybe she'd create one. Maybe she'd forgotten how to relax. Maybe she'd never known.

A scream from the adjoining bedroom brought him back to the present with a sharp jolt.

Cady.

He went still, listening. He could hear a fake coughing. Covering for herself, now that she was awake. She knew he was in here, possibly awake.

Without making a sound, Cole got to his feet and approached the tightly shut bedroom door. He could hear her thrashing around, drawers opening, more fake coughing. "Cady?"

"It's nothing. I'm okay."

Of course. She wouldn't admit it if she wasn't. But Cole admired her intrepidness, her pride. Cady Dye wouldn't give up without a fight.

The door opened, and she emerged from the dark bedroom. With the drapes still open in the living room, the city lights cast long, eerie shadows. She stumbled past him to the dining alcove and stared out at the park, and the skyline beyond. She was shaking visibly. She'd managed to pull on a dark green chenille bathrobe. It hung open, revealing the plaid flannel boxers and oversize T-shirt she must have slept in. Her feet were bare. Her rusty curls hung limply. She looked haggard and shaken, like someone who'd seen too much. Which Cady Dye had.

"Nightmare?" Cole asked quietly behind her.

She nodded without speaking, without looking at him.

"I couldn't sleep myself. You want a drink?"

"That would be nice."

Her voice was hoarse, raspy, distracted. She was probably still seeing the images of her nightmare. Cole went to the kitchenette and found a bottle of chardonnay in the refrigerator and opened it, watching her out of the corner of his eye. She maintained her rigid stance at the window, as if willing herself to stop shaking. He splashed the wine into two glasses. He yearned to touch her. To take her into his arms and chase away the demons.

But he knew he couldn't. No one could. Cady Dye had to deal with her own demons.

She didn't react—she seemed totally unaware of his presence—until he was close beside her, thrusting the wine at her. She took the glass, but her hands were shaking too badly, and she quickly set it on the table. She tried to cover for her agitation with a faltering smile. "I hate nightmares."

"Given your life, I'll bet you have doozies. Come on, have a seat and drink some wine, shake it out of you."

Using one foot, he pushed a chair out from under the table for her and then sat down himself, opposite her. She slid into her chair, looking thinner than she was, more vulnerable than she'd ever admit. She seemed to have difficulty focusing on him, but she again managed a tentative smile. "Thanks."

"No problem. Always nice to have company when you can't sleep."

"Do you have company? At home, I mean?"

He smiled. "Just whatever wildlife's in the area. I don't even have a dog. They chase the ducks."

"I like ducks," she mumbled, distracted.

"Me too."

She tried the wine, taking the glass in both hands. Her teeth had started to chatter. In the semidarkness, her eyes seemed huge. "It's being on vacation, I swear. I never even dream when I'm working."

Not a good sign, Cole thought, but he kept his opinion to himself. He tried some of his own wine. White wine wasn't his favorite, but he'd make do. "Maybe your body won't let you. Not dreaming could be its way of protecting itself. Now that you're safe, away from your work it's letting you dream and clear out all the junk that's stacked up over the past weeks or months or however long it's been."

That brought her back. She scowled at him in a rather charming way—another opinion he kept to himself. "What are you, an armchair psychologist?"

He shrugged. "For all you know, I could be the real thing."

"I doubt that. I may have mistaken you for this Tom character, but I refuse to believe you're a shrink."

"Still like me as a mountain man, huh?"

Her teal eyes fastened on him, betraying the sharp-minded, skeptical reporter in her. Nightmares or not, Cady Dye was no slouch. "I don't usually make this sort of mistake, you know."

He leaned back. "I don't doubt it for a moment. So how impulsive *was* asking me to marry you?"

"I didn't—" She broke off, sighing. Her eyes, even in the shifting shadows, took on a brightness that told him Cady Dye was all there again, alert and on the case. "You're deliberately trying to provoke me in order to help me put my nightmare behind me. Well, you've succeeded. You know damned well I never asked you to marry me."

As if it were beyond the realm of possibility.

Cole stretched out his legs, feeling his fatigue, the strangeness of being in New York with a rusty-haired, internationally known reporter with a whole heap of troubles. She picked up her glass with one hand this time. Provoking her *had* seemed to steady her.

"But to answer your question," she went on, "I've done things far more impulsive than hire you. I trust my instincts. They don't often lead me astray. When I saw you in Maine, I knew in my gut you could get this lunatic who's been calling me off my back, hopefully without either of us having to make a scene. I want to do this thing as quietly and discreetly as possible. So. Here we are."

She surged to her feet. There was no sign now of the shaken, haunted woman who'd just emerged from a bad dream. Thick locks of rusty hair hung in her face. She was all angles and high energy, and Cole knew if he stood up he'd take her into his arms.

He remained in his seat.

"Well, we'd both better get some sleep," she said briskly. "By the way, I'm having lunch with friends tomorrow. I'd like to bring you and introduce you, start getting the word out. But it's not in our contract, so if you don't want to go—"

"I'll go. You're not worried about betraying your friends?"

"I'm not betraying them. I'm lying to them for a noble—well, a reasonably noble purpose. They'll understand."

"You plan to tell them the truth eventually?"

"Maybe. Depends on how this all works out. I haven't planned that far ahead. First things first, I always say. I'm not one to have every tiny little thing figured out in advance. I'm not afraid of winging it."

It was a wonder, Cole thought dryly, Cady Dye hadn't ended up facedown in a ditch in some hellhole. She got the bit in her teeth and ran with it, never mind what lay ahead. "But you don't necessarily intend to tell everyone the truth as soon as you get this bozo off your back?"

"Not necessarily, no. I might just tell them we broke up." She picked up her wineglass, starting back to her bedroom with it. "I haven't decided."

With her safely in the hall, Cole got to his feet. He didn't want to spook her. He didn't want to do anything to bring back the nightmares. But he had to know.

"Cady, you know who's harassing you, don't you? Are you trying to protect him?"

She turned to him, her teal eyes lost in the shadows. "I wouldn't waste my time speculating if I were you, Cole. This is my problem, and I'm solving it my way. I'm paying you well for your role in my solution. Let that be enough."

He noticed she turned all business every time he put her on the spot. But her answer wasn't enough. He'd never have taken this bizarre job just for money.

But he wouldn't push her. Not tonight.

"Sweet dreams," he said.

When she glanced at him, the light caught her eyes, and he saw the spark of fear in them, and he understood. She didn't know whether sweet dreams were possible for her. She didn't know what would happen when she fell asleep again, and she was afraid of what might.

"Thank you," she managed to say in a low voice. "You, too."

Not a chance, he thought. Sweet dreams hadn't been a part of his life in a long time, any more than they had Cady Dye's.

Chapter Three

By morning, Cady felt ready to take on the world. She'd shaken off her nightmare, and the accompanying images. She always had bad dreams after an extended, difficult assignment, like her last. It was nothing that should concern her. Cole Forrest and Billy Del Rio were her most immediate concerns.

Cole had ventured outside for a run in Central Park. It was all of thirty degrees out, but, claiming that was "balmy" for this time of year by Maine standards, off he'd gone. He'd worn old sweatpants and a University of Maine sweatshirt. He was so strong, so competent, so damned big and confident, that Cady had had to suppress an urge to turn all her problems over to him to solve. The physical attraction she felt for him only seemed to intensify with additional contact. She'd hoped it would decrease.

Before heading to the shower, Cady decided to investigate the contents of the hall closet. She didn't know Cole Forrest. She had no reason to trust him. Why shouldn't she take a peek at his stuff?

She'd always been one to solve her own problems, and one of her problems was that Cole Forrest wasn't the man Robin Cross had hired to look after her Maine cabin. Therefore, Cady didn't know *who* he was. Therefore, she was allowed to search his things.

His wardrobe surprised her. It wasn't sleek or sophisticated or anything like that, but it was functional, of good quality, and would look deadly on him. It held no clue as to his identity, however.

She unzipped the side pocket of his otherwise empty suitcase and discovered a cache of foil packages that bespoke preparedness or optimism—or both. They could have been in there for years. She checked the expiration date.

"Then again," she muttered, "the snake could have bought them for this trip."

It didn't have to mean he had any designs on her, or any plans for ringing in the New Year besides sticking to his end of their deal. She didn't object to preparedness. The foil packets could be viewed as akin to the water-purification tablets she carried with her. One never knew when the unexpected might arise.

But the little cache did stay on her mind through her long, hot shower.

When she came out of the shower, she found herself toweling off the steam on the full-length mirror that hung on the bathroom door and gazing at her reflection.

On assignment, she seldom gave her appearance a second's thought. She'd put on her signature outfit and head out to do her job. Her unusual lifestyle kept her in relatively decent shape. Although her diet was catch-as-catch-can, she simply didn't care, so long as she had the energy to get whatever story she was determined to get.

But standing naked in a New York bathroom, she could indulge in wondering what a man like Cole Forrest might see in her.

Water dripped from her wet hair down her front. She'd lost weight in the past month. Her rough night of bad dreams had left dark circles under her eyes, her cheeks pale. When was the last time she had relaxed in a man's arms?

She imagined Cole's touch on her breasts, and shut her eyes.

This is madness....

The telephone rang, jerking her back to reality. She grabbed her robe and picked up the extension in the bedroom.

"Who's the new boyfriend, Cady?"

"Bill, I'm going to string you up. I swear to God I am. My private life is none of your business. I— Wait." She tightened her grip on the phone. "How do you know—? Billy, are you *here?* Have you been spying on me?"

"I don't know why you keep calling me Billy."

She snorted, incredulous that he, of all people, would be up to such despicable tricks. "Because I recognize your voice, you ass. We've worked together for years. Come on, Billy. Snap out of it. If I report you, you'll be ruined."

It was as if she hadn't spoken. "We're meant for each other, Cady Dye. I know that, even if you don't."

"Billy—"

"Stop calling me that."

"Billy, I'm losing patience with you. The only person you're going to hurt with this nonsense is yourself—"

He hung up on her.

Cady resisted the impulse to throw the phone across the room. Billy Del Rio needed help. In her own convoluted way, she *was* helping him. The harassing phone calls were horrible, but she owed him at least the chance to mend his ways. He would see she had absolutely no romantic interest in him and give up, and they could go back to the way things were.

If that was possible. It might not be, and not just because of Billy's shenanigans. There was network politics to consider, and there was Billy Del Rio's state of mind.

"Who's Billy?"

Cady flew around, startled, her robe falling half-open. She quickly retied it as Cole gazed at her, his dark eyes narrowed, all business. He wasn't even breathing hard from his run.

So much for thinking about his hands on her body. He couldn't have looked less interested.

"Billy?" she asked innocently.

"On the phone, Cady. You're losing patience with him, he's only hurting himself. Billy."

Cole's voice was hard-edged, no hint of the casual, slow-witted property caretaker she'd thought she'd hired. Everything about him suggested self-restraint and intelligence, coupled with obvious physical strength. Not a good combination in someone she needed to control.

"Who is he, Cady?"

If there was one thing she hated, it was being backed into a corner. Cole Forrest wasn't *asking* her about the phone call he'd overheard, whether deliberately or by accident. He was demanding. As if he had a right, which he didn't. He had agreed to pose as her fiancé, knowing she wouldn't volunteer any details about why she was undertaking such a ruse.

"Billy Del Rio," she said, matter-of-factly.

"The war correspondent?"

She nodded. "We've worked together for years. We're both taking a breather—he's throwing a cocktail party on the thirtieth, remember? He's just been getting on my nerves, and I told him so."

"He's not the guy harassing you?"

"I don't *know* who's harassing me."

Not for absolute certain, anyway. It wasn't as if it were something she could report. And if she couldn't put it on the air, she didn't know it for a fact.

So she hadn't actually lied to Cole.

But he was looking at her as if she had. She manufactured a smile. "How was your run?"

He didn't answer at once. She could see him weighing his options. Demand she fess up? Pin her to the wall until she talked? Plead? No, she thought. Forget pleading. Cole Forrest wasn't the type. Appeal to her natural compulsion to tell the truth and not keep secrets? But he wouldn't know about that. Whatever he might know about her public self, the Cady Dye of international repute, he would know very little about *her*.

"My run was fine," he said, tight-lipped, obviously choosing not to press her, and not thrilled about it. Cady had no illusions he'd given up. He was like a damned bobcat who'd missed his prey, only to lie back and pounce later, when the time was right. He moved away from the door. "There wasn't as much bad air as I expected, but a hell of a lot more dogs. I'm getting some juice. You want any?"

"Not right now, thank you. I need to get dressed."

"That you do," he muttered, and headed down the short hall to the living room.

Cady felt the heat spread through her, along with a certain unsettling satisfaction. So he hadn't been oblivious when her robe fell open.

She kicked the bedroom door shut, annoyed with herself for even caring. She had enough on her mind, without Cole Forrest stirring up her hormones.

The inadvertent peek he'd had of Cady Dye's silken, naked body when her robe fell open did not bode well for Cole's concentration. Being cooped up with her for a week in New York wasn't proving to be easy. If she thought the money she was paying him would keep him from being attracted to her, she could add *that* to her list of mistakes.

"Hell," he muttered, buckling his belt as he put the finishing touches on his meet-my-fiancée-lunch outfit. He'd opted for casual. Weathered canvas shirt in a deep charcoal, dark pants, boots. He didn't give a damn if it passed Cady's inspection. It was what he was wearing.

He had to stop thinking about that enticing body of hers. It wasn't right. Wasn't going to help him find out what was going on with her and Billy Del Rio. Wasn't going to do a damned thing but frustrate him.

He returned to the living room, where she was on the sofa, reading the *New York Times*. She'd been reading it when he went into the bathroom. She was either reading every word or not succeeding in reading any words, just faking it, preoccupied with other matters.

Or maybe she'd gone through his things while he was indisposed, in an attempt to find out what he might be, if not a property caretaker.

Nah. She'd have done it while he was out for his run. Knowing her, he'd say she *had* done it.

He was under no illusions that she might not be that devious. Cady was a goal-oriented reporter, a woman of tremendous independence and nerve. She might have ethical standards, but they wouldn't include resisting a look through the things of a man who'd broken out of the nice little box she'd put him in. She would feel she had the right to know everything there was to know about him.

Well, that was a sword that cut two ways.

She rose, taking his breath away. She had on a simple deep green knit dress, with her trademark gold-buckled belt cinching her waist and dark brown leather boots. Her rusty curls were pulled back with a wooden barrette, a few escaping to frame her face. There was no evidence of her troubled night. It wasn't just the effects of her natural-looking cosmetics, Cole realized, but that she was anticipating going out, getting back among people.

There was another area where he and Cady Dye were different. He was satisfied with his life on the lake, and its inherent isolation. He didn't need the excitement of lunches, parties, dinners, cities, wars. He needed nothing more than to watch a lone loon feed on the lake, a moose wander out into the bog.

Yet he couldn't deny a rush of anticipation at passing himself off as Cady Dye's lover.

"Ready?" she asked, pulling on the same four-in-one coat she'd worn in Maine. As far as he could see, she hadn't brought a dress coat.

"Sure." But he gave her a long look, not moving. He had to know. "Cady, are you sure you're not using me to make some guy jealous? Because that wouldn't sit well with me. I'd quit."

He could see his words ride right up her spine, irritating the hell out of her. "I would never stoop to manipulating a man to fall in love with me. I'm not that desperate for romance."

"Ah, Cady... We're all desperate for romance."

She shot him a look, as if she couldn't be sure whether he was serious. "The way I figure it, I have my work, and a full life. If the right man walks onto the scene, I'm not going to turn him away. But I'm not a dewy-eyed twenty-year-old. I'm thirty-five years old. I've made my peace with not having a traditional home and hearth."

"No little feet running down the hall in your future?"

"Kids, you mean?" Her teal eyes narrowed, and her cheeks colored. "That's a very personal question."

Cole grinned. "I'm your fiancé. I should know if children are in our future."

"How would I know? I just take life as it comes." She headed for the door, her pace brisk. But she stopped abruptly, casting a sardonic grin his way. "Let's just say that so long as you're in my future, I'll take whatever comes with it."

"I'm beginning to think you don't have a romantic bone in your body, Cady Dye."

She laughed. "Good. I feel safer spending the week with you that way."

He chose not to respond to that provocative statement. Let her feel "safe."

"By the way," she said, pulling open the suite door, "we need a profession for you. I like the idea of your being a Maine native. Gives you a certain rugged appeal. And the Indian ancestors are a nice touch. But it'd be hard for anyone to believe I'd fall for a guy who shovels snow off roofs—not that I'm denigrating your friend Tom, but you know what I mean."

He did indeed. "We can say I'm an ex-reporter who's gone back to Maine to write screenplays."

She shook her head at once, critical, matter-of-fact, absolutely convinced she was in charge. "An ex-reporter among reporters? They'd sniff you out in ten seconds. You don't know the jargon, and—well, you don't really look the part. What *do* you do for a living?"

He was an ex-reporter who'd gone back to Maine to write screenplays. But Cady wasn't ready to hear that. He shrugged. "This and that."

She sighed. "Typical. Robin Cross told me a lot of people in rural Maine carve out livings with a variety of odd jobs, everything from picking wild blueberries to logging and seasonal tourism work. I guess it doesn't matter, if you like the woods." She paused, thinking. "Suppose we tell people you're a naturalist? If they ask, you can say you're researching the moose population or something. But they won't ask."

As they walked down the hall to the elevator, Cole turned that one over a few times in his mind. A naturalist researching the moose population. Cady did have a way with improvisation.

"We don't need to have every jot and tittle of this thing worked out," she said, banging the down button. "Everyone will know it's a whirlwind romance. I'm willing to wing it if you are."

He gave her a lazy, utterly confident smile. "Sure."

That unsettled her. He could see her sudden nervousness as she stepped onto the elevator. "You could be a *little* ill at ease, you know."

"Make you feel better, would it?"

She made a face, then sighed again, her shoulders slumping. "No, I suppose it wouldn't. My friends would spot you as a phony immediately. They know I'd never fall for someone who quaked in his boots around me."

"Let me assure you," Cole said in a low, amused voice, "I do not quake in my boots around you, or anybody else."

She did not look reassured.

Chapter Four

Lunch was an unmitigated disaster.

It wasn't that Cady's friends didn't take to her new "fiancé." On the contrary. They took to him instantly. He was handsome, charming, rugged. He was smart. He wasn't the least bit intimidated by her.

"I just knew you'd end up with someone like Cole Forrest," one of her friends whispered to Cady as an aside.

The deeper meaning of her comment went right over Cady's head. She'd thought her friend was referring to Cole's physical presence.

But no.

She'd *recognized* him.

It hadn't been until Cole, in spite of her veto, pulled his ex-reporter-turned-screenwriter routine that she finally figured out what was going on.

Cole Forrest was claiming to be an ex-reporter-turned-screenwriter because he *was* an ex-reporter-turned-screenwriter.

"How long have you been back in Maine?" another friend asked. "It's been three or four years, hasn't it?"

"Almost five," he said.

The questions kept coming. Had he sold anything? Yes, he'd done a couple scripts for a popular, reality-based cop show to get his feet wet, then moved right into scripts for the big screen. Casting had just been completed for his first action thriller.

He said he went out to Hollywood only when he had to. He preferred his quiet life in Maine.

This, Cady thought, from a man who dressed like a lumberjack and had shoveled her roof and plowed her driveway and stacked her wood.

She could have kicked herself. She was a reporter. She knew not to make assumptions about people.

More to the point, she could have kicked *him*.

"You could have told me," she said through clenched teeth in the cab back to their hotel.

"I did tell you. You just didn't believe me."

She gave him a scathing look. Having him so close, so damned sexy and good-looking, so *amused*, didn't help matters. "You did not tell me. You did not say, 'Cady, I'm a former reporter, I've got a movie in the works. Half the people I meet in New York are going to recognize me.'"

She flopped back, disgusted with him, disgusted with herself. Billy Del Rio, she thought. It was all his fault for bugging her.

"You *let* me believe you were just an ordinary mountain man."

"That's what you wanted to believe, Cady."

"It is not," she said, sounding petulant even to herself.

Cole, of course, wasn't perturbed in the least by his scolding. "Hoist on your own petard," he said.

"Well, the deal's off. I'm packing you up and sending you back to Maine."

"We have a written agreement."

"Tough. I'll tear it up. I'll even pay you, if that's what you want."

He settled back against the cab's ragged seat. She'd resisted the urge to shove herself up against the passenger door, as far away from him as she could get. He would only take it as a sign she was affected by his physical presence. Which she was. Sitting close to him, she couldn't seem to stop herself imagining leaning her head against his shoulder.

All through lunch he'd insinuated a physical intimacy between them that didn't exist, playing his fiancé role to the hilt. He would invade her space in every way he could, brushing her hand, touching her with his knee, draping an arm over the back of her chair. He seemed comfortable with such displays of closeness, as if it came easily to him and their relationship. Of course, that was his job. Just because she was a wreck from his pretense of desire and affection, that wasn't his fault.

But lying to her was.

"What about Billy Del Rio?" he asked calmly.

Yes, she thought. What about Billy? But Cady felt a rush of pure stubbornness. She wouldn't tell him her suspicions about Billy. He didn't deserve to know. "What about him? We're not having cocktails with him until the thirtieth. If he's heard about a supposed fiancé, I'll just say things didn't work out and you went back to Maine."

Cole leaned toward her, his thigh brushing up against hers, sending warm shivers all through her. "Cady, I'm not going back to Maine. I don't care if I have to get a room. I'm sticking to you until whoever's pestering you stops.''

She thrust her chin at him, refusing to back down. ''Why?''

Another mistake. She saw it right away. His eyes darkened, and he traced her mouth with one finger, closer than she had any business letting him be. ''You don't see yourself as I see you, Cady Dye.''

She swallowed. Her mouth had gone dry. Her entire body seemed sensitized, as if every inch of her skin were electrified. She tried to rally. ''What's the old expression? Don't bury yourself in the part, Cole. You're not my fiancé. You're not even my lover.''

''It makes you more comfortable to believe I'm acting, doesn't it?''

I'll be more comfortable,'' she said stiffly, ''when you're back in Maine.''

He smiled, leaning back. ''Are you firing me, Cady?''

''Yes.''

''You don't want to,'' he said.

She snorted. ''Your arrogance is staggering!''

''It's not arrogance, Cady. It's watching you. You liked having me there last night, after you had that nightmare. You liked it after those phone calls yesterday and this morning. You liked it at lunch. Admit it, Cady. You enjoyed having me play your fiancé—me, Cole Forrest, reporter-turned-screenwriter, the guy your friends recognized. It was better than passing me off as a naturalist studying moose."

"That's a noble calling—"

"I know that. It pretty much describes one of my closest friends. But it's not for you."

"I don't get involved with reporters," she said.

"I'm not a reporter anymore."

"Well, you were one." But she knew already it wasn't going to work. She crossed her arms on her chest. "Anyway, this isn't about who I'd *really* fall for. It's about you and me and our business arrangement."

"It's about your ego, Cady," he said, matter-of-fact. "You didn't mind hiring some poor bastard like Tom for your little scheme. Figured you could keep him under your thumb, tell him just what you wanted him to know. You wouldn't worry about him knowing you'd hired yourself a fiancé. How could he hurt you? But me..." He leaned toward her again, his charred-wood eyes boring through her. "I'm another story."

She frowned. "You're enjoying this, aren't you?"

He gave her a broad, unrepentant, sexy grin. "Immensely."

When they arrived back at their hotel, Cole automatically started to pay the cabdriver, but Cady insisted on taking care of the tab herself. She didn't know how much Cole Forrest was worth, and she didn't care. He was in New York on her nickel. She'd said it was an all-expenses-paid week, and she meant to stick by her word and insist he stick by his or go on back to Maine.

"The nerve of *you* accusing *me* of manipulating people," she muttered, not the least bit mollified by their conversation. Talking to Cole Forrest, being near him, set her on edge. It didn't matter if he was a moose expert or a lumberjack or an ex-reporter-turned-screenwriter. She couldn't seem to pull herself together and approach the situation calmly and rationally. She just wanted to hurl accusations at him—to say, do, anything that would ruffle his self-control and help her reassert hers.

He followed her into the lobby, everything about him relaxed, even languid. Her frenzy didn't seem to affect him. "I'd probably be out snowshoeing today if you hadn't asked me to marry you."

She whipped around at him, ready to call security.

Then it hit her.

"You're not doing this for the money. You don't need money. You probably don't even care much about money."

Unperturbed he walked past her to the polished brass elevators and pressed the up button. "See," he said, "you are beginning to know me."

She remained several paces off to his side, studying him warily. Good Lord, she thought, had he been playing her for a fool all along?

"Robin Cross. You two must know each other. She owns the cabin next to your place."

"She bought it from me," he said without guilt.

"Why? How?"

"She was looking for a getaway, knew I was back home in Maine, and contacted me to see if I could point her in the right direction. As it turned out, the cabin had just become available."

Cady nearly choked. She couldn't believe it. She could *not* believe it. Robin had mentioned none of this to her. Not a word. Of course, there'd been no reason. Robin couldn't have anticipated Cady going out and hiring Cole Forrest to play her fiancé in New York.

"You two knew each other before Maine?"

"Yep."

The doors to one of the elevators opened. Cole stepped in. Cady hesitated. He grinned at her. "You know you're coming, Cady. Your reporter's curiosity, if nothing else, will get you into this elevator with me."

He was right and he knew it, which only further unsettled her. But she acquiesced, glad that at least they were alone, without witnesses. He punched the button for their floor. The elevator started up with a small jerk, nearly propelling her into him. He caught her elbow. It was an automatic move, and no doubt had nothing to do with what she was paying him, or capitalizing on the moment, or knowing how physically attracted she was to him.

Yet she could feel the spark of awareness flare right to her very core. Her situation would be a whole lot easier, she knew, if she would only stop thinking about making love to him. She tried to tell herself it was a natural by-product of having him pose as the man she had fallen in love with over Christmas and planned to marry. But she knew it was more than that.

"I hope this doesn't bruise your ego," she said, "but I've never heard of you. Obviously Robin Cross has, and a lot of my friends, but I haven't. Blame it on my work keeping me out of the country most of the time, if you want. So, do you mind enlightening me?"

He shrugged, his ego apparently quite intact. "I was an investigative reporter for the *New York Dispatch,* then for a New York network affiliate."

Cady sank against the wall of the elevator. She hoped Cole would attribute her unsteadiness to her bad night. But New York! The *last* thing she'd have expected was New York. She thought of him in Maine, with his beat-up shovel on his shoulder, his black-and-red checked wool vest, his hunting boots.

"You're sure this isn't some kind of scam Robin and some of my other friends have cooked up to amuse themselves?"

"Check it out."

A New York investigative reporter. "How long were you in the city?"

"A dozen years, not counting college."

"But you're from Maine," she said hopefully. It was about all she had left.

"Yep."

And now he wrote scripts for movies. She was in over her head. *Way* over her head—and Cole Forrest had known it all along.

Breezing ahead of him, she burst into their suite.

A huge vase of red roses greeted her. There was a card, but she didn't read it. Tension ripped up her spine, like some wild animal she couldn't control. She picked up the vase, stormed to the kitchenette and dumped it—water and flowers and card—into the trash can. If Cole hadn't been there, she might have smashed it onto the floor and stomped it into a million pieces.

"Remind me never to send you flowers," he said mildly.

She flew around, and he was there, solid, steady, unruffled by her outburst. She realized she was breathing hard, as if she'd run several miles. *You've got to pull yourself together. You're out of control....*

"It's okay," Cole said. "You can throw a fit if you want, let off some steam. Probably do you good."

"I don't want to throw a fit. I want—" She stopped, catching her breath. Every muscle in her body was tensed, rigid; every nerve seemed on hyperalert. She pulled the wooden barrette from her hair, just to give her shaking hand something to do. And she said, her voice constricted with tension, "I want this all to stop."

Cole took her by the elbows and held her at arm's length until she stopped shaking. His calm presence helped steady her. She averted her eyes, not wanting to let her confused feelings toward him get in the way. She needed him right now. She needed to infuse herself with his rootedness, his self-control.

"I should have told you about myself sooner," he said. "I'm sorry."

"It served me right."

"Not with everything else you have going on, it didn't." Releasing one elbow, he tucked a knuckle under her chin and turned her head so that her eyes were locked with his. "Cady, you've come off a hell of an assignment. The whole world knows it. Plus, you've got some bastard pestering you. You can cut yourself some slack. *Anyone* would be on edge under those conditions."

"I can handle it," she said stubbornly.

"Of course you can. But it doesn't have to be without friends."

He brushed his knuckle across her lower lip, sending a delicious warmth through her. This time, she didn't fight her attraction to him. Instead, unexpectedly, she relished it. She could feel her muscles loosen, almost as if they were turning liquid. She felt no urge to tear her gaze from his or to pull back from him.

"Cady, I've wanted to kiss you since you asked me if moose were dangerous if provoked."

"That was last week—"

"It was the day you arrived in Maine."

She swallowed. "I had no idea."

He smiled, and said, "I know." As his mouth closed over hers, all the anxiety and strain emptied out of her, replaced by a desire so immediate and so powerful that she could think of nothing else, feel nothing else. His hand dropped from her other elbow, and she slid her arm around his hard middle, their kiss deepening. It all seemed so natural, so curiously meant to be.

She'd been mad enough she could have pitched him out a window fifteen minutes ago, but now she was relishing the feel of his body against her.

"Cole, I'm not sure you can trust me," she whispered. "I don't trust myself. This— I don't know what it means—"

"Does it feel right, Cady? Right now. Never mind tomorrow or the next day or six months from now. Just right now."

She nodded without hesitation. "It feels very right."

"Good."

And that was that.

Releasing her, he walked into the kitchenette and pulled the card from the discarded roses. Cady warned herself she should stop him. Her relationship with Billy Del Rio was none of his business. He wouldn't understand why she was protecting him. She didn't expect anyone to understand.

He read the card aloud. "'Cady, you know you can't live without me.'"

She sank onto a padded chair at the table in the alcove. Outside, New York seemed to glisten in the bright winter sun. Kissing Cole Forrest had somehow made her feel less frantic, if no less concerned—deeply concerned—about Billy Del Rio.

But Cole had a different take on the card. "Sounds like a threat to me," he said, dropping into the chair across from her.

"A threat? Oh, come on. He just wants me to fall for him."

"Maybe. But what if he means—literally— what he says? You can't live without him. If you go with someone else, he won't let you live. Seems straightforward to me."

She scoffed. "No way. Billy would never—"

She stopped herself, but it was too late. Cole pounced. He leaned toward her, his dark eyes blazing. "Billy Del Rio. He's your man, Cady. You know he is."

Sudden tears sprang to her eyes, annoying her because she prided herself on being able to handle any situation. She wasn't one to get all emotional. She swore under her breath, as if that would help.

"You two have worked together a long time," Cole said, no softness in his voice now.

"Ten years. He was my mentor. He taught me so much—"

"Now he figures you owe him."

"No!"

Cole didn't relent. "Then explain it to me, Cady. Explain to me why a friend would harass you this way."

"Because he needs help," she blurted. With the words—the truth—out, she instantly felt calmer, something she hadn't expected. "He's burned out. I think he's just latched on to me because subconsciously he's reaching out for my help."

Cole snorted, giving his low opinion of her scenario.

"No, it's true. I *know* him, Cole. Billy Del Rio would never hurt me. We've been through too much together."

"Cady," Cole said impatiently, "Billy Del Rio *is* hurting you."

She refused to back down. Arguing her case—explaining what she knew, in her heart, Billy Del Rio was doing—only confirmed to her that she was right. "If I go to my boss about Billy, he'll be ruined. His reputation will go right down the toilet. Cole, Billy Del Rio's one of the finest, most courageous reporters I've ever known. He's covered Vietnam, Iran, Beirut, dozens of terror-ist attacks, the Gulf War, Eastern Europe, Africa—for thirty years, he's been among the best there is. If he's going all to pieces now, I'm going to be there for him."

"You're his target, Cady. Let someone else be there for him."

She shook her head. "No, it has to be me."

"Why?"

His question propelled her to her feet. She didn't want to answer. She wanted to pretend she had no idea, that it was the cumulative effect of thirty years of seeing the worst humanity had to offer—that it was anything but what she knew it to be.

The images flooded her, sickened her.

"Cady?"

"I'm all right."

But she'd already collapsed to her knees.

To his credit, Cole didn't leap to her aid. He moved toward her, not touching her, not hovering, as she climbed up onto the couch. Her head was pounding. A wave of nausea came over her, then passed.

"Billy and I witnessed a massacre about a month ago." Her voice was oddly even, almost as if someone else were speaking. "Women, children, old men. There was nothing we could do. We reported it. But it was another massacre in a long, bloody civil war that the world basically regards as none of its business, and the story was buried. Nobody paid attention.''

"Billy Del Rio did," Cole said quietly. "And you did."

"We've uncovered atrocities before, and we've witnessed some pretty terrible things, but nothing like that. Billy came home a couple weeks before I did. The calls and messages started soon after. I know it's him, Cole. I recognize his voice." She met Cole's eyes, still convinced she was right. "He's gone off the deep end, and I intend to help him pull himself together."

Cole gave a long sigh, raking one hand through his dark hair.

"I figured having a whirlwind love affair and ringing in the New Year with a fiancé would snap him out of it. So far, no go. But he hasn't met you yet."

"Be interesting to see what happens when he does."

Cady managed a small smile. Cole Forrest was nothing like her hard-living, nomadic, out-in-left-field colleague. "It will be." She got to her feet, feeling somewhat better. "I'm going to put on jeans and sneakers and head to a matinee, get all this stuff off my mind. A couple of comedies I hear are pretty good are playing. You want to join me?"

But he seemed not to hear her.

"Cole?"

His dark eyes leveled on her. "I'd love to join you, but there's one more thing you need to know about me."

"What, you eat raw moose meat?"

"No."

The intensity of his expression gave Cady pause. She licked her lips, feeling the blood drain from her face. "What, then?"

He smiled, touching her hair. "Never mind. It can wait. You've had enough for one day."

"Cole—"

"Let's go see that movie, Cady."

Chapter Five

Cole had his own ideas about how to knock some sense into Billy Del Rio, but he deferred to Cady's wishes.

At least for the time being.

The cretin wasn't at Angie's post–Christmas, pre–New Year's dinner on the twenty-eighth. Angie turned out to be a caterer with three daughters ranging in age from eight to thirteen, all of whom were at the party, all of whom *loved* the idea of living in Maine and investigating the moose population. They helped their mother, who seemed to have known Cady since college, whisk every manner of hors d'oeuvre and holiday delight from oven and refrigerator. Their father likewise had nothing to do with the journalism industry; Cole gathered he did something with municipal bonds. They lived in a spacious town house in Brooklyn that would have dispelled anybody's worst stereotypes about raising a family in the city.

Angie, too, had heard of Cole, which disgusted Cady. "How come *I'd* never heard of him until last week?" she demanded smoothly, stretching the truth only a little. She hadn't heard of him until yesterday. She'd *met* him last week.

"Because," Angie, a sturdy, fit woman with very short dark hair, told her friend unsympathetically, "you're never in the damned country long enough to hear of anything."

Cady wasn't mollified. Cole was beginning to recognize when she was truly satisfied and when she was faking it. After their matinee yesterday, they'd had a quiet dinner, their conversation limited to favorite foods and restaurants and films, the kind of nonthreatening chat that made getting to know someone really possible. In some ways, he'd felt more intimate with her sitting across a red-checkered tablecloth discussing Tom Cruise and Paul Newman than he had kissing her.

But only in some ways.

There had been no repeat of their kiss. When they arrived back at their suite, she'd quickly retreated to the bedroom. As far as he knew, she'd had no nightmares, at least none that made her scream out in the darkness. He would have heard. He had slept little himself, contemplating what to do about his growing attraction to a war reporter he knew could never be satisfied in his life.

In the morning, she'd received another call from her harasser. She continued to be convinced it was Billy Del Rio. She displayed only annoyance and concern, no fear of him and what he might do. A remarkable trust seemed to exist between the two of them. Her contention was that was why he'd chosen her to harass. The logic defeated Cole. It all had something to do with picking your friends to fall apart on, rather than a perfect stranger.

But what if she was wrong? What if the man harassing her *wasn't* her trusted colleague and friend, gone off the deep end? What if it was someone other than Billy Del Rio? That was a scenario Cady seemed unprepared even to consider.

Angie's small gathering broke up before midnight. On their cab ride home, Cole accused Cady of pouting.

"I am not pouting," she said.

"People aren't as shocked about the idea of the two of us being engaged as you'd expected," he said. "You were hoping for a little more drama mileage out of this phony-fiancé bit than you're getting."

"That's not true. I hired you because you look like my type. I mean, you look like someone I might marry. No, wait, I mean—" She made a face. "Oh, never mind."

Cole laughed. "You mean you meant to capitalize on the chemistry between us to make it believable that you'd fall for a moose expert. Instead, I'm an ex-reporter, and you're not getting the raised eyebrows you were hoping for."

"I wasn't hoping for raised eyebrows. I was merely hoping to persuade Billy that he ought to come to his senses and realize he's not in love with me."

"Don't deny it, Cady. You love a good drama."

She laid her head back against the seat, suddenly tired. Cole had resisted telling her how beautiful she looked tonight, not to keep from unsettling her, but to keep from further unsettling himself. He couldn't take his eyes off her, couldn't stop thinking about her. She wore a simple, flowing dress of a knit the same color as her hair, which she'd pulled up and twisted into a knot that managed to be at once elegant and casual. All evening he'd imagined slipping her out of the soft fabric—something else he'd neglected to mention.

When they arrived back at their hotel, he suggested a drink in the lounge. To his surprise, she accepted. They slid into a dark booth, Cady deciding on a decaffeinated cappuccino, the thought of which turned Cole's stomach. He had a beer.

"How would you handle Billy?" she asked. He'd have expected a note of challenge in her tone, but there was none. She seemed to want to know.

So Cole told her. "A left hook to the gut, probably."

She gave a small smile. "The direct approach. I've tried confronting him, but he denies everything—and I have no proof. I just wish he'd stop. Ultimately he's only hurting himself."

"You don't owe him anything, Cady. He's violated your trust in him and abused your loyalty."

"I know," she said softly. "But if I really believed he was just being a lecherous swine, I'd probably take a different course of action." Her eyes, luminous in the dim light, leveled on Cole. "I'm not being naive. I hope you understand that."

Cole grinned as their drinks arrived. "If there's one thing you aren't, Cady, it's naive. Blinded by your loyalty to Billy Del Rio, perhaps, but not naive."

She tried her frothy cappuccino, her mood lifting visibly. "He's always said I had a pathetic love life. Maybe he's just trying to liven things up."

"Think he figured you'd turn to some guy for help?"

"No! That's not what I'm talking about at all. He's not manipulating me to turn to a man to rescue me—he knows better. You're not the one livening up my love life, Cole Forrest."

He leaned back in the tall-backed wooden booth, eyeing Cady. "I don't know. Things were getting pretty lively yesterday afternoon."

She reddened, just slightly. He wondered if he was the only man in America—maybe the world—to have seen Cady Dye blush, however faintly. "You're not what Billy had in mind when he started harassing me, I assure you. I only meant that he might have thought having someone obsessively in love with me would make me—I don't know, feel wanted, needed. It's a twisted way of thinking. A woman doesn't feel wanted because some jerk keeps calling her anonymously and declaring his undying love. Obsession isn't love.''

''What is?'' Cole asked.

She lifted her shoulders and let them fall in an exaggerated display of bafflement. ''I don't know. I don't think about that sort of thing much. But for sure it's not obsession, power, control, dependency. I don't think there can be real love without the two people involved being independent, responsible human beings. I guess I'd have to say real love brings out the best in another person, in yourself.'' She grinned suddenly, unexpectedly. ''Not that you'd never fight. But the fights would be good ones.''

Cole drank his beer, thinking of it. Bringing out the best in Cady Dye. Arguing with her. Loving her.

Dangerous thinking. She was from a world he'd rejected. She was immersed in it, even trapped in it. She couldn't imagine life outside it. He knew, because he'd once been like that himself.

"Is that your idea of love?" she asked.

"Pretty much."

She gave him a wry grin. "Probably why we're both single, huh?"

He smiled. "Could be."

"I'm not an easy woman, Cole. I'm not an Angie. I adore and respect her, but I can't cook, I couldn't care less if the bathroom towels match, I don't notice holes in my own socks, much less anybody else's. I'm impatient and restless. I speak up when I disagree with something." She shrugged, taking a sip of her cappuccino. "You know, after a while you get to know yourself. You accept what you are and what you aren't."

"But the men in your life—"

Again, virtually out of nowhere, came the devilish grin. "What men?"

Cole abandoned what he was going to say. He wasn't even sure anymore what it was. He only knew that, as impatient, restless, driven and unpredictable as Cady might be, she was also deeply compassionate and principled. She undermined his cynicism about her world, eroded the ground beneath it.

Suddenly she was flagging down the waiter, throwing bills on the table. She got to her feet in a torrent of energy, as if she'd just seen a tornado on the horizon.

Maybe she had.

Cole smiled, in no hurry himself. He wasn't like the other men in Cady Dye's life. Instead of scaring him off, her little personality quirks only intrigued him more. And he had a feeling she'd just figured that out.

"All this stuff with Billy must be making me nuts," she muttered, gathering up her coat. She glared at him. "You coming?"

"Think I'll sit here awhile, have another beer."

He wondered if Cady had ever looked so relieved. Well, it wouldn't last. He had to come upstairs sometime.

Ten to one, when he did, she'd be shut up in her bedroom.

He was wrong.

She was at the windows overlooking Central Park, staring at the glittering skyline, in her T-shirt and plaid boxers. She didn't even turn when he came in. He could see fat snowflakes falling from the darkened sky.

"Can't sleep?" he asked softly.

"All this partying must be getting to me. I didn't have as much trouble sleeping in Maine."

He heard the qualifier. He took off his jacket and laid it on the sofa, thought of his log house on the rise above the lake; he could almost smell the fire he'd have going in his wood stove. "But you had some trouble," he said, moving behind her.

She nodded. "I thought it was just being alone. I'm not used to such solitude, not with the schedule I keep." Without warning, she turned to him, her eyes bright even in the shadows. "It seems to get harder and harder to come home."

"Do you regret spending Christmas alone?"

"No, I needed the time. My family all decided to do Hawaii this year. I could have gone, it's not that, but it was a long way, and I'd been through a lot, and then with this thing with Billy—" She shrugged. "No regrets. I had offers from friends, too. I'm not the pain-in-the-neck reporter nobody wants to be around, if that's what you're thinking."

He grinned. "It had occurred to me. Cady, maybe the job's getting to you."

"Are you kidding? I can't imagine doing anything else."

"That could be part of the problem," he said seriously.

She scowled, turning back to the view. "Just because you're a burned-out reporter doesn't mean I am."

He took no offense. He wasn't defensive about what he was. This was Cady being Cady, calling them as she saw them.

But she said, "I'm sorry. I didn't mean to insult you."

"I have no regrets about quitting, Cady. I'd seen enough, and I'd promised myself when I started to get cynical—when I started taking stupid risks—I'd quit. Luckily, I've had some success in screenwriting."

"And you had Maine to go back to," she said.

"Yes. I had Maine."

"Do you ever miss the work?"

"Sometimes. I'd be lying if I said otherwise. The adrenaline rush, getting the story, fighting for balance and thoroughness, for people's attention—yeah, sometimes I miss it. But I've crossed the bridge. I took what I wanted from my old life and moved on, and there's no going back." He suppressed an urge to touch her; she looked so damned alone. "Anyway, more often than not, though, I find it's the city I miss—not enough to move back on a permanent basis, but enough for me to remember the good times I had here.''

"I never thought about living in New York. I don't have a place of my own. When I'm not working, I usually mooch off friends—the cabin in Maine, this suite. There's always somebody willing to offer me a place to sleep. I never really wanted more than that.''

"Do you now?''

She raised her eyes to his, and he could see the fear in them. ''I don't know what I want.''

He touched her cheek. ''That would scare you more than most things.''

His mouth found hers, and the taste of her, the softness of her, took his breath away. Desire pulsed through him, hot and insistent. He had to repress an urge to scoop her up and carry her into the bedroom and make love to her all night. Cady had enough on her mind without him in her bed.

Yet it was what he wanted. More than that, he knew it was what she wanted, too. And it would happen. It was just a matter of time.

As their kiss deepened, she sank against him, wrapping her arms around his middle. He could feel the ache in her. He raised her shirt, felt her skin, smooth and warm. He thought he heard her moan with wanting.

"Cady," he whispered.

"Don't talk. Please."

"Cady."

She sighed, slipping from his arms. His regret was so fierce, he felt as if he'd been kicked by a horse. A willing woman, the old year waning, snow falling—and he knew he couldn't take advantage of the situation.

"I guess that wasn't part of our bargain," she said. "It's been sort of fun having a 'fiancé,' surprising people—surprising myself. Maybe it's the lure of normality, I don't know. Anyway, I got carried away."

Brisk, analytical, she was—but also not embarrassed. Cole liked that. She started for the bedroom. "I almost got carried away, too."

She glanced back at him, the devil back in her eye. "Almost?"

He laughed. "You'll know when I get really carried away, Cady. Trust me. You'll know."

Cady ended up sideways in the king-size bed, with the blankets twisted around her and two of her four pillows on the floor—probably no worse a mess than if Cole had spent the night with her.

She wondered if she'd have had fewer nightmares.

Well, she'd never been one for flings. She did not lead the life of the mythical foreign correspondent. She wasn't sure that was what Cole Forrest was offering her—fantasy sex to go with their fantasy romance—but that was part of the problem. Until she knew what he expected from a night with her, it wasn't going to happen.

Not that she'd been the one to pull back last night.

"Egad," she mumbled, unrolling herself. Even her flannel boxers were twisted. She frowned at them. "Very sexy, Cady Dye. Very sexy indeed."

Feeling the onset of a dreaded morning headache, she crawled out of bed. A peek out the window told her last night's snow had culminated in two or three inches that blanketed the city streets, giving Central Park a postcard effect. Maybe she'd grab Cole and go for a walk. He could pretend he was back in Maine.

Tonight was another dinner, one she dreaded, in a way, as much as she did Billy Del Rio's cocktail party tomorrow night. She hadn't explained its intricacies to Cole. Among the "colleagues" she'd mentioned to him were a network executive and a popular young anchorman, both of whom had their own ideas about how to profit from the work she'd done, especially in the past two years.

You're a phenomenon, Cady....

She'd given some flip reply about how she'd always thought she was a reporter, but they'd corner her eventually. Maybe having a new fiancé with her tonight would deter them.

"Ha!" she muttered, staggering out into the hall.

She immediately noticed the quiet. It was almost as if she could *feel* his absence, which was totally unnerving.

"Cole?"

But he wasn't there. She checked the clock: almost eleven. Had she slept that late? Her heart pounded. How could she have slept that late? She was *always* up early. She'd had plenty of time to get rid of her jet lag, so it couldn't be that. She'd taken a while to fall asleep, and she'd had nightmares, but that couldn't possibly explain *eleven o'clock*.

"You're losing it, Cady. You're as bad as Billy."

Was she?

She noticed Cole's sneakers in the bathroom. He couldn't have gone running. She could imagine him snowshoeing through Central Park, but she'd have noticed if he'd packed a pair of snowshoes. He hadn't.

Had he packed up and left?

Stemming a rush of panic, she tore open the closet door. No. His things were still there.

"What's wrong with you?" she muttered aloud. "He'll be going back to Maine in a few days, anyway."

Suddenly, she couldn't imagine it.

When she went to the refrigerator for orange juice, she found his note. He had a reporter's hasty scrawl.

Gone out for a bit. Back soon. Hope you slept late. CF

Ten minutes later, the telephone rang. It was as if all the world knew she was finally awake.

"Did the nightmares come last night, Cady Dye?"

She gripped the phone, not liking the voice, not hearing Billy Del Rio in it so clearly this time. "Billy?"

"I can be your worst nightmare."

Chapter Six

Billy Del Rio was just as arrogant, pigheaded, fatalistic and irritating as Cole remembered.

"It's been a long time," Billy said, when he reluctantly let Cole into the Greenwich Village apartment he'd had for nearly thirty years. Cole doubted Billy Del Rio had stayed there more than seven days running in all that time.

"Not long enough," Cole said.

"Yeah, well, that goes without saying."

"Thought you'd be dead by now."

Billy gave him a gallows-humor grin. "So did I."

The place reeked of cigarettes. Billy chain-smoked. He drank. He womanized—or used to. Cole didn't know what woman would have the old war correspondent these days. He'd once been reasonably good-looking, but now his body seemed ready to cave in on him—sagging, brown-splotched, even his skin gray. He stuck a cigarette between his lips and lit it with a cheap lighter, automatically, and, of course, without asking Cole if he objected.

"Heard you and Cady Dye hit it off in Maine," Billy said.

"That's not why I'm here."

"Didn't figure it was." His watery blue eyes, still alert and incisive, a reporter's eyes, narrowed on Cole. "You hurt her to get back at me, Forrest, and there'll be hell to pay. I promise you. One way or another, I'll kick you to Kathmandu and back."

Cole resisted the temptation to nail the man's hide to the nearest wall. "You're the one who's hurting her."

Billy nearly choked on his cigarette. "Me? I love that kid!"

"Yeah. That's the problem, isn't it?"

"What are you talking about? Me and Cady Dye, we've been through thick and thin, We've saved each other's lives. That time in Sarajevo—"

"Knock it off, Billy. I know."

Billy scoffed, smashing his cigarette into an overflowing ashtray. His apartment was surprisingly well furnished, probably thanks to one of his dozens of lovers over the years, and his long absences. He hadn't had a chance to wreck the place with his bad habits and hard living.

"What the hell do you know, Cole? You snuck out of this town years ago. I hear you've gone Hollywood. That ought to be fun to watch, a recluse like you writing movies. Hell, even the moose avoid you."

Cole felt every muscle in his body tighten, but Billy Del Rio seemed oblivious. That was one difference between him and Cady. Where she would be aware of every nuance of what was going on around her, Billy just barreled ahead. It was a wonder he hadn't been killed years ago.

Instead, Cole's father had.

He shut off the thought before it could go further.

"I didn't come here to rehash ancient history, or to hear your opinion of me," Cole said coldly. "I want to know if you've been making those phone calls."

Billy's reporter instincts kicked into gear. He fished another cigarette out of his pack, lit it, more thoughtfully, his eyes not leaving Cole. He inhaled deeply, exhaled a huge cloud of smoke. He was the most unreformable man Cole had ever encountered. If Billy Del Rio was Cady

Dye's idea of men—or reporters, ex or otherwise—it was no wonder she didn't trust her attraction to Cole.

Yet Billy was her friend, someone she trusted with her life. Cole had to remember that.

"Hell," the old reporter breathed.

Cole maintained his self-control. "Talk to me, Billy."

He collapsed on a black leather chair, motioning Cole to take the one opposite him.

"Billy, are you harassing Cady?"

He shook his head, looking as tired as any man deserved to look. "No. I swear to God, Cole, no."

"Then what's going on?"

"I don't know." He inhaled again on his cigarette, stubbed it out slowly, methodically, as he exhaled a lungful of smoke. "That last assignment did us both in. I haven't seen anything that bad since Cambodia. Cady—she's a pro. Don't get me wrong about that. I've never seen anyone as tenacious, as thorough, as willing to dig into whatever muck she had to dig in to get the story. But she's been at it a long time, and instead of caring less every day, she cares more. She's got a big heart. She just doesn't want to admit it."

"She's losing it?"

"*I* lost it a long time ago. Cady— No, she's not losing it. Not what's important, anyway. She just doesn't see it that way." The old, experienced eyes fastened on Cole, the son of one of his oldest friends. "They're pulling the plug on me, Cole. All these suits running the joint, they figure it's time to put me out to pasture."

"Maybe it's time," Cole said, feeling an unexpected twinge of sympathy.

"Yeah, maybe it is."

"What about Cady?"

He shrugged. "Her star's rising. She gets the ratings, Cole, and that's what it's all about now. What I hear, they're trying to get her to join one of those prime-time newsmagazines." He sank back into his chair, the energy that had propelled him all over the world for thirty years nowhere in evidence. "She won't want to hear it. But she ought to. She's done her tour. It's somebody else's turn."

They were words Billy Del Rio had never been able to say about himself. Cole said quietly, "You think she should quit."

"I think she deserves a better life than I had." He shot upright with a sudden urgency, leaning forward, intense. "She deserves to have kids, a husband—if it's what she wants. I know other reporters can do what we do and manage, but I couldn't, and she can't. It's all or nothing with us. It's the way we think, it's the way we are. Hell, Cole, if anybody knows what I'm talking about, it's you."

Yes, he thought. If anyone knew, he did.

"What about the calls?"

"Tell me about them," Billy said.

Against his better judgment, Cole told him.

"And she thinks it's *me?* That little pain in the butt! She knows she's too damned skinny for my tastes."

Bravado. Pure Billy Del Rio bravado. He didn't like the idea of the anonymous phone calls any more than Cole did. "Any ideas?" Cole asked.

"Like I say, her star's on the rise. If I had to make a bet, I'd say somebody's hoping to blow it out of the sky."

They arrived at the elegant Park Avenue restaurant right on time. Cady wore a black wool crepe dress and a full-length cashmere coat she'd picked up on an afternoon shopping spree because her four-in-one parka wouldn't do for dinner with the boss. She simply didn't own much stuff. She stashed her income in various safe investments and left it there. She didn't do what she did because of the money. It was something the people she was meeting tonight didn't necessarily understand.

Cole wore a dark suit that was devastating on him, and yet he was still every bit the man who'd shoveled off her cabin roof. He seemed totally unruffled at the prospect of meeting a network muckamuck. But Cole Forrest, she'd discovered, didn't let much rattle him—including her. He'd been back at the suite when she returned from her afternoon out. He hadn't mentioned where he'd gone. She hadn't asked. She had, however, noticed how free she felt wandering the streets of New York. After shopping, she'd gone to the Metropolitan Museum and taken herself out for hot chocolate. She'd put aside her worries about her career, she hadn't felt restless, and she hadn't had to repress nightmarish images. Cole's influence at work on her life?

He'd heard from her harasser while she was out. "He didn't want to talk to me," Cole had said.

Cady would bet not. Billy Del Rio wasn't stupid. He'd have figured out by now that he didn't want Cole Forrest on his case. It wasn't the ending she'd had in mind, but it would work, provided Billy quit calling.

Donald Huntington, the network executive, greeted them and introduced George Alston, the man Huntington was considering "matching" Cady with for a prime-time newsmagazine. In his late fifties, Huntington had been around the business for a while. Alston was relatively new, and exceedingly handsome in a cleft-chinned, slicked sort of way.

Both men immediately recognized Cole. Cady would have preferred passing her fiancé off as a moose expert, but she supposed that was just her perverse nature revealing itself. They'd even heard about his latest movie deal. Cole's charred-wood eyes gleamed knowingly whenever they met hers, as if he knew what she was thinking. Probably he did. He was having a good time at her expense. She wished she'd put playing a moose expert in their agreement. But obviously Cole Forrest wasn't posing as her fiancé for money.

Then for what? She really hadn't figured that one out yet, at least not to her satisfaction.

George Alston seemed acutely aware that people in the restaurant recognized him. Cady had the feeling he assumed they *ought* to recognize him, but attributed that to fame having only just come to him. He wasn't used to it yet. Its newness made him more aware of the looks he was getting. Such recognition usually came as a surprise to Cady—possibly, she thought, because she was so seldom in the country and was always so preoccupied with her work. Not that she was oblivious to being picked out in a crowd.

Within ten minutes of meeting him, she'd decided she'd been too generous in her interpretation of George Alston's attitude. The man had an outsize ego. She couldn't imagine working closely with him—or working with him at all. Give her Billy Del Rio and all his obvious bad habits and cynicism any day!

They were just finishing their first glasses of wine when she got her wish.

Billy Del Rio marched into the upscale restaurant in the ragged safari jacket that had become his trademark. Only Cady knew how rarely it got washed.

The maître d' quietly asked him to put out his cigarette. Billy loudly told him to go to hell.

"This is outrageous," George Alston said, offended.

Donald Huntington inhaled sharply, looking vice presidential and obviously waiting for someone else to handle Billy, who was a notorious brawler. The network had bailed him out of jail and discreetly paid damages after more than one barroom mix-up, always careful to blame his actions on the stress of his job.

Cole didn't look the least bit disconcerted. But then, Cady thought, he wouldn't.

"So," Billy said, taking no pains to lower his voice, "what a nice, happy, dysfunctional family we have here. Cady, they're going to put me out to pasture and stick you next to this weasel to boost their lousy ratings. You know that?"

"Billy," Cady said in a low warning. She hated to see him self-destruct. "That's going to be a self-fulfilling prophecy, if you don't behave yourself."

George Alston got all puffed up. "I hardly need Cady, or anyone else, to boost my ratings."

Billy snorted loudly. Cady thought she saw Cole smile. She realized she liked having him there. It was a curious feeling. He wasn't a part of what was going on, but he wasn't exactly a detached observer. He was an ally. *Her* ally.

"Mr. Del Rio," Huntington said formally, insistently, "I think you should leave before you land us all on the front pages of the morning papers."

"Yeah, I know, I don't get invited to dinner with the big shots anymore."

Alston rolled his eyes.

Cady started to her feet. Her loyalty to Billy put her in an awkward position, when he was behaving like such a jerk. "Billy, what are you doing here? If it's got anything to do with me—"

"It does, kid."

She held her breath. "Don't do this, Billy. Please."

He turned to Cole in disgust. "Didn't you tell her?"

"Figured I'd let things unfold first," he said calmly, without guilt.

"Tell me what?" Cady demanded, instantly suspicious. She glared at Cole. Not even a flicker of discomfort crossed his face. He must have snuck off to see Billy earlier, without telling her.

She turned back to Billy, who was regarding her with an expression of unrivaled disgust, as if she'd done sloppy journalistic work and he wasn't about to entertain any excuses.

And she knew.

Billy Del Rio wasn't the one harassing her.

"Cady," Huntington said, "we can leave if you'd like—"

She shook her head. Blood pounded in her ears. Cole and Billy must have put their heads together. Without including her. Without confiding in her.

"If it wasn't you, Billy, then who?"

Huntington hissed impatiently. "I would like to know what's going on here."

So would I, Cady thought.

Cole, however, had grown quiet and serious. His eyes were virtually black as he turned to George Alston. "Maybe you can tell us, Alston."

"Me?" He seemed appalled. "I haven't the slightest idea what you're talking about—"

"I have proof," Cole said simply.

"Yeah," Billy said. "He's got proof."

Huntington was enraged. "Proof of what? Mr. Del Rio, I *insist*—"

"I have proof," Cole went on, in a low, deadly voice, "that George Alston has been harassing Cady Dye with anonymous phone calls and messages."

Alston had gone pale. He didn't speak.

Cole didn't relent. "You knew what kind of hell she and Billy had been through on their last assignment, and you hoped to put her over the edge, shake her confidence enough that she'd do something stupid and the network would withdraw its offer. You didn't want the competition from her. You knew she could outshine you. You wanted people to perceive Cady as burned out."

Billy clapped one beefy hand on Alston's shoulder. "Should have covered your tracks, George, but you were too arrogant, figured Cady would never investigate because she'd be too busy trying to protect me."

Cady slid in beside him. "But it sounded like you, Billy. I swear—"

"Yeah. George here used to be the life of the party, doing imitations of all the old war-horses like me. I was his best. We got him going one night in Saudi, back when we thought he might serve time as a real reporter, getting a little seasoning, before sitting behind a desk and going for the big bucks.''

Given Billy's peculiar take on life, he wouldn't get too upset by what he considered a second-rate reporter making nasty phone calls to a colleague, which he'd regard as a sort of professional guerrilla warfare.

Cole, however, was another matter. He hadn't moved.

''I traced the flowers you sent to Cady,'' he said.

Huntington sat in stunned silence. Alston rose unsteadily, getting more stares now than he probably wanted. ''I don't intend to say another word without the presence of my attorney. This is the most ridiculous accusation—''

''You let arrogance and ambition get to you, George,'' Billy said, not totally unsympathetic. ''You let it make you do something stupid. You used Cady's loyalty to me to try and keep her from upsetting your applecart.''

''I'm calling my lawyer,'' he croaked, heading for the exit.

Billy made a loud noise of pure disgust. He liked playing the wise old reporter, but George Alston wasn't listening.

"You need help, Alston!" Billy yelled, uninhibited by any sense of decorum, turning what few heads in the restaurant hadn't already turned. "This business has killed better reporters than you, you pompous twit! Call your lawyer—then call your psychiatrist!"

Breathing hard, he dropped his cigarette butt in Alston's water glass.

Cady touched his shoulder. "I'm sorry, Billy. I never should have suspected you."

"Forget it. I've heard Alston's imitation. It was good. He's always been a twerp, but it would've gotten knocked out of him if he'd stayed in the field a few more years. You going to press charges?"

"Probably not. The flowers aside, it'd be hard to prove anything. My word against his—he could claim he called to discuss the show. It wouldn't do either of us any good."

"Stupid jerk should have realized you'd help his career, not hurt it. A rising tide raises all ships." Billy seemed tired suddenly, the energy drained out of him. He patted Huntington on the shoulder. "I could have handled this with more subtlety, like Cole here asked. But you know me, I need the adrenaline. Guess I'll have to satisfy myself with the thrill of catching fish. My resignation's on your desk."

Huntington cleared his throat. "Billy, we can talk in the morning, after I've had a chance to sort out this situation—"

"Nah. I've made up my mind." He grinned, and winked. "Happy New Year."

Cady noticed a spring to his step as he left the elegant restaurant. Billy Del Rio was free.

"I never thought he'd retire," Huntington said, following Billy with his eyes. Finally he turned to Cole. "Your father's death haunted him, you know. We all thought he'd have to die with his boots on, or be forced out."

"I know," Cole said.

Cady went still. No, she thought. It couldn't be.

Then Donald Huntington said, "Edward Forrest was one of the greats. I was privileged to know him when I first got into this business."

But it was true.

She flew around at Cole. "Edward Forrest—he was your *father?*"

Cole's eyes had darkened. He gave a curt nod. "Yes. I wanted to tell you yesterday, but I didn't."

She hadn't made the connection. In her own way, she'd been as arrogant as George Alston, just as determined to get her way—and willing to use Cole to do it. Never mind her motives, she'd been willing to maneuver and manipulate and use people.

Cole Forrest was Edward Forrest's son. She should have known. There was no excuse for not knowing.

"Cady?"

It was Huntington. She couldn't talk to him. She was just as loony for passing off a phony fiancé as George Alston was for pretending to be Billy Del Rio to turn her into a wreck. She couldn't take any more. She fled without even bothering with her coat.

Cole caught up with her out on the sidewalk. He seemed calm as he slid her coat over her shoulders. She was already shivering with the cold. She didn't look at him. "Your father was one of the great war correspondents. He's a legend. It never occurred to me you might be his son. I knew he and Billy had worked together.

They were friends. But I didn't think— I never even knew he was from Maine, had a family."

"There was no reason for you to know. His work was everything to him."

Cole's tone was deceptively matter-of-fact. Cady plunged out onto Park Avenue and flagged a cab. Cole followed her without waiting to be invited, and she was glad; she had known, deep down, that he would.

"Billy's felt for years he could have done something to save your father," Cady said quietly.

"He couldn't have," Cole said, sadly but with certainty. "My father was the only one who could have saved himself. He was burned out. But he kept going, he refused to quit. Billy would have had to break his legs to stop him. He'd lost his edge, took a stupid risk, and was killed."

"He's why you agreed to play my fiancé for a week?"

"No, Cady. You're why."

Her eyes were hot with unspilled tears. "You recognized the signs of burnout in me."

"I recognized the signs of a determined reporter with tunnel vision and not much of a life—who likes it that way. I wasn't planning on

falling for you. I swore I wouldn't fall for someone bound to go out and get herself killed one
day. But I knew you were in trouble, or you
wouldn't have come up with a kooky idea like
hiring a phony fiancé. I thought it might have
something to do with Billy. I knew you two were
friends.''

"So it was Billy that made you say yes, not
me.'' She spoke without self-pity. She was simply stating the facts.

"I didn't want to see him go out the way my
father did. He deserves to go fishing for a few
years and write his memoirs. But, no, you're the
reason I'm here, Cady.'' He smiled at her. "If I'd
just been worried about Billy going off the deep
end, I'd have marched down to New York and
asked him what the hell was going on. I wouldn't
have played fiancé for your friends. But you
hooked me, with your rusty-colored hair and two
versions of *A Christmas Carol* and your obvious conflicts over the future.''

"It wasn't pity?''

He looked at her, amused. "It wasn't pity.
Trust me on that.''

"You could have told me the truth.''

"Uh-uh. I'd never have gotten the job.''

True. He wouldn't have.

When they arrived back at the hotel, he asked the driver to wait. He had his bags checked. "I'm going back to Maine, Cady."

She nodded. She understood. He'd made his choices a long time ago, and she wasn't the woman for the life he wanted—needed—to lead. "Good." She could hear the bravado in her own voice. "I'm glad you're saving me the trouble of packing your bags myself."

He grinned. "Stubborn to the bitter end."

"I'll send you a check for services rendered."

The bellhop looked around at them, eyes wide. Cole laughed. "Suit yourself. I'll donate it to moose research in your name."

"Fine."

She breezed past the bellhop and tore open the front door herself. She was dangerously close to tears. Her throat was tight. But she'd be damned if she'd cry.

"It's almost a new year, Cady Dye."

Cole's voice was soft behind her.

A new year. A new life, even if she didn't want one. No more Billy Del Rio. Nothing ever stayed the same.

"I should have gone to Hawaii," she said, "and spent the holidays with my family."

"Then you wouldn't have had me to bring out your best self," Cole Forrest said, just as he shut the cab door.

Chapter Seven

New Year's Eve was a snowy, windy day in Maine. The car Cady had rented at the Bangor airport skidded twice on the icy, snow-packed dirt road down to Robin Cross's cabin. She supposed she'd have to get herself a four-wheel-drive vehicle, if she planned to spend any time at all in Maine, which she did.

About three inches of snow had fallen already. Tom, the caretaker, would still be at Disney World with his family. Cady made her way through the snow, the wind whipping her face, into the cabin, where she turned up the heat and built a fire in the wood stove. She checked out the window at the snow-covered, frozen lake. Someone must have been out snowshoeing. She could see the tracks.

"The poor bastard's besotted with you," Billy Del Rio had told her just yesterday morning. She'd visited him while he pulled together fishing gear he'd bought in the seventies; it still looked new.

"Besotted? What kind of word's that?"

"An old-fashioned one, m'dear. I don't have to worry about keeping up, now that I'm retired."

"Well, I doubt a 'besotted' man would leave the woman of his affections—"

"Sure he would. Let you stew awhile, figure out you're besotted with him."

Cady had scowled in a lame attempt at denial. "You know me, Billy, I'm not one to get all weepy and obsessed just because I've taken a fancy to some guy."

He laughed. "Taken a fancy, have you? Cady, I've known you a long time. I know you probably better than anyone else. You haven't just taken a fancy to Cole Forrest. You're—"

"Besotted," she said dryly, then sighed. There'd never been any fooling Billy. "But he's asked me to choose between him and my work. That's not fair."

Billy snorted in disbelief. "He's done no such thing!"

"He certainly has!"

"No, you ass. He's asked you to imagine your life with him in it, just as he's imagining his with you in it—which is something I ought to warn him about, by the way.''

Incorrigible as ever. Cady had seen Billy off to the Florida Keys. He had, of course, canceled his party. Any excuse.

After she put a few things away, Cady pulled on her four-in-one parka and a pair of fleece stretch pants she'd just bought that Cole would disdain. One thing she'd learned during her years on the road—she hated to be cold. She followed Robin's driveway up to where it joined his, then headed toward Cole's snow blowing into her face. She had no idea how much snow was forecast. She hadn't had time to listen to the weather.

Snowshoes were the way to get around during the winter in Maine, she decided. She had to learn. There'd be canoeing and kayaking in the summer, too, probably. Fishing. They could invite Billy up. It was stuff she hadn't done since she was a kid. *It'll keep you fresh,* Billy would say.

Cole apparently didn't apply the same zeal to his own walkways as he had to hers. Cady slipped twice on the narrow path up from the driveway to the side door of his log house, a cozy place with a huge porch overlooking the lake. Smoke was curling from the chimney. She could smell it in the frigid air.

But she was curiously unafraid as she knocked on the door. She knew what she was doing, what she wanted. She'd figured out, finally, that Cole wasn't asking her to know the future, only to imagine its possibilities.

He came to the door in jeans and a worn chamois shirt, and she'd never seen him look so sexy, so ridiculously irresistible. His charred-wood eyes dropped to hers, unreadable. "I was just about to come looking for you."

"You knew I was on my way?"

He smiled.

"Billy squealed, didn't he? This was supposed to be a surprise."

Cole motioned for her to come inside, and she peeled off her snowy coat, welcoming the warmth of the fire in the wood stove. The big main room was all wood and leather, comfortable. Cady felt immediately at home.

"Would Billy doubt your ability to negotiate a blizzard, after what you two have been through together?" Cole walked over to the wood stove, which was of an efficient, updated Franklin style with a visible fire, and put on another log. "No, it was Robin Cross. She was still laughing over the idea of you mistaking me for Tom."

Cady wasn't surprised. "I had to tell her when I bowed out of her party tonight. She roared. You should have heard her. It was embarrassing. I've got to meet this Tom character."

"You will," Cole said, and his words warmed her further.

She came and stood beside him in front of the fire. "Robin knew your father, too, back when she was still fetching coffee for the big boys. How come I'm the only one who didn't know you were Edward Forrest's son?"

"Because you're oblivious to that sort of thing. Who's related to whom, who's sleeping with whom—it all sails right over your head, because you're one of the few journalists I know who's not an unredeemable gossip." He turned to her, touched a rusty curl with a tenderness that Cady found intensely provocative. "Just as you couldn't imagine anyone trying to intimidate and manipulate you out of professional jealousy."

"Speaking of George Alston," she said, trying to stem some of the desire that seemed ready to overwhelm her, "it turns out he has an alcohol problem. He's checked himself into a rehab center. Billy likes him better already. People without flaws make him nervous.''

"He wasn't the one Alston was harassing.''

"The way I figure it, the whole thing would have been more unnerving if he hadn't tried to pass himself off as Billy. He knew I'd never believe Billy would hurt me.''

Cole looked dubious. "If you say so.''

He stirred the fire with an ancient wrought-iron poker, and it was as if he were stirring the fires within her.

"I've taken the newsmagazine job,'' she said.

"I know. I heard it on the news.''

She groaned. "I called Huntington ten minutes before I left. He promised he'd keep it quiet—''

"He probably did.''

"Damned reporters,'' she muttered.

Cole laughed. "I'd forgotten how much I enjoyed being around them.''

"Then you don't hate reporters?''

"No.''

She knew then that she'd done the right thing in coming. Not that she'd had any doubts. "Being based in New York will be a change. I won't be as nomadic—I can have a place of my own, a wardrobe. Even if other people can swing being on the road for forty years, having a family and roots, a balanced life, I couldn't. My approach to the job is different, I suppose."

"You're one to do what you have to do," Cole said, "the way you have to do it."

She licked her lips, staring at the flames. "When you left New York, it was so I could decide what I needed to do, wasn't it?"

"I wanted you to be your best self.

Tears welled in her eyes. She didn't know where they'd come from. "I can get to Maine a lot, Cole. I'll buy my own plane, if I have to, and learn to fly."

He smiled. "A can-do woman. I like that about you. But no need to worry. Maine will be here. We'll get back often."

"Cole, I'm not asking you to return to New York—"

"I know," he said. "I'm asking it of myself. If love is bringing out the best in someone, Cady, then I must be in love with you, because I'm imagining things that I couldn't have imagined before I met you. I'm not going back to the job, but a place in New York would be fun. Good for me, good for my career. Who knows what'll happen, where we'll end up five years down the road." He drew one finger along her lower lip. "We'll keep our options open."

"And imagine the possibilities," she whispered as he lifted her into his arms, kissing her softly.

When he scooped her all the way up and carried her into his first-floor bedroom, Cady didn't protest. There was a maple four-poster bed. A starburst quilt hung on one wall. "My greatgrandmother stitched it," he said, following her gaze as he laid her on the bed.

"I have another one," Cady said. "It's meant for me, anyway. My mother's been holding on to it. *Her* great-grandmother stitched it. Apparently she had a touch of wanderlust, as well."

Cole pushed back Cady's hair, trailed the back of his hand along her jaw. "You can hang it on any wall you want."

She smiled, draping her arms on his shoulders. "I already feel like I belong here."

They kissed again, deeply, hungrily. She could hear the wind picking up outside, see the snow falling through the window.

"It's supposed to be a hell of a storm," Cole said. "We could be stuck here for a few days."

"I don't mind."

His mouth covered hers once more, tasting her, stirring up their own private storm. She was aware only of his lips, his tongue, the feel of his body on hers. Desire swirled inside her, something she welcomed, relished. He peeled up her flannel shirt, discovered a turtleneck underneath, then expensive long underwear.

"How many layers do you have on?"

"Daunted, are you, Mr. Forrest?"

He grinned. "Not in the least."

He set about proving it to her. Slowly, tortuously. When finally their clothes were heaped on the floor, the northern air did nothing to cool Cady's overheated skin. Just Cole's eyes could make her hot with wanting him. He ran his palms up her sides, covering her breasts, teasing her nipples with his thumbs, then following that same path with his mouth. She could feel his own arousal throbbing between them, exulted in the warmth and strength of his hard body.

"I love you, Cady Dye," he whispered, trailing small kisses up her throat. "I must have been waiting for you to storm into my life."

She smiled, running her hands through his dark, shaggy hair. "It seems everyone's been waiting for you to storm into mine."

"One of those things that's meant to be, aren't we?"

"Robin Cross told me she earmarked you for me when she bought the cabin."

He laughed, his mouth close to hers. "Do you mind?"

"No—no, I don't mind. I have no sense about these things. Everyone knows it. I only know that I love you, Cole Forrest." She dragged one finger along his jaw, up along his lower lip, mimicking what he liked to do to her. "I always will."

He entered her then, joining her with a power and force that robbed her of all thought, filled her with new possibilities, new hopes.

A long time later, when they'd made love again and sat quietly talking by the fire, when they were snuggled together under a billowing down comforter and the storm was still piling up the snow outside, Cady noticed that it was almost midnight.

"I almost forgot," she said. "Happy New Year, Cole."

He rolled onto his back, bringing her with him. "Happy New Year."

"I always wanted to ring in a New Year this way." She lay her head on his chest. A howling wind lashed at the windows. "I can imagine a moose wandering around out in the bog, can't you?"

"With you, Cady," he said, "I can imagine anything."

*   *   *   *   *

HARLEQUIN®

AMERICAN ◆ ROMANCE®

Dear Santa,

This year I want you to bring me a mommy!

Love, your friend,

JENNY

This Christmas, some of the most precocious kids team up with Santa to play matchmaker for their unsuspecting moms and dads.

By popular demand, Christmas Is for Kids is back—with four brand-new stories to warm your heart this holiday season!

Don't miss

THE CHRISTMAS HUSBAND by Mary Anne Wilson
MERRY CHRISTMAS, MOMMY by Muriel Jensen
IT HAPPENED ONE CHRISTMAS by Jackie Weger
WANTED: CHRISTMAS MOMMY by Judy Christenberry

HARLEQUIN® Available this December wherever Harlequin books are sold.

XMASKIDS

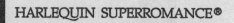

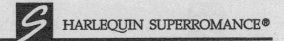

a heartwarming trilogy by *Peg Sutherland*

*Meet old friends and new ones on a trip to
Sweetbranch, Alabama—where the most unexpected
things can happen...*

Harlequin Superromance #673 *Double Wedding Ring* (Book 1)

Susan Hovis is suffering from amnesia.

She's also got an overprotective mother and a demanding
physiotherapist. Then there's her college-age daughter—and
Susan also seems to have a young son she can't really
remember. Enter Tag, a man who claims to have been her
teenage lover, and the confusion intensifies.

Soon, everything's in place for a Christmas wedding.
But whose?

**Don't miss *Double Wedding Ring* in December,
wherever Harlequin books are sold. And watch for
Addy's Angels and *Queen of the Dixie Drive-In*
(Books 2 and 3 of Peg Sutherland's trilogy)
this coming January and February!**

Harlequin Romance ®

New from Harlequin Romance
a very special six-book series by

MIDNIGHT SONS
DEBBIE MACOMBER

The town of Hard Luck, Alaska, needs women!

The O'Halloran brothers, who run a bush-plane service called **Midnight Sons**, are heading a campaign to attract women to Hard Luck. *(Location: north of the Arctic Circle. Population: 150—mostly men!)*

"Debbie Macomber's *Midnight Sons* series is a delightful romantic saga. And each book is a powerful, engaging story in its own right. Unforgettable!"

—Linda Lael Miller

TITLE IN THE MIDNIGHT SONS SERIES:

HARLEQUIN®
A M E R I C A N ◆ R O M A N C E®
®

"Whether you want him for business...or pleasure, for one month or for one night, we have the husband you've been looking for. When circumstances dictate the need for the appearance of a man in your life, call 1-800-HUSBAND for an uncomplicated, uncompromising solution. Call now. Operators are standing by...."

1♥800 HUSBAND

Pick up the phone—along with five desperate singles—and enter the Harrington Agency, where no one lacks a perfect mate. Only thing is, there's no guarantee this will stay a business arrangement....

For five fun-filled frolics with the mate of your dreams, catch all the 1-800-HUSBAND books:

Coming to you only from American Romance!

HFH-1

Harlequin® Historical

WOMEN OF THE WEST

Don't miss these adventurous stories by
some of your favorite Western romance authors.

Coming from Harlequin Historical every month.

Don't miss any of our **Women of the West!**

WWEST-1

HARLEQUIN®
Temptation

'Tis the season...for a little Temptation

ALL I WANT FOR CHRISTMAS
   by Gina Wilkins #567

MAN UNDER THE MISTLETOE
   by Debra Carroll #568

Treat yourself to two Christmas gifts—gifts you
know you'll want to open early!

Available in December wherever Harlequin books
are sold.